Staten Island Publishing Co.

Great Republican Speeches of the Campaign of 1880

Staten Island Publishing Co.

Great Republican Speeches of the Campaign of 1880

ISBN/EAN: 9783337425760

Printed in Europe, USA, Canada, Australia, Japan

Cover: Foto ©Andreas Hilbeck / pixelio.de

More available books at **www.hansebooks.com**

GREAT REPUBLICAN SPEECHES

OF THE

CAMPAIGN OF 1880.

"But I know that if one speak, even in a whisper, in the cause of his country, and for love of it, the people of the United States will catch up the sound · and wherever patriotism has not died out, and wherever liberty is not suppressed, and wherever suffrage is honored and respected, they will carry on that voice, though lost in the final decision which has triumphed, or has faded away."—Hon. WILLIAM M. EVARTS.

STATEN ISLAND PUBLISHING COMPANY,

STAPLETON, NEW-YORK.

—

1881.

PREFACE

This volume contains some of the best speeches delivered by eminent Republicans in the Cities of New-York and Brooklyn, during the Campaign of 1880. It will be seen by a glance at the contents that this volume contains concise, noble, generous, instructive, soul-stirring words, which will live when those who have uttered them have passed away.

Possibly the reading of these speeches may make us more patriotic, fill us with greater love of country, of home, of all that goes to make up home, of love for the best and grandest form of government that has ever existed.

Let us all hope that the career of the Great Republic will be one of uninterrupted prosperity and peaceful progress. We believe that the Republic of the United States of America is the strongest form of government, so far as respects cohesion and self-maintenance, that the world has seen. We believe in a prosperous and honorable future; we want concord at home and peace and respect abroad; the good citizen cherishes an equal confidence in regard to the destiny reserved for our beloved country. We are at the dawn of a day of prosperity, such as has never been measured out to this land.

CONTENTS.

——— ••• ——

GREAT CAMPAIGN SPEECHES.

The great Speech of Senator Roscoe Conkling, *in the Academy of Music, New-York City, Friday night, September 17, 1880.*

Whoever is given greeting and audience in such a presence ought indeed to have something worthy —something fit and wise to say. Inadequate in all, save only grateful and respectful appreciation, must be my return. We are citizens of a Republic. We govern ourselves. Here no pomp of eager array in chambers of royalty awaits the birth of boy or girl to wield a hereditary sceptre whenever death or revolution pours on the oil of coronation. We know no sceptre save a majority's constitutional will. To wield that sceptre in equal share is the duty and the right, nay, the birthright, of every citizen. The supreme, the final, the only peaceful arbiter here is the ballot-box ; and in that urn should be gathered, and from it should be sacredly recorded, the conscience, the judgment, the intelligence of all. The right of free self-government has been in all ages the bright dream of oppressed humanity—the sighed-for privilege to which thrones, dynasties and power have so long blocked the way. France seeks it by forced marches and daring strides. Mr. Forster, Secretary for Ireland, tells the peerage of England it must take heed lest it fall, and Westminster and England ring with dread echoes of applause. But in the fullness of freedom the Republic of America is alone in the earth ; alone in its grandeur ; alone in its blessings ; alone in its promises and possibilities, and, therefore, alone in the devotion due from its citizens. The time has come when law, duty and interest require the Nation to determine for at least four years its policy in many things.

Two parties exist ; parties should always exist in a Government of majorities, and to support and strengthen the party which most nearly holds his views is among the most laudable, meritorious acts of an American citizen, and this whether he be in official or in private station. Two parties contend for the management of national affairs. One or the other of these two contestants is sure to manage the Nation's concerns for some time to come. The question is, which of the two is it safer and wiser to trust. It is not a question of candidates. A candidate, if he be an honest, genuine man, will not seek and accept a party nomination to the Presidency, Vice-Presidency or Congress, and after he is elected become a law unto himself. Few things are more despicable than first to secure elevation at the hands of a party, and then, in the hope of winning pretentious non-partisan applause, to affect superior sanctity, and meanly to imply that those whose support and confidence were eagerly and deferentially sought are wanting in purity, patriotism, or some other title to respect.

The higher obligations among men are not set down in writing and signed and sealed—they reside in honor and good faith. The fidelity of a nominee belongs to this exalted class, and, therefore, a candidate of a party is but the exponent of a party. The object of political discussion and action is to settle principles, policies and issues. It is a paltry incident of an election affecting fifty million people, that it decides for an occasion the aspirations of individual men. The Democratic party is the Democratic candidate, and I am against the ticket and all its works.

The general issue confronting us is in itself and in its bearings sectional. I would, and you would, it were not so, but it is so. If in one portion of the country one party outnumbers the other even by overwhelming odds, the fact need not be blamable, nor proof of sectional aggression. But if in any section a party gains and keeps control, not by numbers, not by honesty and law, and then, stifling free discussion and action, attempts to grasp the government of the whole country, the proceeding is sectional, guilty, and monstrous. In twelve States of the Union the approaching election is to be no more than a farce, unless, as has sometimes happened, it be turned into a tragedy. There is to be no free debate, no equal rights, no true expression in these States ; and in several States the clear majority is to have no deciding power—not even a chance in a raffle, such as that in which lots were cast and the booty divided the other day between Tammany Hall and the upper air and solar walk reform Democracy. Senator Hampton largely promises 40,000 Democratic majority in South Carolina, where the actual majority is 40,000 the other way. In several Southern States there is a large, well-known, often ascertained Republican majority, but all Southern States alike, without exception or doubt, are relied upon to count on the Democratic side, and to score 138 Electoral votes—lacking but 17 of a majority of all.

The causes of such a condition and the consequences, if it succeeds, are matters which no sane, intelligent man can put out of view, and yet he who discusses them must be told, in the coarse parlance of the day, that he waves " the bloody shirt." It is a relief to remember that this phrase and the thing it means is no invention of our politics. It dates back to Scotland three centuries ago. After a massacre in Glenfruin, not so savage as has stained our annals, 220 widows rode on white palfreys to Stirling Towers, bearing each on a spear her husband's bloody shirt. The appeal waked Scotland's slumbering sword, and outlawry and the block made the name of Glenfruin terrible to victorious Clan Alpine even to the third and fourth generation. I am not going to recite horrors, nor to allude to them, nor to the chapter of cruelty they fill ; nor to retry the issues of the war. My purpose is quite different. It is to show, if I can, what is actually at stake now, who and what the contending forces are, how much the result may mean, and which way prudence and wisdom point.

The Testimony of Gen. Grant.

You have listened to a letter from one to whom at least as much as to any other man the Nation owes its preservation, prosperity and primacy. This letter, instinct with common sense, hits the nail on the head. Its writer generally does hit nails, rebellions and pretenders on the head. He says :

" This meeting should awaken the people to the importance of keeping control of the Government in the hands of the Republican party until we can have two national parties, every member of which can cast his ballot as judgment dictates, without fear of molestation or ostracism, and have it honestly counted ; parties not differing in opinion as to whether we are a nation, but as to the policy to secure the greatest good to the greatest number of its citizens. Sincerely believing that the Democratic party, as now constituted and controlled, is not a fit party to trust with the control of the general Government, I believe it to the best interest of all sections, South as well as North, that the Republican party should succeed in November.
Yours very truly,   U. S. GRANT."

Lord Chesterfield said that a letter shows the man it is written to, as well as the man it is written by. This letter bears Lord Chesterfield out. It is written to Gen. Arthur, and it reveals the confidence and esteem in which the writer holds him. Informed by many years of intimate acquaintance, Gen. Grant knew and felt, as we know and feel, that he was writing not only to a friend, but to one of the most genuine, patriotic and honorable of men.

There is a vast number of upright, patriotic men in it—a vast number of men who gave all and did all they should have given and done to uphold their Government and their flag in the supreme and dire hour of trial. A vast number who imperiled their lives, as other Democrats laid down their lives for their country. Many Northern Democrats who cast all their weight and sympathy on the Nation's side, after the war was over returned to their former party association ; many others never did so return. Were such Democrats to guide and influence a Democratic Congress and a Democratic Administration their party would not be "constituted and controlled " as it is. Because such men and their views and interests will not and cannot control, in the event of Democratic success, much grave peril arises.

As the Democratic party is constituted, not the men of the North, not the men who were for the Union and the Constitution, but the men of the South, who were against the Union and the Constitution, men whose policy and purposes are still hurtful to the country, are bound and predestined to control a Democratic Administration and a Democratic Congress. In the Senate and in the House the South has an overwhelming majority of the Democratic members, and most of them are men who led in the rebellion. Every party measure in Congress is settled in party caucus by a party majority ; thus the Southern members hold absolute sway. In possession of the law-making power, of the purse, and of the power to confirm or reject treaties and appointments, the South is also to furnish all the votes to elect the Democratic candidates, save only the 17 votes which must be raffled, or counted, or certified, or produced from the Northern States, particularly not excepting Oregon. Should the election be close, there is no knowing but the two Democratic houses may find ground on which to throw out a part or all of any State's Electors. With much unemployed leisure on their hands, with the danger which the Electoral Commission of 1877 alone overpassed, for that time, staring the country in the face, these Democratic houses have adopted no measure to insure order and right in ascertaining the result of the Presidential election. Should controversy arise, and the election be thrown into the House, there, the vote being taken by States, the South would cast nearly all the Democratic votes, and in the Senate the vote for Vice-President would come from the same source. In every event of Democratic success, the Southern end of the Democratic party must be to the Northern end as the locomotive is to the tender, as the horse is to the cart. This is as plain as any truth in gravitation or arithmetic.

All this commanding power is exerted by the representatives of a small fraction of the country's population, and of a still smaller fraction of the country's property.

How the Democratic Party is Constituted and Controlled.

The letter furnishes a text for many sermons. "The Democratic party as now constituted and controlled." How is it constituted, how controlled ?

Swelling the Southern Vote.

Perhaps this point will seem to you to challenge some attention. For the population of Southern States we must go back to the census of 1870. That count of the people was made by enumerators not selected by Southern Senators and members of the House as "non-partisans" and professional reformers. It was made by the regular Marshals and their deputies, and the compensation was so adjusted as to induce thorough visitation, and, at the same time, to guard against exaggeration of numbers. No imputation of fraud was ever cast upon the work. Such a thing as a plot to fabricate a monstrous increase of the population in one section, in order to baffle the course of nature and the logic of events in another—a plot to change the balance of power and population in order to aggrandize one section by establishing a false basis of representation and apportionment, thus robbing other sections of their share in governing the country, in levying taxes, and appropriating money—had not at that time occurred to the conservative foes of radicalism. That particular spoke in the wheel of deviltry had not turned up to the shifty patriot of that day. Now, such schemes seem to wax apace. We read of producing false heirs to thrones and estates, but to multiply false heirs without any one to personate them on a scale so grand as seems now in process, would stupefy the ingenuity of a French novelist, or anybody else except a thorough-going, non-partisan conservative disciple of the Democratic persuasion, wanting nothing for himself, but ready to do and suffer for a white man's government with "reform" and "a change."

The suggestion now is that the census takers of 1870 under-counted their neighbors. Paid by the head and by the mile, not by the day, it is now alleged they robbed themselves; they neither travelled nor counted, nor charged for doing it. They were "carpet-baggers," too, many of them, in the South; their States were Republican, they had their ambitions and motives for increased political numbers and power, there was not the remotest danger of any direct tax; and yet, with nothing to gain and everything to lose, they wronged and swindled themselves for the sake of being dishonest. This all may be. It is the only way of accounting for the awkward wonders of the census now progressing. It cannot be called ingenious, because it is plainly the only possible explanation, and it limps badly. Ecumenical councils may sit on these recent fabulous census revelations, but men will still wonder how 43 per cent. was added to the population of a State in ten years, during which she received exactly 137 foreign immigrants—a fact established without the aid of any census. Such an increase of population anywhere would crop out in unnumbered directions. Production, consumption, buildings, tilled acreage, railway traffic, postal returns, immigration, would tell the story of such growth. Whether these tell-tale tests, which cannot be smothered, sustain or demolish the proposed count in the Southern States will incidently appear further on, if your patience shall endure.

I was speaking of the population of the eleven States, now twelve by the division of Virginia, which seceded from the Union, and now constitute the chief power of the Democratic party. In 1870 it was: white, 7,067,213; black, 4,179,222; total, 11,246,435. The total was 29 per cent., or three-tenths of the population of the United States. The whites were one sixth of the whole population of the country; the blacks one-ninth. The Democratic majority in all these twelve States represents about six million people, or fifteen per cent. of our whole people. If to this number be added all the people of these States, of whatever color, then they represent not more than seven per cent. of the industrial, commercial, tax-paying, property interests of the country; the other States of the Union representing ninety-three per cent.

Rebels Controlling the Nation.

Let us see how much National control is now in the hands of the South, scant as it is in numbers and interest. Upward of thirty members sit in the House of Representatives and in the Electoral Colleges, by reason of counting the whole colored population as citizens, with full political rights, equal in all things with the whites. This is a double wrong and double robbery, to just the extent to which the freedmen are hindered or defrauded of their vote and their voice. To what extent this is true, the election returns too clearly show. This representation, based on stifled rights, is a plain violation of the Constitution and of common honesty; but there it is, and there it votes and speaks in the Nation's councils.

The sixteen lately Slave States (including Delaware, Maryland, Kentucky and Missouri, which did not secede) have thirty-two Senators. Thirty-nine is a majority of the Senate; so that the South needs only seven Senators from the other States to make a majority of all. She will never fail to get them if seven Northern Democrats are there. There are twelve there now.

In the House of Representatives there are 293 members. A majority is 147. The South has 106 members, lacking only 41 of a majority of all.

The Electoral College consists of 369; a majority is 185. The South has 138, lacking only 47 of a majority. Consider the sway these numbers have. In the Senate there are twenty-eight committees, and committees not only prepare but virtually control legislation in both houses, and this must be so more and more as the houses and the business grow larger. Of these twenty-eight committees the South has the Chairmanship of seventeen, and the control of all. The Southern chairmanships are of important committees. Delaware, with 140,000 people, about as many as the City of Cleveland, Ohio, or a single rural county in New-York, has the Chairmanships of the Committees of Privileges and Elections and of Finance—both very important committees. The great State of New-York, with five million people, and her enormous interests and tax-paying, has for her Democratic Senator the Chairmanship of the Committee on Patents. West Virginia has the Chairmanship of the Committee on Appropriations, which holds the purse strings of the country. The great State of Pennsylvania has the Chairmanship of Revision of Laws, a committee whose business was finished years ago. Virginia has the Chairmanship of the Committee on Pensions, Georgia of Commerce, Texas of Post Offices and Post Roads, Missouri of Claims, North Carolina of Railroads, and so on.

I have said the South has control of all the working committees. This is true in this way: On every committee there is a majority of Democrats, and of these a majority in all cases consists of Southern Senators.

The same conditions prevail in the House. There are forty-two committees. The Chairmen of twenty-two are from the South. All the committees are so constituted that the majority is Democratic, and of the majority more than half is Southern.

During the two years while this absolute power in both Houses has been so lodged, the existence of the veto power, and the approach of the Presidential canvass have suggested urgent reasons for "going slow." Many expected bills have not been introduced, many that have been introduced have not been "pressed," some that have been "pressed" have run against such obstinate opposition as to secure present postponement or some modification. But whenever the hour strikes that the veto power is in Democratic hands—put there by Southern votes—whatever the "solid" caucus decrees will be written.

The South and the Property Interests of the Country.

That caucus will be controlled by those who represent less than one-seventh of the people of the Union. I have said also that they represent not more than one-fourteenth of the producing, commercial, industrial, tax-paying and property interests of the country. Let me prove this by the official figures of the Bureau of Statistics:

Revenue.

1879—Customs duties, $137,250,048. Collected at Southern ports, $2,115,505.

This is 1½ per cent., or one-sixtieth part.

1879—Internal revenue, $116,818,221. Paid by twelve Southern States, $20,332,364.

This is 17 per cent., or one-sixth part.

Since the war, Ohio alone has paid more internal revenue than all the late Confederate States united. So has Illinois. New-York alone has paid nearly twice as much. If customs duties were added, the comparison would be more striking still.

Commerce.

Our domestic commerce exceeds our foreign commerce twenty-fold. Railways move 90 per cent. of it. In 1879, 423,013 freight cars carried this traffic. Of these cars, the late Confederate States employed 31,248. This is 7 1-25 per cent., or one-fourteenth part.

In 1879 the tonnage of vessels engaged in internal traffic was 2,678,067 tons. The late Confederate States employed 242,518 tons. This is 9 per cent., or one-eleventh part.

In 1879 (to June 30, 1880) our exports were $8,5,63',595. The South exported $188,629,717. This is 22½ per cent., or two-ninths part. Of this, 84 per cent. was cotton, and the New-York Cotton Exchange reports that very little of it was moved by Southern capital. All that came North was handled by Northern capital. That exported directly was moved mostly by Northern and foreign capital.

In 1879 (to June 30, 1880) our imports were $667,954,902. The South imported $15,934,391. This is 2½ per cent., or one-forty-third part.

Exports and imports together were $1,503,586,897. The share of the South was $204,564,108. This is 13 3-5 per cent., or one-seventh.

In 1879 (Oct. 2) bank loans were $878,503,097. Loans of Southern banks, $46,360,057. This is 5 per cent., or one-nineteenth.

In 1879 (Oct. 2) State and national bank circulation was $314,103,223. Southern banks, $23,478,426. This is 7½ per cent., or one-thirteenth.

In 1878 (six months, ending May 31, latest returns) deposits in savings banks were $879,135,817. In Southern banks, $2,527,423. This is four-tenths of 1 per cent., or one two hundred and fiftieth part.

In 1879, cost of rail-roads in the United States was $4,166,331,921. Cost of Southern rail-roads, $556,274,979. This is 13½ per cent., or one-seventh.

The latest returns show weight of mails carried on railways was 551,970,158 pounds. On Southern roads, 94,394,853 pounds. This is 17½ per cent., or one-sixth part.

In 1870 our manufactures were $4,232,325,412. Southern portion was $277,720,637. This is 6½ per cent., or one-sixteenth part.

In 1870, production of our mines was $152,598,991; of Southern mines, $4,996,052. This is 3½ per cent., or one-thirty-first part.

From June 30, 1870, to June 30, 1880, the number of immigrants who came to the United States was 2,812,177. Of these, 2,602 came to Southern Atlantic ports, and 47,299 to ports of the Gulf of Mexico, making for the whole South, 49,901. This is 1 77-100 per cent., or one-sixtieth.

The latest report of the Commissioner of Education states the total income for the public schools of the country at $86,678,301. The South paid for public schools $8,536,797. This is 9 1-12 per cent., or one-tenth part. This item is presented here because it belongs to the industrial interest.

Looking into this mirror of the country's business we see impartially and exactly reflected the respective proportions and features of the two sections. By analysis and average we see that production, industry, commerce, capital and revenue are found one-fourteenth in one section of the country and thirteen-fourteenths in the other sections.

Industry and Capital Disfranchised.

These are hard, stubborn facts. They are not recited with pleasure—far from it. They are recited with deep regret, yet their recital will be denounced as evincing a spirit of exultation, of hostile, invidious criticism. It will be said the South was taunted with her poverty. All this will be untruly, unjustly said. As an American, profoundly do I deplore the languor, the misfortunes and the wasted opportunities of any and every portion of our land.

The ruinous course of affairs in the South comes home to every citizen of this great State, whose interests and whose grandeur are so dear to me. The welfare and interest of the South and of the West, and of every portion of the country, is the interest of New-York. Whose capital helped to build Western and Southern railways? Who holds the bonds and obligations of Southern communities? When petitions are presented to Congress praying some action to stay repudiation in Louisiana and other Southern States, who sign these memorials as holders of the dishonored bonds? Who sells on credit to the South? Who buys her cotton and tobacco? Who would gain by her increase of production and wealth? Who loses by her inertness and distractions? Do men wish to injure or destroy their own investments? Whoever will answer these questions will know that New-York and her people, from love of self and love of gain, saying nothing of other reasons, earnestly long that the South may be peaceful and prosperous, and able to pay her share of taxes and bear her share of the public burdens. From the wheat-fields of Minnesota to the pastures of Texas there is not an acre whose fertility does not benefit New-York, nor could she profit by the misfortunes or poverty of a hamlet in all our borders.

It is not needed to the argument at this moment even to relate the causes of the mildew and sterility of the South, sunny, fertile and blessed by nature, as she is. Were I speaking to Southern men, with a hope that they would listen, it would be well indeed to beg them to reflect upon these causes. When the war was over, had there been hearty, manly acceptance of the most generous, magnanimous terms the world ever saw accorded by victors in any case—not in any like case, because there is none like it in history; had politics and thirst for power played less part, wasted less time and done less wrong; had industry, enterprise, thrift and humanity ruled the hour; had there been more mending and building, and planting and sowing; had there been less ostracism and hate to repel Northern capital and keep back and drive back Northern men; had a fair day's wages been paid for a fair day's work; had there been no prosecution or exodus of labor; had repudiation been loathed and shunned and not embraced—how high in the firmament of the Union would glitter the constellation of the South?

But, as already said, I deal at this point with consequences and results as they are, not with causes. Deploring as we do and as we should whatever of misfortune falls on any section, when that section comes forward as a claimant of control and management of our general affairs, it is right to look—we are bound to look—into the scope and ground of the claim, and into the motives, method, fitness, situation and standing of the claimant.

Light is thrown upon these inquiries by the facts already presented, but much light may be gained from other facts of kindred import. One thing for which we fought was the freedom of the Mississippi River. As some one expressed it, we were determined the father of waters should go unvexed to the sea. The building of jetties at the delta of this great stream to deepen a channel in which seagoing ships might reach New-Orleans, has also attracted wide attention and stimulated the belief that New-Orleans must be a vast outlet to the markets of the world and a port of entry of commanding importance.

The river commerce of the Southern Mississippi is regarded as a great tie of interest, a great safeguard and assurance against purposes sectional or inimical, and a large foundation for the claims set up for Southern influence in national affairs. The canvass in some portions of the country already blossoms with literature in this behalf.

This theory, as far as it ever was true, belongs to the past. The tread of man in all ages has been on lines of latitude, not on lines of longitude. Rivers and mountains on this Continent run north and south; men bridge and tunnel them, and move east and west. This is the ordinance of a power higher than a South Carolina census-taker. The enterprise which in its youth and helplessness floated the way the water ran, has changed its course. Trade has veered from one point of the compass to another, and permanently altered its relations.

The construction of railways has revolutionized traffic and transportation. Four trunk lines of steel roads, of which the sea ends are Boston, New-York, Philadelphia and Baltimore, now carry, each one of them, more freight than ever moved on the Mississippi River. The great companion and competitor to this transcontinental movement is the lakes and the Erie Canal. Besides handling a vast traffic this water route acts as a check on railway freights, keeping them down by force of competition. To this vast comprehensive modern current of business, tributary streams flow in by rail and rivers, from the North, South and West. The tonnage across the Mississippi on bridges above St. Louis is twelve-fold the tonnage to that city by river. Twenty-five years ago the commerce of St. Louis was all by river; last year, as shown by the records of the Merchants' Exchange, the railway tonnage was 6,918,794, and the river tonnage was only 1,366,115.

The single bridge at St. Louis has a capacity for ten-fold the traffic that ever floated on the Mississippi River. The actual commerce crossing this one bridge is four times as great as that of the river beneath. Traffic south of the Ohio River and of the State of Missouri is but tributary now to the east and west current. The St. Louis Merchants' Exchange reports that last year the number of tons moved to and from the East by rail was 2,950,858; tons moved to and from the South by river, 6,2,230; tons moved to and from the South by rail, 1,952,008. Commerce takes the rail, even with the river by its side. New-Orleans is 652 miles further from Liverpool than St. Louis itself is. Baltimore is 940 miles nearer than St. Louis to Liverpool, making a difference in favor of Baltimore as a point for shipping to Europe of 1,572 miles as against New-Orleans, saying nothing of the disadvantage of carrying products through the tropical exposures and risks of the Gulf of Mexico. Philadelphia, New-York and Boston are still nearer than Baltimore to Liverpool.

Trade's Convincing Argument.

But this is not all. The commercial forces of seven great cities have grasped this vast carrying trade, and hold, propel and direct it. Boston, New-York, Philadelphia and Baltimore at the East, and St. Louis, Chicago and Cincinnati at the West, command the machinery and the outlets and inlets through which the surplus products of the United States reach the markets of the world, and through which the merchandise of Europe is brought here and distributed. Geographical and natural advantages are favorable, but alone they would not be decisive; the vital fact is the genius, energy, enterprise and capital of merchants, farmers, manufacturers and railway managers, aided by wholesome adjustments of tariff and other laws in the interest of American labor. Could science deepen the mouths of the Mississippi till the Great Eastern could load at the wharves of the Crescent City, the achievement would no more arrest or divert the movement of commerce and population East and West than it would control the tides of the sea, or change the courses of the stars.

Southern commerce is simple, tardy and dependent. Northern commerce is complex, intensely active, highly organized and independent. Northern methods and progression have constantly increased their fruits. The reverse is true of Southern methods. In 1860 the imports of New Orleans were $22,922,773. Last year they were only $10,840,254. They were less last year than in any year from 1856 to 1878. In 1860 exports from New-Orleans were $107,812,580. Last year they were only $90,249,874—less than in 1870 and 1874. The tonnage account varies this statement apparently, but only apparently, because steam vessels have been more used of late, and steam vessels count more rapidly in tonnage than in cargoes. Like retrograde and stagnation appear at other Southern ports. Baltimore is not treated as a Southern port because it is the ocean terminus of a great East and West line of traffic. Now turn to Northern ports:

	1860.	1880.
Boston's imports,	$39,366,560	$68,619,638
Boston's exports,	13,530,770	58,033,587
New-York's imports,	233,692,941	543,595,898
New-York's exports,	120,630,975	388,441,064
Philadelphia's imports,	14,625,801	35,961,392
Philadelphia's exports,	5,512,755	49,612,105
Baltimore's imports,	9,784,773	19,956,256
Baltimore's exports,	8,864,600	76,290,870

The imports of these four ports in 1860, were $279,191,075; their exports, $148,479,096. Total, $545,950,161. In 1880 their imports were $668,122,604; their exports, $572,294,315. Total, $1,240,420,420. In 1880 the foreign commerce of New-Orleans was 24 per cent. of that of the four ports just named. In 1880 it was only 8 per cent., falling of from $130,735,359 in 1860, to $101,092,129 in 1880. The foreign tonnage of New-Orleans in 1859 was 659,083. In 1860 it was 632,398. In 1880 it is 769,910. Foreign tonnage of Charleston in 1859 was 129,764; in 1860, 126,411; 1880, 116,283. Foreign tonnage of Savannah in 1859, was 86,521; in 1860, 92,648; in 1880, 183,895. Foreign tonnage of Mobile in 1859, was 131,600; in 1860, 105,909; in 1880, 61,471. Foreign tonnage of Boston in 1860, was 718,587 tons; in 1880, 1,341,457. Foreign tonnage of New-York in 1860, was 1,973,812; in 1880, 7,651,382. Foreign tonnage of Philadelphia in 1860, was 185,162 ; in 1880, 1,351,312. Foreign tonnage of Baltimore in 1860, was 186,417 ; in 1880, 1,502,713. In 1860, (year ending June 30,) tonnage of vessels entered at seaports south of the Potomac was one-third as large as the tonnage of all Northern ports, both Atlantic and Pacific. This year, (ending June 30, 1880,) it is only about one-seventh. Democratic orators bid us look at the exports of cotton. I have looked at them, and find these facts touching cotton and breadstuffs:

	Value.
1860, Bales of cotton exported, 3,812,345	$191,806,555
1870, Bales of cotton exported, 2,005,323	227,027,624
1880, Bales of cotton exported, 3,810,150	211,535,905

Fewer bales this year than 20 years ago.

In 1860 breadstuffs exported sold for....	$24,492,320
In 1870 breadstuffs exported sold for....	72,250,913
In 1880 breadstuffs exported sold for....	288,036,835

Cotton has stood still, while surplus breadstuffs have multiplied twelve-fold. Look again—look at the value of all exports as they have risen and fallen in one part of the country and in others. The value of all exports from ports south of the Potomac was, in 1860, $199,959,775; in 1870, $192,889,920; in 1880, $187,140,553. Here is seen a steady decline. The value of all exports from Northern ports was, in 1860, $173,279,469; in 1870, $346,102,428; in 1880, $616,153,673. Here is a steady increase of nearly four-fold. The value of imports of all kinds to all ports south of the Potomac was, in 1860, $30,790,343; in 1870, $22,774,573; in 1880, $17,975,796. Here, again, is steady decline. The value of imports at Northern ports was, in 1860, $331,376,021; in 1870, $439,633,014 ; in 1880, $713,613,360. Here is an enormous constant increase. The value of imports at the ports of South Carolina was, in 1860, $1,539,570; in 1870, $505,394; in 1880, 231,535. Here is sad decay. The value of exports at the ports of South Carolina was, in 1860, $21,193,723; in 1870, $10,818,619; in 1880, $21,660,763. Here is stagnation for 20 years.

The North's Paramount Interest.

These unerring proofs map and locate the bulk and substance of the Nation's wealth and business. But some man may say what has all this to do with electing Garfield and Arthur and a Republican Congress? I answer, it has everything to do with it. Again, some man may say all these vast enterprises and transactions are managed by individuals and corporations as private business, and what are they to politics or politics to them? I answer that the good of every one of them depends on just and friendly laws and wholesome administration of the Government.

I say this, speaking in the great commercial metropolis of the Western hemisphere, and speaking to men whose wisdom, integrity and enterprise have made this one of the greatest, and, in my belief, the most generous, benevolent city on the globe. I affirm that the broad issue at this election is whether our colossal fabric of commercial, industrial and financial interests shall be under the management and protection of those who chiefly created and own it, or shall be handed over to the sway of those whose share in it is small, and whose experience, antecedents, theories and practices do not fit them or entitle them to assume its control.

Tariffs, tax laws, finances, currency, banks, courts, appropriations, the maintenance and enforcement of national as well as State laws—these are the things upon which prosperity depends, and these are the things at stake in this election. The party which represents the tax-paying portions of the country is the party whose representatives can best be trusted to vote upon drafts on the Treasury. A Congressman whose constituents "foot the bills," may not stand up alone, or with a few others, against his party and its caucus; but if he belongs to the party all of whose Congressmen represent tax-paying constituencies, they may be trusted to stand together against raids on the Treasury which they know all their districts would condemn. It is still more certain that if you place the tax-laying power in the hands of those who do but little of the tax-paying, your situation is like that of the man who sat on a limb and sawed off the limb between himself and the tree.

The consideration of disparity of interest, if it stood alone, ought to turn the scale in deciding whether to put the Government into the hands of the Democratic party, "as now constituted and controlled," in the language of Gen. Grant. But inferiority of interest or antagonism of interest is, unfortunately, not the only consideration. Banded sectional resentments and sterile hates disfigure and pervert the political policy of those who dominate the South, foreboding immeasurable peril and evil should they come to wield the whole forces of the national Government.

Intolerance of free action, and of equal rights in political or even business affairs, is too patent and flagrant to be denied or doubted. One glance at Southern elections proves ostracism, tyranny and wrong, in monstrous proportions. In 1868 eight Southern States gave majorities for Grant. In 1872 seven States did the same thing. The Republican vote was very large. Only four years afterward 200,000 of these votes disappeared from the count. In the nine other Southern States, in the same four years, 300,000 Republican votes disappeared from the returns also, making an absence of 500,000 votes. Most of these stifled votes were the votes of men who had been slaves—freedmen, only just crowned with the crown of American citizenship, and proud and eager—more proud and eager than the most of us—to exercise the right to vote. Does any sane man doubt that they would have voted if they could, or that those who dared and could, did vote, and that their votes were not honestly counted? If any man does doubt it, let him look at the spectacle presented in individual States.

Fraud, Cruelty and Deviltry.

The voters of Georgia were registered before the election in 1866. The white voters numbered 95,363, the colored, 93,458.

In 1876 the whole Republican vote counted was 50,446. Only two years later the whole Republican vote counted was 5,257. Pretences have been made that the freedmen of Georgia do not care to vote, and often vote the Democratic ticket. Only read the savage laws of Georgia under the fiction of vagrancy and prison management, and then learn of their sickening, beastly administration, and human nature will tell you that the freedmen of Georgia do not support the Democratic party, but would cast it out if they could.

In 1876 the Republican vote of Louisiana was 77,174. Two years afterward the Republican vote disappeared from the election returns. Yet in 1867, in this same State, the registry of voters showed 45,159 white voters and 84,431 colored voters; and in 1876, the registration showed a Republican majority of 22,314. In North Carolina, in 1876, the Republican vote cast was 108,417. At the next Congressional election Republican votes scarcely appeared in the count. In Alabama, in 1872, the Republicans cast 90,272 votes. They elected five of the seven Representatives to Congress and the Legislature by a large majority. In 1876, 68,230 Republican votes were counted—two years later, when a Governor and members of Congress were elected, not one Republican vote was counted. In South Carolina the registration showed that the colored voters outnumbered the whites by 32,721. In 1872 Grant received 72,870—49,587 majority. Every Congressional District elected a Republican. The Legislature was Republican by 95 majority. In 1876 the Republican vote cast was 91,870. Only two years afterward, when a Governor and Congressmen were elected, all the Republican votes counted in the State were 213.

This was a very carnival of fraud, cruelty and deviltry. Voting-places in Republican regions had been established twenty-five miles apart, and the Republicans of South Carolina do not ride by night or by day—they go on foot. They are poor and ignorant, but they know what emancipation meant, they know what the ballot-box means, they know which side they prayed and fought for in war, they know which side they would vote for in peace.

Force and tissue ballots took care of the election of 1878 in South Carolina. It was testified before a Committee of the Senate that one man put about 700 votes into the ballot box. This makes politics one of the "exact sciences," much more certain than the dice or lots with which offices and nominations were raffled off here the other day. In Mississippi more than half the population is colored. Every year until 1874 the Republicans had a majority in all elections. In 1876 the Republican vote returned was 52,605. The next year it was but 1,168, and the year after 2,085. In all these States the Republican vote, and even the Republican committees and newspapers, have been utterly suppressed.

Alabama has just held an election. The Greenback candidate for President went there and realized the embarrassment of the bull who butted against a locomotive. The whole proceeding was a shameful wrong, and Mr. Weaver says that the enforcement of the national election laws is the only thing which will make a fair election possible. Arkansas has just voted—Arkansas, where, until recently, Republicans always elected members of Congress and the Legislature; where, at the last Presidential election, 38,669 Republican votes were cast, and where now in no part of the State does the Republican vote appear. Repudiation and Democracy prevail mightily.

I repeat here, as I said in the Senate, when the Government was taken by the throat and threatened with strangulation unless the election laws were stricken down, that the Democratic party would have to-day no majority in either house of Congress except for elections dominated and decided by violence and fraud.

Ill-Gotten Power Badly Used.

What use is made of all this ill-gotten power? One of its chief uses has been the repudiation of honest debts. Every Southern State but Texas has lately repudiated its obligations. This aggregate repudiation of State and municipal debts amounts to about $300,000,000. In 1872 the debts of Southern States were $242,500,000. Now these States recognize and pay interest on only $53,978,945. A large part even of this is unpaid and funded interest. On $20,000,000 interest has been scaled down to 2 per cent. Whether the residue of debts are also to be foresworn is now an open issue.

Is there excuse or palliation for this? We are told so. What is it It is that "carpet-bag Governments" contracted these obligations. One difficulty with this excuse, and not the only one, is that it is not true. The anti-war debt, contracted before the "carpet-bagger" ever visited the South, either with knapsack or without it, was $90,000,000. No part of this debt has been paid ; a large part has been repudiated. The "carpet-bag Governments" paid the interest on it regularly.

The increase of debt since the war was largely for public improvements. But the most damaging fact for this excuse is that all the alleged illegal issue of bonds charged upon the carpet-bag Governments put together does not equal the sum repudiated by Georgia alone.

What are we to think of men and communities who go into wholesale repudiation as gayly as the troubadour touched his guitar? When Mr. Weaver brought forward in the House of Representatives a bill to issue "fiat money," and make it a legal tender for all debts public and private, man after man from the South openly declared that if the word "private" were stricken out, he would vote for the bill.

They had no objection to paying off public debts with chaff, but private debts they thought should be paid in money.

State debts are sacred above national obligations in Southern ethics—a "sovereign State" is of higher essence than the Nation, and this was the standing defence in rebellion for "going with their States." Moreover, State and municipal obligations are for home purposes. If their own State faith and credit is not inviolate with Southern leaders, what in their hands would be the fate of obligations which were the means, the cause, the memorials of their defeat?

But we are told Gen. Hancock would watch them! An angel might watch a tiger; a child might attempt to divide a beefsteak with a bloodhound; a lamb might lie down with a lion, but the lamb would lie inside. The peril of Democratic ascendency in all the branches of the Government is deeper rooted than any measure within the scope of existing public questions. Statesmen abroad talk of the "balance of power," and of "changing the map of Europe." These sayings mean not much more than might easily occur here.

The resolution admitting Texas to the Union in

1845 provided for erecting out of Texas four additional States. The area and population are both sufficient. The area is 274,000 square miles, the population a million and a half. Such a proceeding would add eight to the number of Southern Senators, and add to Southern power in the Electoral College. From New-Mexico and other Territories, whose traditions and prejudices have descended from slave-holding influences, several new States may also be made. Schemes exist, not in embryo, but far advanced, to obtain "a slice of Mexico." Cattle stealing on the Rio Grande border has been and is a fruitful occasion for incursions into Mexico. Special cavalry regiments, of unusual size, have been raised and stationed on the Texan frontier. It is an open secret that not long ago much exertion and alertness were needed to keep us out of another Mexican war.

Without violating the Constitution or transcending the usages of the Republic, at least seven new States could be brought in, and, in the case of some of them, a very plausible case could be made. The project would become a high party measure. Its success would assure complete Democratic ascendency in the Nation for a generation at least. It would put the Government not merely in the hands of the Democratic party, but of the Southern Democratic party.

Why should this not be done? Who and what is to prevent it if the Democratic party is elected? The Northern wing could never resist the Southern wing in Congress, were these new States brought forward for admission. The Northern wing never could, never will and never can withstand the pressure of the far stronger Southern wing. Gravitation and arithmetic make such resistance impossible, just as a pound cannot outweigh a ton, just as one man cannot outnumber a regiment. The past is pitiful in its warnings in this behalf. Despite pledges and Northern indignation, Northern Democrats in Congress united in voting down the Wilmot proviso in order to make California a slave State; united in voting for the Fugitive Slave law ; united in the mighty perfidy which overthrew the Missouri compromise in order to fasten slavery on Kansas and other States, and united in defeating the Homestead law—all at the behest of the Southern majority.

Mr. Van Buren at last, like Macbeth, would "go no further in this bloody business," and political destruction was his reward. Mr. Douglas at last made a brave stand against sectional aggression, and he was hunted to his grave. Caucus is king, and the avenging angel is hardly more inexorable in decree or more unerring in retribution.

Attacking the Judiciary.

One of the main bulwarks of the Republic is the Judiciary. The courts of justice are umpire, conservator, citadel. The Supreme Court is the final arbiter of many momentous controversies. This great tribunal is very obnoxious to Southern leaders in Congress and out. It is in their way. It does not always decide as they think. The halls of Congress rang last year with assertions, uttered with passionate vehemence, that the laws for protecting elections are unconstitutional. Soon afterward a case, on the docket of the Supreme Court, involving the validity of these laws, was reached, and the Court decided them valid. A Register in Bankruptcy not long ago overruled the Chief Justice on the construction of a statute, and so it often happens that the Court is not able or recondite enough to get at the "true inwardness" and profound depths of the law as understood on the hustings, where the moonshiner thrives and the fire-eater reigns. Mutterings deep and loud, breathings of dire longings to "go for" the Court, have for years been gathering in volume.

In the House of Representatives, for two or three years, this feeling has now and again found harsh voice in unseemly sinister words. Not only Kentucky, through the Chairman of the Judiciary Committee, Mr Knott, but Missouri, North Carolina, and other States, assisted, I regret to say, by a representative from this City, have uttered language, gross and calumnious of the Court, aspersing its integrity and its decisions. "Mere drivel," "plausible sophistry," "packed, partisan and demoralized," "packed tribunal" decisions to be observed "*pro tempore*" only, "dirty work of its masters," "made a political decision to order," "fiery indignation of an inflamed people"—these are some of the buffetings to be found in the *Congressional Record*, delivered sometimes from carefully written speeches, and sometimes received, the *Record* says, with "loud applause.'

To what does all this pave the way? The *Congressional Record* will inform you. On the 26th of January, 1880, Mr. Manning, of Mississippi—a State well known to be jealously sensitive to the pure administration of justice and the rigorous punishment of crime—especially hideous, cowardly murder and massacre—introduced a bill to place 12 new additional Judges on the Supreme Bench. What an easy, effectual, and with all, plausible, disposition this would make of the Court. Increased business would be such an innocent excuse—the Court could sit by sevens for some purposes and meet in banque for all large purposes when State sovereignty and State rights amendments to the Constitution and cotton taxes and the like are at stake. The bill passed to a second reading, and was referred to a Committee, whose Chairman, a few days afterward came into the House and denounced the Court, and said a majority of the present Judges were "hopelessly lost in a fog." For the present it would be premature and bungling to pass such a bill; a veto might spoil it, and it might spoil the result in some close Northern State. But let the Democrats elect their President, or rather their party—for the party is running—and who will say that this bill will not find its way to the statute book. You can all say what sort of Judges the 12 new ones would be.

But no new law is needed; nature's law, and the statutory limit of age at which Judges may retire, will, during the next four years, vacate at least four seats on the Supreme Bench. These four appointments will decide the political complexion of the Court. With what Judges would the Democracy fill them?

The Circuit and District Courts are obnoxious also. They are still more easy to deal with. Like

the Judges of the Supreme Court, these Judges hold their places during good behavior, but legislation, as has often been seen in States and in the Nation, has ways to plow around this stump. Abolishing a circuit or district, or adding to it another, takes his seat out from under a Judge and gets rid of him finally; he is "legislated out."

Thus the whole judicial establishment of the Republic is at the disposal of the law-making power.

With Courts revolutionized to conform to reactionary notions and dogmas, prejudices, and interests, what may be the fate of questions affecting "commerce among the several States," revenue, bank and legal-tender currency, the taxation of Government bonds, the currency in which these bonds are payable, civil rights acts, election laws, claims growing out of the war, claims for refunding the war tax on cotton, the late amendments, and many other grave matters, no man can predict.

Bourbon Hatred of the Army.

The Army, too, is envied—its "offence is rank." Less than four lines of the Revised Statutes are all that denies commissions in the Army to men who, educated at the country's cost, and presented with their country's sword, drew that sword against their country's life. A bill to repeal these four lines is now pending in the Senate, already passed by a third reading by the solid Democratic vote. On the 25th of February last, Mr. Heiskell, of Maryland, was relieved from the operation of this exclusion, and a Senator from Arkansas moved as an amendment its total repeal. The yeas and nays were demanded, and 36 Senators, every Democrat who was present, voted yea. Ohio, New-Jersey, Pennsylvania and New-York contributed their Democratic votes to this Southern proposition of "reform." Subsequently the mover and all concluded to reconsider and drop the amendment—a sagacious conclusion in a "Presidential year."

Mr. Tucker, of Virginia, moved in the House the repeal of this safeguard to the Army as a rider to an appropriation bill, but it was huddled out of sight on a point of order—a judicious point in a "Presidential year." The Democratic majority put in the Army bill a provision that officers now in the Army might receive advanced rank and pay if they would retire—a benevolent, thoughtful provision certainly. But if a body of Army officers could thus be coaxed out of the service, there would be so many vacancies to be filled, and filled by the President, by and with the advice and consent of a Democratic Senate. When this free-will offering was presented a cry arose about "gift bearing Greeks," and other ungracious symptoms were manifested on the Republican side, and so brevet rank and brevet pay stand over at least till the season of Santa Claus.

Meanwhile the Army has been reduced to a skeleton, and whenever a scare, a pretence, a speck of war on the Mexican border or elsewhere can be discovered or invented, the Army must be increased and filled up. Filled up by whom? That depends on the approaching election. If Garfield and Arthur are chosen, by Union men always for the Union to the core. If Hancock and English and the Democratic party get in, by men who," went with their States." Confederate soldiers would flock to the standard of military as well as of civil service reform, and flock in a fervor of magnanimity and devotion, ready to let by-gones be by-gones, and to forgive the "usurpations of Lincoln" and the "unconstitutional coercion of sovereign States." Why shouldn't they?

Who would be warranted to assert that a Confederate soldier was false or immodest in professing patriotic intentions while seeking rank in the Army of the Republic? No man ought to assert it, and yet all fair men would agree that, other things being equal, preferments in the Army should be given to those who fought in that Army rather than to those who assailed it in the dread extremity of the Nation's life.

The present tariff and revenue laws are deemed very bad by the dominant element of the Democracy. They want to change them. They will change them radically whenever the way is clear. There is a whisky rebellion now in several States, and the officers of the law are powerless to suppress it. In Alabama the law is resisted, and the process of the Courts destroyed and defied. Recently a warrant was issued for the arrest of one Penton, charged with such an offence. A Deputy Marshal went with a posse to execute the warrant. In his report to the Marshal he says Penton assembled from 25 to 50 armed men, and set him and the law at defiance. When cautioned to desist, Penton replied, "When Hancock is elected this damn foolishness will stop."

The thing to stop, thus piously predicted, is the collection of the tax on whisky—that mild beverage so sacred to the Democratic heart, so grateful to the Democratic stomach, and so nourishing to Democratic principles. The law is defied in Arkansas, and the officers apply to the Governor for the use of the arms of the United States loaned to Arkansas, and the Governor replies that he dare not permit the arms to be used, because if he should, and if a moonshiner should be killed, he would have to leave the State.

Washington raised an army when he was President; and marched at its head to put down such lawlessness; and he kept the army in Pennsylvania three months after it was put down to see it did not get up again. Now, there are 32 soldiers of the United States in Alabama and 57 in Arkansas, and if a hundred more should be ordered to either State, the country would not be big enough to hold the noise. Hancock's Order No. 40 would leap from the Democratic scabbard, and we should hear how "the military must be always subordinate to the civil power," and how "the Courts are open." These obnoxious laws are marked for "reform" and "a change" whenever the Democratic hand can reach them.

Defying the Constitution.

The recent amendments to the Constitution and the laws made in pursuance of them are objects of unabated Democratic wrath—a wrath going to such excess as to compel the belief that free fraud in elections is deemed the only adequate means to party success. These amendments of freedom, especially the thirteenth and fourteenth, were established in the Constitution against the most desperate opposition the Democracy could make. As they gained power in States which had already ratified them, in impotent passion the farce was enacted of formally re-cinding and withdrawing the irrevocable assent which had been finally given. This was done in Indiana and New-Jersey, and Mr. Tweed did it in New-York.

From first to last, the organs of Democratic doctrine have declared these amendments illegally carried—illegal, because Democratic States that were out fighting were not in to vote. They never yet have said or admitted that the amendments were legally adopted. They did say in National Convention, in 1872, that they opposed re-opening the questions settled by the amendments, and they did say, in 1876, that they would accept them; but that they were legally valid they have never said.

These amendments are constantly and flagrantly defied in more than half the Democratic States, and have been for years. The laws enacted under them have been denounced in every form, and denounced as null and void, even since the Supreme Court has solemnly decided otherwise. It was to get rid of these laws that the revolutionary plot was laid last year to stop the wheels of Government, to close the Courts and Post Offices, and put out the beacon lights on the sea and on the lakes unless a repeal was yielded. With a thorough-bred Democratic President, whatever may happen in form to the amendments, they will become more a dead letter than a quickening spirit, and the laws made to enforce them will be swept like leaves before a gale. Should these laws be swept away, and should the spirit which assails them in the South, and which called them into being, continue to rage, mildew will follow in the wake.

When Lincoln issued his proclamation of emancipation, men and women in this city were maddened by being made to believe that the slaves set free would swarm to the North, crowd out white labor, and cut down its wages. The draft riots were largely incited by this wicked, insane pretence. Throughout the North this was the appeal to the laboring man, and many members of Congress who had supported Lincoln were defeated at the ensuing election. Vainly we pleaded for reason. We said no, men do not fly from liberty; they fly from slavery and wrong. Events have vindicated the logic of freedom.

Once more I repeat the argument and the warning. The black man wants to remain by the graves of his fathers, but let persecutions go on, and the story of Pharaoh and of Egypt will be repeated.

An exodus, not of a few despairing souls, but a real exodus, will begin, depriving Southern fields of the hands that should and would till them, and bringing to the North and the West a population not inured to Northern climes, and not adapted to usefulness and advantage here, which, fairly treated, would come from them in the South.

The national banking system is another eyesore to the opposition. Their National Conventions have denied all power of Congress to authorize banks. By votes and speeches in Congress, by declarations of conventions and leaders, by studied amendments offered to the bills under which the national debt has been refunded, the national banking system has been struck wherever a blow could be put in. This fabric of banking is now inwrought not only with the business of the country, but with the maintenance of specie payments—it stands a lion in the path of flat money, inflation, and all the long train of financial heresies which possess the Democratic mind, especially in the South. In unnumbered ways, direct and indirect, this vast interest is constantly exposed to the action of Congress.

The Cincinnati Convention seems to have felt the need of a little caution on this point when it nominated Mr. English for Vice-President. He is President of a national bank. They nominated a Union General as a blind to the soldiers and a bank officer as a blind to the bankers. Evidently it is thought the Northern Democratic team drives better with blinders. But even blinders do not always answer. In 1864, after solemnly asserting, just when the rebellion was gasping its last, that the war for the Union was a failure, the Democratic Convention, at instigation coming then from the sheltering refuge of the Canadian shore, the same instigation which prompted a like expedient now, put up a Union General. That General did not issue order No. 40 in the midst of lawlessness and butchery, which civil authority could not arrest. No, he issued orders arresting the Legislature of Maryland, a State which had not seceded, and he issued orders proclaiming martial law and suspending the habeas corpus at election time, and placed soldiers as Supervisors of the polls. But even with such a Union General the disguise was too thin.

Seeking to Plunder the Treasury.

War claims upon the Treasury have been and will be a subject fruitful of much agitation. I am moved to refer to it by the wholly groundless assertion in regard to it now going the rounds of party journals. The fashion of this assertion seems to have been set by Mr. Randall, Speaker of the House of Representatives. Mr. Randall is one of the ablest and most intelligent, as he is one of the most courageous, men of his party, and I speak of him with much respect. In several speeches he has taken up the matter of Southern claims, always to say that they are barred by the fourteenth amendment of the Constitution. It puzzles me to see how so discerning a man can have fallen into such an error. The proceedings over which he presides constantly refute the assertion.

In the fourteenth amendment stand these words: "Neither the United States, nor any State, shall assume or pay any debt or obligation incurred in aid of insurrection or rebellion against the United States, or any claim for the loss or emancipation of any slave, but all such debts, obligations, and claims shall be held illegal and void." The claims which stand in staggering totals in bills already before Congress, and in other bills said to be waiting, are not touched by this section of the Constitution.

For example, it is insisted that the direct tax imposed by the Nation on all States in 1861 should, as to the seceded States, be refunded. The amount claimed is $2,192,110. Again, it is said the war tax laid on cotton should be refunded. The argument

is that cotton, like wheat and corn, is a product of the earth, and that wheat and corn were not taxed, and therefore, cotton should not have been taxed. There is plausibility in this; but petroleum is a product of the earth also, and that was heavily taxed, not only during the war, but afterward, and yet Pennsylvania has never claimed that the money should be refunded. The amount of cotton tax claimed is $170,180,220.

Again, buildings were occupied, crops were trampled, fences and wood were burned, provisions were consumed, edifices were demolished, and regions were laid waste by the armies of the Union. The total of such claims dizzies arithmetic. These are not "debts or obligations incurred in aid of insurrection or rebellion"—decidedly not in aid of rebellion. They are claims because of acts done to crush rebellion. The constitutional amendment does not come within gun-shot of them.

The error of the distinguished speaker is the more puzzling because, as reported, he said in another part of his address recently that the Republican majority in Congress had paid $100,000,000 of such claims. This I presume is true, if he means that Republicans have voted to pay Union men whose property was taken for public use the value of the property so taken. But whether correct in the amount or not, he is certainly correct in saying that a vast sum has been so paid. Does not this fact clearly show that such claims are not extinguished by the Constitution? If they were so extinguished, surely the law-making power would not have been so stupid or wicked as to pay them year after year, and this without any member of either house ever suggesting that the Constitution stood in the way. These appropriations for Southern claims also throw light on the question whether Republican action in Congress has been hostile and cruel to the South. The statutes on the subject enacted by Republicans made the loyalty of the claimant a *sine qua non*, and the Democrats have repeatedly voted to repeal the loyalty test, and bills for this purpose are now pending. There can be no doubt that the way is wide open to all the Southern claims which a majority can be found to vote for and a President to sign.

There is as little question that large and ever increasing sums are plucked from the Treasury in the River and Harbor bills to dredge small Southern streams and runs, entirely local and of no possible use as channels of national commerce. The creeks and bayous and ponds thus improved at the general expense, some of them, cannot be found named on the map, and all of them are put into appropriation bills for the pecuniary or political advantage of individuals and corporations.

The erection of public buildings for Courts, Post Offices, and the like, at the national cost, is another serious and increasing drain on the Treasury. From small places where no such expenditure is needed come applications for public buildings; many of them have recently passed the Senate. One place in North Carolina where a public building was voted has not more than 2,500 inhabitants. No one at all familiar with the facts can doubt that, with full Democratic swing, the doors of the Treasury will open, and copious streams will run South and empty into the pockets of no end of expectants.

How Democrats Have Not Saved Money.

Whichever way we turn, reasons rise up before us for keeping the staff in the hands of those who have vastly most at stake in the wholesome preservation of the Government, its revenues, and its laws. Those with the least at stake fought for one-half the Government, and now the question is whether we had better vote them both halves. The Democratic party has had possession of one house of Congress for four years, and of both houses for two years. What useful thing has been done or proposed? They have stricken some millions of tax from whisky and tobacco. They have attempted by revolutionary means to put the Executive under duress, and to cripple the Government in order to overthrow just and time-honored laws. What else? I do not know.

It is said the Democracy have reduced appropriations. I do not so understand it. The claim of economy is no better than a juggle. Here are the exact figures year by year, Republican and Democrat, of sums annually appropriated for current expenses, stated in currency and gold:

For Fiscal Year.	Currency.	Gold.
1874 (Republican)....	$172,290,701 82	$153,855,595 83
1875 (Republican)....	155,917,778 20	137,655,760 28
1876 (Republican)....	147,714,940 81	129,603,718 03
1877 (Democratic)....	124,122,010 92	115,063,104 12
1878 (Democratic)....	88,356,983 13	86,296,415 53
1879 (Democratic)....	172,016,809 21	171,072,775 59
1880 (Democratic)....	162,404,617 76	162,404,617 76
1881 (Democratic)....	154,118,212 64	154,118,212 64

It will be seen that under a Republican majority appropriations steadily decreased down to Democratic accession in 1877. In the first year the Democrats continued reduction, omitting, however, needed appropriations. In their second year—the year preceding Congressional elections—they badly neglected to provide for many obvious and indispensable appropriations. This was exposed on the spot as an electioneering device, but the figures went forth and had their effect. There they stand in the tables of 1878 as a great apparent saving, loudly bragged about at the time. But as everybody familiar with the workings of the Government knew beforehand must be, the pretended saving which had been purposely left out of the regular appropriation bills came in as "deficiency bills" after the election, at the next session. There stands the proof in the tables of 1879. The appropriations that year were much greater than in 1876, the last year of Republican rule—greater in currency by $24,301,868 40; greater in gold by $41,979,057 56.

For last year the appropriations exceeded the last Republican year more than $15,000,000, and for this year they are considerably larger; and in both years appropriations were purposely omitted in cases in which they are sure to be supplied at the next session.

Before speaking of finances it may be well to read a telegram sent it seems by General Hancock to General Plaisted, of Maine, when it was said that the result of Tuesday's election was a fusion victory in that State:

"GOVERNOR'S ISLAND, N. Y., *Sept.* 14, 1880.

"To Hon. H. M. PLAISTED, Bangor, Maine:

"Accept my congratulations on the glorious result of your campaign." *Your* campaign—it seems really when we think of it to have been in one sense very much Mr. Plaisted's campaign. This way of putting it reminds me of the end of an Indian as related by a man who said he shot him. Said he: "I shot an Injun, and I wouldn't believe an Injun could spread so—I shot him, and he spread down four blankets and a Buffalo skin and just got down and died all over them."

Mr. Plaisted seems to have spread a good deal of canvass and just got down and died all over it—there is truth in calling it his campaign. General Hancock proceeds: "It will inspire *our* friends with confidence and strengthen them in the preliminary battles which remain to be fought elsewhere, and which need all *our* forces.

"W. S. HANCOCK."

This last statement I believe—"*need all our forces*," that is to say, all the inflationists and all others who can be induced to vote the Democratic ticket—the indications are that it will require more than all these forces.

Now read along with this dispatch the address of the Secretary of the "National Democratic Labor party," on the same day. Says this address: "Our victory in Maine surpasses expectations." The sageness of that remark reminds me of Isaac Newton, who used to be Commissioner of Agriculture—an excellent old man, but not as able as his giant namesake. Had he been a South Carolina census taker, he wouldn't have been handy at all. They thought the old gentleman was spending too much money, and they brought him to book before a committee to give an account of himself. They badgered him awhile, and then he said: "The fact is the expenses of my Department has exceeded my most sanguine expectations—and I knowed they would all the time."

"Our victory in Maine exceeds expectations. A straight Greenback candidate for Governor has been elected, and two or three Congressmen with the Legislature. The party of Solon Chase is victorious over the hard money Republicans and Bourbon Democrats." After some further pleasant allusions to the Bourbons, the address adds: "Their own party having fallen to pieces, they lent our ticket their support in hopes to usurp the credit of our victory." The address closes by predicting "the coming disintegration of Bourbon Democracy, and their final surrender to the despised 'rag baby.'" "By order of the National Executive Committee.

"LEE CRANDALL, *Secretary.*"

I ask honest money Democrats to consider the spectacle here presented. General Hancock, the spokesman and exponent of his party, sits down in seriousness, when he supposed Maine had elected as Governor a man never a Democrat, and now snake-bitten with the delusion of fiat money inflation, and offers his congratulations and rejoicing over such a result. Last year the avowed inflation vote in Maine was about 48,000, and the Democratic vote only about 22,000; so that Mr. Plaisted's support was two-thirds of it from out and out avowed paper money expansionists. On this state of case, the man the Democrats propose for President makes lightning his messenger to exclaim: " Accept my congratulations on the glorious result of your campaign."

Looking around on the men seated on the platform, and remembering the lineage of which they come, I remind them of ancestral teachings and achievements. What would be thought of such an episode and of such a posture of a great party, by the illustrious men of many nationalities—men profoundly learned in the science of government and national prosperity—who came to these shores, and building, not in the gray twilight of dawning experience, but with the beams of all the centuries streaming upon them, laid deep the foundations of a government of the people, for the people, and by the people.

What would they say of such a predicament of a party whose name descended from grand epochs in our history, seems the only ancient possession that remains—a party which, spurning the teachings of Jefferson, Jackson and the rest, seeks such affiliations and resorts to such shifts. What would they say of a party whose leader and mouthpiece in the last quarter of the nineteenth century publicly applauds the event, when he supposed that a State has given a vote in favor of National degradation, National dishonor and National absurdity?

The Great Work of Resumption.

In the face of the facts, bald and arrant as the claim is, the country is gravely told of wondrous Democratic economies, and it now begins to be stated, that the resumption of specie payments was really brought about by the frugality of a Democratic Congress. If a race was to be sailed on the sea of fiction, the inventor of this statement would surely take the cup.

The resumption of specie payments was a transcendent achievement. The credit of it belongs to some party, and to that party future generations will look back with grateful admiration. Whoever would know the truth about it can easily do so.

Clamoring for Repudiation.

After the war we had afloat well toward a thousand millions of paper currency. It fluctuated in value from 38 to 70 cents in the dollar. The public debt was more than $2,800,000,000, and more than $2,300,0,0,000 of it bore interest. The annual interest charge was $150,000,000. The first Presidential election afterwards was in 1868. The two parties, of course, arrayed themselves on the greatest financial issue which has ever arisen in this country, or perhaps in any country. The question was, what should be done with the colossal debt inflicted by the rebellion, and with the sea of paper promises we had been compelled to put out. The Democratic party pronounced for repudiation. The declaration was covert and indirect, but it meant repudiation. They resolved that all debts should be paid in paper promises unless the obligation expressly on its face said otherwise, or unless the law mentioned that coin should be paid. They resolved that " Government bonds and all other securities " should all be taxed. They resolved that " every species of property " should be taxed, and taxed at its "real value." They resolved that there should be but one currency for the Government and the " bondholder." Taken together, these declarations were plain repudiation.

Nobody pretended that the obligations of the Government were payable in honest money, for the reasons which alone could allow them to be so paid under the Democratic resolution. Had their payment in honest money been specified literally and technically in the way required by the resolution, there would have been no efficacy of meaning in such a resolve; and declaring that the bondholder should have only the same currency that the Government received, clearly and conclusively meant that payment of bonds was to be made in legal-tender notes.

The bonds had been sold on an express agreement that they should never be taxed, and exemption from taxation had entered into the transaction and been discounted as an element of value, and paid for in the price given for the bonds. To tax not only the bonds, but " every species of property at its real value," would have taxed a barrel of flour as well as a barrel of whisky, would have taxed land, and all else. Such a scheme would not only have worn a frontlet of repudiation, but would have thrown into chaos the whole revenue and business of the country. This was the Democratic position.

The Republican Position.

The Republicans in their National Convention declared two things: First, that repudiation is a national crime; and that every debt must be paid to the uttermost, not according to the letter, but the spirit of the law. Second, that the wise course was to improve our credit so as to refund our bonded debt at lower interest, and that this could not be done if repudiation, open or covert, partial or total, was threatened or suspected. On this platform Gen. Grant was elected. His first Presidential syllable was spoken on the portico of the Capitol to assembled thousands, and spoken with lips which only an instant before had touched the Bible to solemnize an oath of faithfulness in office. In his inaugural address then delivered, stand these words:

" A great debt has been contracted in securing to us and our posterity the Union; the payment of this debt, principal and interest, as well as the return to a specie basis as soon as it can be accomplished without material detriment to the debtor class or to the country at large, must be provided for. To protect the national honor, every dollar of Government indebtedness should be paid in gold, unless otherwise expressly stipulated in the contract. Let it be understood that no repudiator of one farthing of our public debt will be trusted in public place, and it will go far toward strengthening a credit which ought to be the best in the world, and will ultimately enable us to replace the debt with bonds bearing less interest than we now pay."

Public Credit Act—1869.

This significant declaration produced a deep sensation. Both houses of Congress were Republican.

Immediately a bill was introduced in each house "to strengthen the public credit." In less than a fortnight it had passed both houses and was approved by President Grant March 18, 1869. It was the first act he ever signed. It declared that "the faith of the United States is solemnly pledged to the payment in coin or its equivalent of all the obligations of the United States not bearing interest, known as United States notes, and of all the interest-bearing obligations of the United States, except in cases where the law authorizing the issue of any such obligations had expressly provided that the same may be paid in lawful money or other currency than gold and silver. * * * And the United States also solemnly pledges its faith to make provision at the earliest practicable period for the redemption of the United States notes in coin."

This bill was resisted by the solid Democracy in both houses. They voted against it, they voted against considering it, they voted for amendments to pervert and reverse its meaning. Senator Thurman, of Ohio, moved to add to it: "Provided that nothing herein contained shall apply to obligations called 5-20 bonds." Every Democratic Senator present voted for this, every Republican voted against it. The 5-20 bonds then constituted the great bulk of the public debt, and this proviso would have frustrated and vitiated the whole act. Senator Davis, of Kentucky, moved to amend so as to scale down the bonds to the coin value at the time of the currency received for them. This was supported by the Democrats, Senator Bayard, of Delaware, among others, speaking in its favor. Senator Vickers, of Maryland, moved to amend so as to prevent coin ever being purchased to be used to pay bonds. Senator Bayard denounced the bill as wrong, unwise, and as a "stock jobbing operation." After all this the bill passed, and not one Democrat voted for it in either house.

Funding Act of 1870.

The next step in this progress was the Funding Act of July, 1870, the act authorizing the redemption of the 5-20 or 6 per cent bonds by negotiating bonds bearing lower interest. All the Democrats resisted this bill also, and voted against it. Exempting the new bonds from taxation was opposed. In the Senate, Mr. Bayard moved to strike out the provision and to subject the bonds to taxation; all the Democrats voted for it. Again, Mr. Bayard moved an amendment to bring back the State banking system, and all the Democrats voted for that also. The bill was at length carried by Republican votes. By this time our currency had much appreciated, and funding at lower interest began.

Opposing Specie Resumption.

In 1874, by a vote not Democratic alone, an inflation bill made its way through both houses. This bill proposed to keep out permanently twenty-six millions of legal tender notes belonging to the Treasury reserve which had been put out temporarily during the panic of 1873, and to put out eighteen millions more. The suffering produced by the panic drove many Republicans into the support of this measure as an experiment and expedient for relief.

The pressure upon President Grant to induce him to sign it, exceeded anything of the kind I have ever witnessed. Men who should have upheld his hands, not only threw their weight upon him, but industriously criticised and even ridiculed his venturing to set up his opinion against a majority in such a crisis. He vetoed the bill, however. In his Message returning it unsigned, he referred to the declaration of the Republican party, to his inaugural, to the act of 1869 already cited, and he said the proposed act would violate faith, and he was against it. This happened on the 22d of April, 1874.

Foreshadow of the Resumption Act.

About a month later a conversation occurred one evening between the President and his chief adviser, Secretary Fish, and others, about the wise course out of the increased difficulties which had come from the disasters of the year before. One of those present at this conversation was Senator Jones, of Nevada. So struck was he with the views expressed by President Grant, that the next day (June 4, 1874,) he by letter requested that the substance of them should be put in writing and a copy sent him. This was done, and the memorandum made by the President was handed about among members of the two houses, and afterward found its way into print. Here it is. It is the foreshadow of the Resumption act, to which the veto had paved the way. I read two passages:

"I believe it a high and plain duty to return to a specie basis at the earliest practical day, not only in compliance with legislative and party pledges, but as a step indispensable to lasting national prosperity. I believe, further, that the time has come when this can be done, or at least begun, with less embarrassment to every branch of industry than at any future time, after resort has been had to unstable and temporary expedients to stimulate unreal prosperity and speculation on a basis other than coin, the recognized medium of exchange throughout the commercial world. The particular mode selected to bring about a restoration of the specie standard is not of so much consequence as that some plan be devised, the time fixed when currency shall be exchangeable for coin at par, and the plan adopted rigidly adhered to. * * * I would like to see a provision that at a fixed day—say, July 1, 1876—the currency issued by the United States should be redeemed in coin on presentation to any Assistant Treasurer, and that all the currency so redeemed should be canceled and never re-issued. To effect this it would be necessary to authorize the issue of bonds, payable in gold, bearing such interest as would command par in gold, to be put out by the Treasury only in such sums as should from time to time be needed for the purpose of redemption."

The Resumption Act.

It was not long before this advice found the form of law. A committee composed wholly of Republican Senators, of whom I was myself one, prepared the bill now known as the Resumption act. It was not the work of any one Senator, nor did it express literally and in full, perhaps, the views of any single member of the committee. It was a compromise of somewhat conflicting opinions. It was submitted to every Republican member of the Senate, and every one, after consideration, determined to vote for it. It was brought forward in the Senate, and every Republican Senator did vote for it. Every Democratic Senator present voted against it. It went to the House, and there encountered a solid Democratic opposition, but it was carried by Republican votes. President Grant promptly signed it. It fixed the 1st of January, 1879, for the resumption of specie payments; and when the day came, as noiselessly and naturally as night melts into day, specie payments were resumed.

Democratic Opposition to Resumption.

The adoption of this bill for resumption is easier told than it was done. The Democracy rose as one man in both houses against it. It was denounced as an absurdity and a sham, and was called many wild and uncleanly names. Senator Thurman, Senator Bayard, and other Democratic Senators, vehemently opposed it. This was in January, 1875. Immediately Democrats of all shades, including the Greenbacker, the country over, opened fire on the act. The next year the Democratic party met in National Convention at St. Louis. There the Republican party was denounced for "enacting hindrances to a return to specie payments." The climax of the resolution was in these words: "As such hindrance we denounce the Resumption act of 1875, and we here demand its repeal." Mr. Tilden, the nominee of the Convention, in his letter of acceptance, stood up to the platform, and also railed against the act, and throughout the canvass reasons were given which no man could number why resumption never would, never could, take place under such a law. At the next session repeal bills were brought forward, and the Democrats voted for them separately and as riders to appropriation bills.

Prosperity Despite the Democrats.

Meanwhile, the world seeing that we meant to be honest after all, notwithstanding repudiation at the South and threats in the North, and vicious declarations in national conventions, it became easy to negotiate 4½ and 4 per cent. bonds at par and above par. This was done, and the debt has melted away at the rate of $2,000,000 a month; the interest charge has been reduced one-half, and when the bonds of high interest rate still outstanding fall due, in 1881 and afterward, they also will be replaced by 4 or 3.65 per cent. bonds, and then the interest charge will fall much lower still. This all looks pretty well—very well by the side of the exploits of the last Democratic Administration—Mr. Buchanan's—which increased the debt tenfold in time of peace, paid 12 per cent. interest on Treasury notes, and sold 6 per cent. 20 year bonds for 89 cents on the dollar. It is well to add that during the last five years of their Congressional control the Republicans dismissed one hundred and twenty millions of annual taxes, thirty-one millions of tariff duties, and eighty-nine millions of internal revenue. I hold up the record since 1860, when the bloody drama of the rebellion opened, and I say that the Democratic party has been wrong and beaten on all the great issues of the century.

Cry for a "Change."

A triumphant Nationality—a regenerated Constitution—a free Republic—an unbroken country—untarnished credit—solvent finances—unparalleled prosperity—all these are ours, despite the policy and the efforts of the Democratic party.

Along with the amazing improvement in National finances, we have amazing individual thrift on every side. In every walk of life new activity is felt. Labor, agriculture, manufactures, commerce, enterprise and investments, all are flourishing, content and hopeful. But in the midst of this harmony and encouragement comes a harsh discord crying, "Give us a change—anything for a change." This is not a bearing year for "a change." Every other crop is good, but not the crop of "change"—that crop is only good when the rest are bad. The country does not need or wish the change proposed, and the pressing invitation of our Democratic friends is much like "Will you walk into my parlor? said the spider to the fly." A good-natured but firm "No, I thank you," will be the response at the polls.

The Candidates.

The candidates we support, besides being Republican, are largely fitted for the stations which await them.

Some service with him in Congress has made me well acquainted with Gen. Garfield. That he has the intelligence, experience and habits of mind which fit a man for the Presidential office, I think I know. Without early advantages, he, years ago, achieved prominence among the leading men in public life, and that prominence he has maintained ever since in all the collisions between individuals and parties. That he is competent to the duties before him, there seems to me no reason to doubt.

Of Gen. Arthur it seems needless here to speak. Most of you know him, and all who know him know a high-souled, honorable man—honorable in every position in which he ever stood—a man to be trusted in every relation of life. If the character, the popularity and personality of the candidate can add strength to the Republican cause, Gen. Arthur will add that strength wherever he is known, and most where he is best known.

Upon its record and its candidates the Republican party asks the country's approval, and stands ready to avow its purpose for the future. It proposes to rebuild our commercial marine, driven from the sea by Confederate cruisers, aided and abetted by foreign hostility. It proposes to foster labor, industry and enterprise. It proposes to stand for education, humanity and progress. It proposes to administer the Government honestly, to preserve amity with all the world, observing our own obligations with others, and seeing that others observe theirs with us, to protect every citizen of whatever birth or color in his rights and equality before the law, in cluding his right to vote and to be counted, to uphold the public credit and the sanctity of engagements; and by doing these things, the Republican party proposes to assure to industry, humanity and civilization in America the amplest welcome and the safest home.—*From the New-York Semi-Weekly Times, Tuesday, September 21, 1880.*

The Address of Hon. WILLIAM M. EVARTS, in the Academy of Music, New-York City, Wednesday evening, September 29, 1880.

MR. CHAIRMAN, FELLOW-CITIZENS, LADIES AND GENTLEMEN: The kind reception which you have accorded, in advance, to whatever I may be able to contribute in the canvass now pending, to the proper judgment of the American people on the great issue before them, inclines me to think that I was wrong in an opinion which I have intended to espouse, that it was the press that was the only potent orator in these popular discussions. By their magnificent enterprise and apparatus they speak to millions where we speak to thousands. By their perpetual possession of the public ear they lay down, line upon line, precept upon precept, in season and out of season, whether men will hear or whether they will forbear. The orator has no such hold upon the attention or the respect of the people. But I know that if one speak, even in a whisper, in the cause of his country, and for love of it, the people of the United States will catch up the sound; and wherever patriotism has not died out, and wherever liberty is not suppressed, and wherever suffrage is honored and respected, they will carry on that voice, though lost in the final decision which has triumphed, or has faded away.

The question before the country, the question before this vast representative assembly, is, to which of the two parties that divide the United States the conduct of its affairs for the ensuing four years may be safely, may be wisely, may be hopefully, may be dutiably trusted by a people loving its honor, respecting its duty, and the value of the institutions which we have inherited from a noble ancestry. Twenty-four years ago the people of this country intrusted the management of their affairs to the Democratic party of the United States. Twenty-four years ago they trusted to a Democrat of Pennsylvania, Buchanan, [laughter and hisses.] the management of her affairs. To-day it is proposed to you that you shall restore the same Democratic party in the hands of another Pennsylvania Democrat. Twenty years ago the people of the country intrusted the management of their affairs to the Republican party, born of patriotism and devoted to liberty. [Applause.] Twenty years ago they thus intrusted their affairs to the hands of an Illinois Republican. [Applause.] And, substantially, the people of this country are to answer to-day the inquiry to their conscience, the test of history, the judgment of the world, whether they repent of taking power from Buchanan, and repent of giving power to Lincoln.

The People Rebuking the Democrats.

Active fault-finders may, in this process of 20 years, have had private or public grievances. There may have been failures of equality always to the greatness of the demands, but as history reads it, as foreign nations read it, as the great God-fearing people of the United States read it, if, next November the Pennsylvania Democrat is restored to power, it is a verdict that the people have tired of patriotism and are weary of liberty. ["Good, good," and great applause.] Now, in these 20 years, the Democratic party, made up as it was when it was trusted under Buchanan, asked—five times asked—to be restored to power, and five times the people have answered in the same way: "Never; no, never." [Applause.] They tried it during the war, when the Nation was in the throes of desperation, when every coward had joined the Democratic party—if he had a party—when every coward in the whole North was arrayed in the army of non-fighting traitors, and the people said: "It is sad to us that our youth have perished, and that our youth must perish; it is sad to us that mourners are to go about our streets for a whole generation; it is sad to us that the substance of this people, thrifty, industrious, fond of the pursuits of gain, should be poured out like water, and that, so far as we can see, the last dollar may be put forth. But we know what made our population what it was; we know what made our waste, and we will maintain 'Liberty and Union, one and inseperable,' though the last man should fall in his lot, and the last dollar should be spent in the conflict." [Applause.] They asked again after the war was over, and after the resistance to the loyal Government had taken the form of controversies about reconstruction, and the appeal to the people was that the Republican party, having fallen into a quarrel, and having on their hands a great impeachment and a great struggle within their own ranks, would now, at least, under this experience of vicissitudes of concord and union among themselves, trust power to the Democratic party united—no longer divided between combatants in arms and non-combatants in treachery—the united Democratic party—and the people said: "No. [Applause.] The party that carried us through the war, when you said it was a failure, shall conduct the Government now, and you shall submit to it. [Applause.] And that you may understand what we mean, we put the great captain, who received your surrender, in charge of the Government." [Applause.]

Well, four years went on and they said: "Now, our people are fond of a change." [Laughter.] So you thought when you took up arms in 1860, and we showed you that we were not fond of a change. We loved our Government as it was. We adored our country as it was. You then proceeded to try and inaugurate a change, and enforce it by the most telling arguments that the Democratic party ever issued [applause]—powder and shot and shell. [Applause.] No; we will keep the Government so long as the Democratic party holds out the threat and presents the array, and avows the principles we have resisted up to this time. We will keep it in the hands of the same Captain of our armies that we trusted before. [Applause.]

Well, they said: "Now we have had long peace and prosperity." Long peace and prosperity! Think of the emphasis the Democratic party put upon that in the year 1876. "We have had long peace and prosperity." [Laughter.] Why, do they suppose that we are a nation of red Indians to whom a few years of peace seem irksome and tiresome, and who desire a change. [Applause and laughter.] Did they suppose that when the laborers of the country, under the desperate tangle of our finances that the rebellion had brought upon us, were working upon half time and upon half wages, did they think that that was the complete prosperity that the laboring people of the Nation should enjoy? We answered: "No; we will elect a volunteer soldier [applause] that never hid behind his charming family, but went to the war and served to the end, and we will trust him." [Applause.] Well, then, they said, "What can we do to please these people? We have offered them a change four times since they trusted Lincoln, and they said they would not change at all. Why, they must be a people of fixed principles. [Great laughter and applause.] They must be a people that understand their own minds, [laughter,] and it must be they think they can take care of their own interests. What an extraordinary people! A people, they say, wedded to such a continuance in well doing and with such a sagacious and persistent selection of the means of carrying out their purposes is on the very brink of despotism. What can save them—a people that chooses Republicans for 20 years? Why, what can save them from the very abyss of military despotism?"

Saved from Military Despotism.

We thought that when, in 1865, we had ended the greatest war that modern times have ever seen, and when it waged against free and equal institutions by a great military power, we thought that was nearer a threat of military despotism than anybody had ever dreamed possible in the United States, and when we got out of it we thought we were rid of it forever, and we are. It is not now by the ranks of war and its armaments that they attempt to overpower you. It is by your own frank, generous, confiding natures, which, like charity, "suffer long and are kind," that they expect us to yield, from an unguarded people, what no powers in the world could take from the people.

Well, they said: "Only look at the alternatives we offered you. We offered you in 1864 a great Union General—Gen. McClellan." Well, he was a great Union General, and the united South, in arms, not voting, and this desiccated Democracy that attended upon their will at the North said: "What, not take a great Union General? Why, what a

pledge of fidelity, when you see as plain as day that if you only put yourselves under that great Union General, McClellan, the South will lay down their arms because they won't have anything to fight for, they will have gained it." [Applause.] An admirable suggestion to a people that is fond of peace and likes commerce and manufactures and a great deal of peaceful industry and development—a charming proposal! The answer was: "This candidate of yours is better than his party. He was only unready, but his party was untrue. But yet the great statesman that the affections of the people had twined about, that has written a more glorious page in our history than any one since Washington, that has made liberty universal, and has dispelled the shades of color and broken the lines of race, was a good enough President for us, though he was not a great General of the Union Army, and had not been either unready or untrue during the trials."

Well, in 1868, they said: "We offer you a candidate now (always from the North)—Gov. Seymour, a candidate better than his party." Well, that we agreed was true. But how under heaven should these people think—when ours is a government, not of men, not of kings, not of nobles, but of the mass of the popular feeling and of public principle that is represented in the Presidency—how, I say, should they think that a party could commend itself to the suffrage by saying its candidate was better than they? What a reason for taking a party, that it is worse than the candidate! [Laughter.] I don't know but our countrymen have eaten of the insane root and have gone mad, but I don't think that any answers they made to that proposition in the past show that they have lost their wits at all. Well, now, Gov. Seymour was better than the party. In fact, as he has gone on increasing in excellence, I think he is better than any party, or, in fact, I don't know but he is better than all his fellow-men. [Laughter.] That may be. I know he showed a very extreme instance of that forgiving spirit and humbleness of soul which are said to mark the Christian when, clothed with the sword of power and speaking in the name of authority, when your streets were red with the blood of innocents, he spoke to the rioters as his friends. Now, that suits a man for some departments of life, but not for the command of the Army and Navy of the United States. [Great applause.]

More of Democratic Offers.

Well, in 1872 they said: "Those people are very hard to please. We have offered them candidates that were better than our party; now we will offer them another candidate, a man who don't belong to our party at all. [Laughter.] These Northern men," they said, "are of rather melodramatic temperament. They like a show, and what could be a finer show than for a great party to take a candidate for the Presidency right off from the top of the other party. [Laughter.] Well," they said, "you must admit that that candidate is better than our party." [Laughter.] They said: "We only presented you before a loyal patch upon a moth-eaten garment of rebellion and Democracy." [Laughter.] "Well," we replied, "we admit that you have not presented a patch, but you have actually clothed yourselves in another man's garment," and we added : " Our notion that the party that is in power ought to be in power, is the transaction which the American people pass upon in their Presidential elections, and we will vote for Gen. Grant and not for Horace Greeley." [Applause.]

"Well," they said, "we have tried everything. Now we will have a man after our own heart, a man that does not come from the Republican party, a man that is *not* better than our own party, who can tell about these fickle, melodramatic Northerners, who are always running into scrapes for want of prudence, thrift and forethought—a people that you cannot keep out of the fire or out of ;the water." And so they presented our distinguished fellow-citizen and my classmate—Samuel J. Tilden.— [Laughter.] Well, that was very fine. Now they say : Look at him ! See how we have come back to our true colors ! Did you ever see," say they, " a pattern that was better matched by a patch on it than the Democratic party was by Samuel J. Tilden. [Laughter.] Now you cannot object to that." " Well," the people said : "Let us look at that. Didn't you have an old ticket and a popular suffrage on it then 20 years ago—1856 ?" (for this Tilden candidacy was in 1876.) Let us look at that. Somehow or other, it strikes us that history is repeating itself, and that the same voters that voted for Buchanan are to vote for Tilden, and we will agree that, so far as we can see, in record and in temper, Tilden and Buchanan are as like as two peas. [Laughter.] Now, we have had that pattern before," the people said, "and we will choose Hayes." [Great applause.]

Well, now, gentlemen, we come along down. At their elections the Democratic party has been made up of the same constituents—the solid South and the dessicated Democracy of the North, [laughter.] and the people have passed upon them as such. And now they present again the same combination—the solid South and the dessicated Democracy of the North, neither more nor less—and they have chosen a candidate, saying : " Having tired ourselves with pleasing you by offering every pattern and patch, we will give you another candidate that is better than our party." Indeed, a very eminent public thinker and writer, who seldom speaks within bounds, has thought to frighten the people of the country that espoused the Republican candidacy by saying that our candidate, God bless him ! Gen. Garfield, [tremendous applause and cheering]—this is the crushing criticism upon him—is no better than his party. Well, we thought so, we thought so. We thought the party was as good as could be, and that, while it could find in its ranks and in its lead many men that were worthy of its honors and its votes, we really must be excused from saying that we could find any one man that was better than the great Republican party. [Applause.]

Now, this is an extraordinary business. The Democratic party, conscious of the beam in its own eye, and knowing that there is not even a mote in the eye of the Republican party, [laughter,] has sought to make a balance of the beam in the Democratic party against the mote in the Republican candidate. Well, that is an extraordinary situation ! A whole party trying to make a balance out of themselves against what they charge as a blemish in our candidate ! They try to make a balance against the enormous iniquities unrepented of and not yet laid aside; every epaulet, every plume, every ruffle, every cartridge-box, every sword-belt, every holster still surrounding the Democratic party in its relation to our institutions and our prosperity, they think to draw attention to what they call a mote in our candidate.

" No Better than his Party."

Well, gentlemen, when Mr. Black, desiring to help his party, said that Garfield personally was one of the honestest, warmest-hearted, most guileless men that he ever knew ; [applause;] that he was a man of genius, of learning, of eloquence, of popular power, he knew where to put the only arrow that could pierce any harness of our candidate when he said : " But, good as he is, he cannot in politics and in government be any better than his party." [Laughter and applause.] Now, Gen. Garfield [applause] stands before the American people as a candidate for its highest honors upon a plane of longer and more varied experience, of better proved capacity, of larger benevolence, of a comprehensive mind, and a tender heart for his countrymen's difficulties and dangers and sorrows, than any candidate that has been presented to the people of the United States by either party since Henry Clay.

I had occasion to remark four years ago on the superciliousness of our Eastern people here—New-York and New-England, and the Atlantic board—of taking it for granted that because the candidate lifted up on the shoulders of the great people of the West was not as familiar to our observation and as clear in our estimate as one of our great men, of assuming that he was not so fit as he should be, and voting in the dark against him as so many did against President Hayes. But now that he has stood in the light for four years ; now that his countrymen and the public men of Europe have estimated his public services, and when our people feel the full rush of honesty, of fidelity, which brought prosperity in the very fingerends of every man in the land, they begin to think that if they had known President Hayes as well four years ago as they do now, he would have had a larger majority. [Great applause and cries of " That's so."] We had the same talk about him then that they would like to engage you in now about Gen. Garfield. They had the same talk about him then, I say, that he seemed to be a good man, but they did not know exactly by what counsels and advisers he would be surrounded. They did not know who was to lead him, and who was to push him, and who was to guide him ; and as they saw various adventurers, leaders of the party, that looked as if they would like to have a large share in the Government, some of whom they liked, and some of whom they did not like, why, people said, they would vote in the dark until they knew who was going to manage him. Nothing has managed him but love of country, an upright nature, a sincerity in the homely virtues of American common life that will long be remembered in the affections of the men and women of the United States. [Applause.]

Now, people begin to say—Democrats—"Oh! If your party had only re-nominated President Hayes, why, we could not have stood against him; he has the hearts of the people. But as for Garfield, we don't feel so sure." In other words, they feel about Garfield now as they felt about President Hayes four years ago. And four years hence, they will feel about Garfield as they feel about President Hayes now. [Great applause.] They used to be, in following the Republican party and adopting its credits as belonging to themselves, at a safe marching distance of about 12 or 8 years behind them, but now they are beginning to crowd us, for they are only four years behind. If they will only keep on and study our step and learn our music, it may bring them abreast of us some time or other. [Laughter.]

Only two "Superbs" in History.

Well now, having discussed Gen. Garfield, who is *not* better than his party, let us look at Gen. Hancock, who *is* better than his party. [Laughter.] Gen. Hancock is a great and faithful General of the armies of the United States. [Applause mingled with hisses.] He was a faithful General in the war, and in his place in the Army he has been a faithful General since, and no Republican seeks either to obscure or belittle his claims upon his countrymen. But when General Hancock is sought to be the "make-way" to bring up the party whose candidate he is to the standard of a party like ours, that has seen a Lincoln, [applause,] a Grant, [applause,] and a Hayes, [renewed applause,] he has got to have a great deal more avoirdupois to weigh us down. [Laughter.]

What do these people think a change of party government means? Is it, as some of these palaverers would have us suppose, a toss of a copper or wave of a hand, and all is over? Is that so? Is that what a change of party means? What a change of parties in a great nation like this means? What a change of parties from the one that preserved the country to the other that attacked it—is that all that it means? Does it mean nothing to the poor freedmen of the South whether, all else being against them, the Federal Executive is to be against them too? Does it mean nothing to the loyal people of the country, to the heroes of your fights, to the leaders in your Cabinets, and to the memories of the great statesmen that have passed away, whether the American people are to put that party and those memories and those living statesmen to an open shame; and whether they are to exalt over their heads the party that, in the name of the people and with the people's power, we have resisted until we saved the country from war and preserved it from disasters of peace? I tell you, gentlemen, that the relations of a people to their public men and of the public men to the people are reciprocal; and when a nation turns its back in prosperity upon those who never turned their backs, in the field or in the Cabinet, against the enemies of the country, the people has gone over to the side of the enemies of the country. [Applause.] Manners change at different ages, but this affair of a transfer of power from one party to another diametrically its opposite is, with a proper allowance for the difference of manners and the ameliorations of life, pretty much the same thing. And, as I remember but one great character in history that received from his countrymen the surname of "The Superb"—only one "Tarquinius Superbus," of Rome—I thought I would see whether history that had repeated itself here with this magnificent title would not find some other traits of resemblance in the transactions of Tarquinius's government.

The King of Rome that preceded Tarquinius had made a change in the Roman Constitution in favor of popular rights. He had endowed with a share in the suffrage and in the commonwealth the plebeians, and it was a thorn in the side of the haughty classes that domineered over them that the poor plebeians should be trusted with the suffrage. Now, I think that Lincoln did something of that kind for the poor plebeians of the South. [Applause.] I think the Republican party has done, not only something, but all that its powers thus far have permitted it to do, to establish those popular rights—to be sure only in the hands of the plebeians. Tarquin came forward and slew Tullius, and the great reformers that represented the people died by the hand of the assassin, and then, when he had thus got power, he at once took away from the very plebeians every vestige of their rights. He put to death all Senators that had voted for it. He took into his hands the whole administration of justice, and he slew or exiled all that were obnoxious to his will. Well, gentlemen, let me say for the Roman people that Tarquinius Superbus was the last king that ever sat upon the throne in Rome, [applause,] and until the time that Cassius and Brutus completed the assassination of Cæsar—down to that time there had always been a Brutus that would brave the eternal devils to be King. Now, as I say, manners have changed. Three hundred years ago, in England, they sent their foreign Ministers to the tower, and beheaded their Archbishops. But the principle of human nature which makes the gulf so wide between the principles of Servius Tullius and Tarquinius Superbus, and so wide the gulf between the principles of Abraham Lincoln and the party of Gen. Hancock, and change of parties do not pass like a summer dream. No, it is to be from our hearts, if at all, and, thank God, it is to be only if we have the will to allow it. [Applause.]

Taking up Mr. English.

Now, gentlemen, we have candidates also called Vice-Presidents, and I take Mr. English first. I have never seen any very open or public avowal of why the Democrats nominated Mr. English. He was not in our minds at all. I do not know that his countrymen were turning him over among the men that they thought the Democrats could nominate. It will not do to put it wholly upon the fact that he is a rich banker, and so we look at the speeches he has made in Congress twenty years ago, when they talked about abolitionists and about the blacks and about the plebeians in the fashion that the old Democrat used to talk about our notions of befriending the people. There did not seem to be a reason for that, and I leave it to his neighbors, who have expressed their minds about him, whether there is any thing in that large liberality of personal character which makes a man popular in spite of the badness of his political principles. I do not understand that there is a very large claim on that score. I do observe in his letter of acceptance that he seems to be of a very sympathetic nature—feels for the sufferings of others—because I observe that he expresses great interest in the toiling millions of his countrymen. Well, these are all trifling matters, perhaps, but yet they do show whether a party is sincere or not ; and when I saw that Mr. English had this yearning of heart for the toiling millions of his countrymen. I could but think of a story that our excellent judge, Judge Brady, is fond of telling at the expense of our profession—for there is one good thing about us lawyers, that we do repeat all the jokes against ourselves that we can pick up. Well, a young man who had lost his father, and had a small estate of $50 from a solvent debtor that yet he needed to collect by law, waited upon a lawyer in the village who, he knew, was a friend of his father, and asked him to collect it. The lawyer received him as only a lawyer knows how to receive a client, [laughter,] and admitted frankly that he did know his father, that he loved him as a father, and nothing would give him greater pleasure than to collect that little bill. So, when the process had brought in the money, word was sent to the young man that the debt had been collected, and he would be glad to pay it to him, deducting the costs, and so the lawyer handed out to the young man, who was full of gratitude, $15 out of the $50, at which he seemed a little dazed in counting it, and the lawyer said, "Why, is it not all right ; are not the $15 there ?" "Oh, yes," says the young man, "there are $15 ; I was only thinking how lucky it was for me that you didn't know my grandfather." [Great laughter.] And I could not help thinking how lucky it was for these toiling millions of our countrymen that only a few thousand of them were within the immediate friendship of Mr. English. [Applause and laughter.]

And now Gen. Arthur, [applause,] our townsman and our friend, is proposed to make one more in the long roll of Vice-Presidents that New-York has given to the Nation. Everybody knows of Gen. Arthur that he never sought an honor, but took only such as came to him by the free will of his fellow-citizens ; everybody knows that in the lead of the great administrations of our political affairs, he has been trusted and honored, and the people of the United States accept this candidacy from this, our great State and City, and, knowing of his character and position, intend to make his term the ninth Presidential term that has been filled by Vice-Presidents from the State of New-York.

The Confidence in Republicanism.

Now, gentlemen, let us see what are the great questions before the people. In the first place, let me submit to your intelligence that the people of the United States do not need to be asked to reconsider any of the decisions that they made in 1864, or in 1868, or in 1872, or in 1876. Those have passed into the judgment of their countrymen, and the people have said that the Republican party should keep power, notwithstanding any thing that could be urged, with reason or without, by hypercriticism or by honest discontent, that the party, the great party and its great and honest leaders, should be kept in power at all those terms. Now, if I am right in this,

what ought always to be the great question for a people practical in their tastes and interested in their prosperity is, what shall we say of the party as it has administered the Government for the past four years? [Applause.] What shall we say of the Democratic party as it has exhibited itself in the last four years? Is it wise, is it prudent, is it for our advantage that the Government should run on for four years more in the conduct of that party that has guided it four years, and in the same way that it has been guided four years? Has the Democratic party, that we condemned during all these previous stages at which our judgment has been called for, has it, in the last four years, helped our credit, helped our peace, helped our public faith, helped our prosperity? We do not need to be told that we live under the Government of a good God. That we knew, even when the Democrats were racking our hearts with sorrow, and rifling our coffers of wealth. It was not a good God that we turned upon and cursed. It was the Democratic party that we turned upon and cursed and defeated, and when this general and universal Providence, protecting us all through a great party, has, in what belongs to Government, in what belongs to prudence, in what belongs to honesty, in what belongs to human wisdom, spread the golden mantle of peace over the whole country, filled our granaries and our warehouses, lit up our forges, set awhirling all our spindles, and asked even for more means to employ the industry of this people, this people are not to be turned aside by saying that it is all a good Providence that did that.

Well, to bring it down a little more concisely in this Democratic devoutness, it seems that we have been living under a financial theocracy for the last eight years, and that John Sherman [applause] was favored by Providence as the best man to carry out the purposes of the Divine wisdom. Well, Mr. Bayard thinks that that, doubtless, was a mistake on the part of Providence, for he ought to have been the prophet under this theocracy. Well, gentlemen, if the Republican party has carried on the Government thus prosperously and to these results by the special favor of Providence, did you ever hear of a more illogical reason to a people than that they should turn them out because Providence was on their side? Do the Democrats expect to get along against Providence or without Providence?

The Republican Party's Work.

But away with these frivolities. No doubt Providence causes His sun to shine upon the evil and the good, and his rain to fall upon the just and the unjust ; but, nevertheless, the farms of the drunkard and the sluggard do not show such a smile of Providence as the farms of the thrifty and the laborious and the temperate. Did not this sunshine and rain fall upon the wide areas of agriculture when our corn was used to burn for fuel, because confidence was destroyed in the country and it could not be moved to the hungry demands of Europe ? But what moves the crops ? Is it the rail-roads and the steamships ? Why, the iron tracks and the trackless paths of the ocean were as open at those times as at these. Why is it that there was no capital, that there was no enterprise ? Why, there was capital and there was enterprise, but the unextricated snarl of our finances, brought about by the war and perpetuated by Democratic obstructions in peace, had frightened capital, and it had hidden itself in the 6 per cent. bonds of the United States. And then, when following in the same path with Abraham Lincoln's Secretary of the Treasury, we set our faces toward John Sherman—favored by his countrymen and favored by Providence as well, no doubt—when he carried through that magnificent financial march to the broad sea of prosperity, which rivals in the fame and in the gratitude of his countrymen that military march that the great Captain, Sherman, took to the sea, [Applause,] then he unbound capital and enterprise, then he dislodged it from its safe shelter under the 6 per cent. bonds and reduced it to the scanty pittance of 4 per cent., and drove it out into the activities of commerce, and the risks of manufactures. And then you had the circle completed as distinctly by this final touch of the human prudence, sagacity, fidelity, and courage of the Republican party, just as distinctly as the natural philosopher completes the circuit of the electric current that surrounds the world.

Now, I would like to know how much the Democratic party did to help Providence out of its difficulties. [Laughter.] I am astonished at this new element in party politics. Why, everybody knows that the conflicts in England and in this country are based upon this proposition—that the party in power is to be blamed for its faults, its errors and even its misfortunes, and that it is to receive the honor of its fidelity, of its wisdom, of its prosperity. [Applause.] And this is the first time that statesmen who valued their public character have gone through the land prating against a party's right to the honor of the things that it had done. Let them say that they will do better—let them say that they will do better *against* Providence than we have done *with* it. Let the country trust them if they will.

Looking at Hancock's Letters.

But they say, that Gen. Hancock, who is better than his party, has always been an excellent friend of the country and its prosperity and faith. Well, now, when a man is a candidate for the Presidency and writes letters, everybody knows that they come substantially from the bottom of his heart. [Laughter.] That is settled. If there is anything that the country can rely upon as true in purpose and in fact, it is a candidate's letters. That we have always known. But, nevertheless, letters are not exactly transactions. When Admiral Coffin, who lived in Cape Cod as a child, had adhered to the British Crown, and risen to a great rank in the Navy, came over to visit this country about 50 years ago, and renew his associations with his people and the familiar scenes of his boyhood, he told his officers that when they got to Cape Cod they would see lobsters that would make them open their eyes—that they would see lobsters that weighed 25 pounds. The rules of the quarter-deck do not permit you to contradict an Admiral flatly, but still some distrust was shown on the faces of those Lieutenants and Captains. "Well," he says, "if you doubt it, I will make you a bet that when we get to Cape Cod I will show you lobsters that weigh 25 pounds." And the bet was made, under this permission of the Admiral.

And when they got there the Admiral scoured the Cape, but he did not find any lobsters that weighed 25 pounds. So he said, "Well, they don't happen to be here just now, but I will get the affidavits of the old fishermen," and he brought a pile of affidavits, that when they were fishermen, in early times, lobsters that weighed 25 pounds were as common as huckleberries are on the Cape. Then it was left to an umpire to decide which had lost or won the bet. And this concise judgment was given by the umpire, which would entitle him to a seat on the Supreme Court of the United States if everything in his life comported with it. His decision was that "Affidavits are not lobsters." [Laughter.] Now, if any one doubted that, they could try to eat an affidavit from any source whatever. People are said sometimes to swallow their oaths, and these written depositions are not very savory food.

Now, candidates' letters are not the decrees of a Democratic caucus, much less the acts of Congress of the United States. If anybody thinks they are, and elects Gen. Hancock in that view, he will have to come back to that sober, common-place judgment, that candidates' letters are not acts of Congress. Now, Gen. Hancock prides himself, and justly, upon having been a consistent and a genuine and earnest Democrat all his life. He was so in 1864. I have never heard that he "kicked," as the phrase was, against the platform at Chicago of the Democratic party. I never heard that he did, and I do not now find that it was made a matter of boast then.

Now, let us look at this party of ours, that has a candidate no better than itself, and the Democratic party, with their candidate that upheld its platform then, and let us see how they compare. It is short reading. The Republicans say in 1864: "We approve the determination of the Government not to compromise with the rebels or to offer them any terms of peace except such as may be based upon an unconditional surrender of their hostility, and a return to their just allegiance to the Constitution and laws of the United States, and we call on the Government to maintain this position, and to prosecute the war with the utmost possible vigor to the complete suppression of the rebellion, in full reliance upon the self-sacrificing patriotism, the heroic valor, and the undying devotion of the American people to the country and its free institutions." [Applause.] I would like to see the Republican now that will not follow his party in that sublime faith through the next election in November. [Applause.] What did the Democratic party say at that very time on this very point? "That this convention does explicitly declare as the sense of the American people, that after four years of failure to restore the Union by the experiment of war, justice, humanity, liberty, and the public welfare demand that immediate efforts be made for a cessation of hostilities, with a view to an ultimate convention of the States or other peaceable means, to the end that at the earliest practicable moment peace may be restored on the federal union of the States." Which was right—the arrogant assumption of the Democrats to speak the deliberate sense of the American people, or the humble faith, in the dark hour and in the shadow of the valley, of the Republican party, that they could rely on the patriotism, the courage, and the undying devotion of the

American people to their country and its free institutions? [Applause.] Now, I think I would rather have a candidate who is not better than that Republican party than a candidate who is a good deal better than that Democratic party.

But in 1868 Gen. Hancock was actively enlisted in the maintenance of the principles then avowed by the Democratic party. He was a candidate before the convention, and received, I think, 144 votes—I will not deprive him of anything—I think 144½ votes. [Laughter.] So, there he is, with his colors nailed to the flag-staff. Now, nothing remained but this war. They had found out that the American people were attached to their institutions. But there we were, with this load of debt, with this embarrassment in the burden of taxation, with a people still tugging and sweating under the burdens that the Democratic party had laid on it. And now, they say, is a time to catch these people in despair. There are no trumpets now, there are no drums, there are no cannon—none of the pomp and circumstance of war to arouse and inflame them. It is the painful, slow drudgery of labor to pay taxes, and of capital to pay tribute to the Government.

The Parties' Records Compared.

Now, we will see how the two parties stand, and how the party that Garfield represents stands by the side of, and in comparison with, the Democratic party. I will read of the Democratic party first: "1868: The bonded debt shall be paid in greenbacks. [Laughter.] Government bonds and all public securities to be taxed equally with all other property." There is the faith of the Nation sacrificed at once. It then arraigns the Republican party "for the unparalleled oppression and tyranny that have marked its career." [Laughter.] Now, this is the smooth-spoken Gen. Hancock, who thinks that the Republican party will not make much of a change if it falls into line behind him. This is the party—our party—that he speaks of as displaying the "unparalleled oppression and tyranny that have marked our career—your career and my career! Let us vote for Hancock! [Laughter.] Again, it announces "that should the Republican party succeed in November next, and inaugurate its President, we will meet as a subjugated and conquered people, amid the ruins of liberty and the fragments of the Constitution!" [Laughter.] Well, I would be very glad to meet Gen. Hancock, as I often have done, almost anywhere. But amid the ruins of liberty and the fragments of the Constitution I would say that I would not recognize him at all. [Laughter.] Then they "regard the reconstruction acts of Congress as usurpations" and "as unconstitutional, revolutionary and void," and yet we are told everything is going on "smoothly"—"in a groove"—in a Republican groove, with only a change of cars and of brakemen, and of engineers, and of conductors, and of Superintendent. [Laughter.] The whole fabric—that splendid fabric—of energy, of courage, of faith, by which the wisdom of the Republicans has drawn the nation out of the horrid, out of the ruinous contacts and destruction of war, and set them on the plane of comparative peace and on the plane of law—all that "usurpation," "unconstitutional, revolutionary, and void!" [Applause.]

What did we say when we were struggling to pay this debt? for I think it must be admitted that the North was to pay, and is to pay, more of that debt than the South. We did not try to "scale it;" we did not try to tax it. What did we do? We speak our mind pretty well. Our platform denounced all forms of repudiation as a national crime. [Great applause.] There is no uncertain sound in that, is there? We did not stop to see whether we could commit a crime and escape punishment in this world or at the hands of Providence. It was enough for us to know that it was a crime. (Reading:) "And the national honor requires the paying of the public debt in the uttermost good faith to all creditors at home and abroad," not only according to the letter, but the spirit of the law under which it was contracted. [Applause.] Lord Coke says, "the letter killeth, but the spirit maketh a lie." And if there was any doubt in the minds of our creditors, whether they were the poor widows and orphans in our land, or the Rothschilds and rich bankers of London, that we would pay a debt that was so sacredly contracted to save all that is worth having in this world, according to the spirit as well as the letter, such a declaration would set them at rest. [Applause.]

Now, let us see the wisdom of the other side. They said, "pay your debt in greenbacks; tax your Government securities." We said that the best policy to diminish our burden of debt is so to improve our credit that capitalists will seek to loan us money at lower rates of interest than we now pay, and must continue to pay so long as repudiation, partial or total, open or covert, is threatened or suspected. [Applause.] Now, there are two ways of getting rid of debt. Which is the true mother of this child of the Nation—the public credit—that bold-faced jade, the Democratic party, that would have cut it in half and left it to perish, or that nursing mother, the Republican party, that sought to cherish and shelter its weakness until it should outgrow it, and become, as it is to-day, the glory and strength of the American people. [Applause.] I am happy to say, Mr. Chairman, that those sentiments of the Republican party were uttered when you were at the head of the finances of the nation. [Applause.]

I am not going to read the later platforms, for they are fresh in your minds. In 1876 they said that the resumption of specie payments was impossible, and would ruin us. Well, as the client said to the lawyer, when he asked him if the magistrate could put him in prison for such and such and such cause, "No," said the lawyer, "he cannot." "But," said the client, "he has; I am in prison." [Laughter.] We did resume specie payments, Did it ruin us? Well, gentlemen, Napoleon used to say that, in the affairs of war, he had noticed that Providence favored the heaviest battalion, and I think that, in the affairs of peace, Providence favors courage, fidelity and faith in the moral government of the world. [Applause.]

The Right of Suffrage.

There are two things that underlie the whole fabric of political society, its interest and its sentiment. One is the suffrage, which is the basis of it all. Another is the largeness and integrity of our country, which this people, for some reason or other, in spite of all the inculcation of Southern dogmas, are insisting upon thinking is greater than any of its parts. Our people know what the elements and traits of free suffrage are, and have resented any attack upon it in any form. What is the education of this people if it be not to value the liberties of others as well as their own? I never knew a King or a noble or priest or rich man that did not value his liberty, and I think some of them were willing even to carry their liberties to the extent of license, as we say. But the question is, whether the strong value the liberties of the weak. The question is, whether the proud value the liberties of the humble. The question is, whether the man of great intellect, of great learning, values the liberties of the ignorant. And when a great section of this country talks about suffrage as an inviolable right, and then, with all its strength, all its pride, all its learning, flaunts itself before this country, boastful that it can intimidate the weak and can deceive the ignorant, I don't think much of their love of liberty, [applause,] except in the sense that Kings and nobles love liberty—for its license—at the expense of the poor, the humble, the ignorant and the weak. That is an old stage of politics in this world, but since the Fourth day of July, 1776, it has not been the politics of the American people, [applause,] and I don't think it will be next November.

Let us see how much the platforms preach, and, at the hustings, the orator's palaver about the suffrage. The platform of the Democratic party speaks of it as the right preservative of all rights, and immediately proceeds to take it away from the blacks. Now, if that right is preservative of all rights, and you take it away from the blacks, cunning as you are, you take away their rights. Now, General Hancock says, in the admirable letter of acceptance, of which his party is so proud, that a free ballot, a full vote, and an honest count is what the people of the United States want. [Applause.] Now, here is a little table that has been used by an accomplished orator throughout the western part of this country, in which he gives the following result of a free ballot, a full vote, and a fair count in 1876:

	Hayes.	Tilden.
Green County, Ala.,	2	408
Walton County, Ga.,	2	1,393
Wilkes County, Ga.,	2	1,139
East Feliciana, La.,	none.	1.786
Lawrence County, Miss.,	2	2,073
Tallahatchie County, Miss.,	1	1,144
Yazoo County, Miss.,	2	3,672
Brown County, Texas,	1	2,525
Eastland County, Texas,	3	1,787
Hidalgo County, Texas,	4	1,629
Buchanan County, Va.,	2	1,330

Now, you see what the Democratic protection of the right of suffrage, preservative of all rights, and a free ballot, a full vote, and a fair count is. [Applause.] Here are 11 counties in 6 different Southern States that have produced in the aggregate 21 votes for Hayes and 16 odd thousand for Tilden. [Laughter.] Now, I think that, under a candidate that is better than his party, and with this printing in the platform, and this palaver at the hustings, the Re-

publican vote in these 11 counties will probably be doubled from 21 to 42. [Applause.] But as the Democrats like to be included in all this talk about a free ballot, a full vote, and a fair count, I suppose their aggregate will rise from 16,000 to 32,000.

Well, gentlemen, I don't know what the American people are made of. I don't know whether they like this palaver. I don't think it is creditable to a candidate that is better than his party, to write such contemptuous imitation of principles as that. I don't think it is creditable to a party, even though it is worse than a candidate, to put forth such a solemn proposition of its love of that suffrage, " preservative of our rights." The only equal for this disparity between principles and practice that I have ever heard of, was that of the man who broke his wife's head with a motto that hung in a frame at their bedside, " God bless our home." [Applause.]

Now, as I say, loving the suffrage, we resent any interference with it. Now, this Democratic party says to us, " Oh, don't mind them ; they are far off ; they are not of your race ; they are ignorant ; they are feeble. Don't distress yourselves about this injury of the poor blacks in the distant parts of the country ; that is our State rights, and we mean to exercise it." But when American liberty accuses the Democratic party of having made a deadly assault upon the first foundation right of liberty and equality, the Democratic party undertakes to reply : " When have we made such an assault ? Why, we have prophesied under the name of liberty, and under the name of liberty we have cast out Republican devils." The answer is, " Inasmuch as ye have done it to the least of these poor disciples of liberty at its feet, ye have done it unto me," [great applause,] and in the scales of justice, and in the eye and in the balance of the Divine scrutiny this is a law of the moral government of the world, and if this people looks with patience on this robbery of the suffrage from these poor freemen, it won't be long before we will have to debate what we shall do to protect the suffrage of these poor plebeians that Tarquin the Superb robs of their franchises.

The Government as it was.

As we then next value the great country that we love, as we have preserved its Constitution unviolated, and this territory unmutilated, we are not afraid to meet and encounter any charges that politics will bring against us. And we are, as lovers of the Union, as lovers of the union of States, intelligent as to what that means. Why, it used to be enough that we were always in favor of the union of the States as Jackson was, as all Republicans ever have been. But when it came to be a matter of judicial scrutiny, the Supreme Court—in the hands, I am glad to say, of the principles of the Union, the Republican party —as lovers of the Constitution, and lovers of liberty and the Union, spoke of it as " an indissoluble Union of indestructible States." And that is Republican doctrine. Now, Democrats have got it up, and are crying it up and down the streets as if it was Democratic doctrine of an indissoluble Union of indestructible States.

What was the Democratic doctrine in 1860 ? What was it up to the end of the war ? What, in equal stress, will it be again ? It is of a dissoluble union of destructible States. Now, that is the difference between Republicans and Democrats. Gentlemen, we must consider, as I have said, the Democracy do not criticize trouble in your affairs, as during the four years the Government has been administered what do they call attention to ? Is it we that go back into the past ? No, it is they ; it is they that go back into the past. Their whole proposition, their whole discussion is made up of the passions of the past, of the interests of restoration, and they wish, with a party made up in the same way, to bring back the Government as it stood in 1856, over the head of the party that drove them from that Government and has kept them out ever since.

Well, now, these Democrats are very devout. Senator Hill said : "Why will you keep up these animosities ? Why don't you let us into the Government ? If you don't think we are fit for it, why just try us ; just try us," with about the same easy air with which a school-boy in the country tries to wheedle a kiss out of a pouting beauty. "Just for once," does he say. [Laughter.] Senator Hill says, "It is only for four years." Well, in an era of good feeling, after an extreme effort of compromise on the part of the North in 1852, we chose Pierce, a Northern statesman—better than his party—and only four years— and just for once ! [Laughter.] And how he did tear the face, the honor, the prosperity of this country to tatters—all in four years—by the repeal of the Missouri compromise ! And we tried another kiss from the Democratic party in Mr. Buchanan—and just for four years—and just for once—and how he did rack and ruin this country only in four years ! And now for the 20 years, by faith in God and faith in the people, we have made the country larger, more populous, richer, more powerful than it was before, and now they want us to put it back, just for once, just for four years. [Applause.]

Well, I think that when the people of this country make a partnership between these leaders and our affairs they had better think a little of that story of the partnership that was made between a somewhat experienced practical merchant and a capitalist who had a good deal of property and not much sagacity "Why," says his friend to this experienced trader, "You have made a new partnership, I understand." "Yes, I have, with Mr. Jones." "Well, what does he put in ?" "He puts in $100,000, and I put in the experience." "Well, how long is this to last ?" "Oh ! only for four years, and then I will have the $100,000, and he the experience." [Great laughter and applause.] Now, these leaders have had a great deal of experience, and we have a great deal of money. But even at the end of four years we would not like to find that we had no money, although we had had some experience. But what good would experience do ? Have you not had the experience of Pierce, of Buchanan, of flagrant war, of treachery to the public faith, of ruin of credit, and obstruction everywhere ? What do they think of us ? That we are light headed to the pitch of lunacy, or rash to the point of self destruction ? Is that the character of this sober American people ? Is that the character of the New-Englanders, of the New-Yorkers, of the Pennsylvanians, of the great West ? Well, November will tell the story. It is as bold as I put it to you,

I said four years ago that this people did not need another eye-opener in one generation. But these experienced Southerners think that we are ready for another eye-opener that will last us fifteen years more.

The Devout Democrats.

But these gentlemen are very devout. Senator Hill, I notice, without having the fear of the example of the Pharisees before his eyes, before an immense crowd of his fellow-citizens, publicly gave thanks to the "God of his fathers" that slavery had been destroyed. Well, the solid South did not destroy slavery, did they ? The desiccated Democratic party of the North did not destroy slavery, did they ? It was the Republican party that destroyed slavery. And thus far all that Senator Hill has found occasion publicly to thank God for, is something that the Republican party did. [Laughter and applause.] Senator Bayard says, in 1880, in a public speech in Brooklyn, that the war to save the Union has been a success, and, for one, he thanks God for it. Well, it was not the solid South that made the war a success, nor the desiccated Democratic party of the North. It is the Republican party that made the war a success. [Applause.] And Senator Bayard thanks God that this was done. Well, these great statesmen are right in being devout, are right in assuming the humility of David in one of his most celebrated Psalms—Non nobis domine—"Not unto us, O Lord, but unto Thee be all the praise." [Laughter and applause.]

Well, gentlemen, we do abhor sectionalism. The Union men of this country, the great body of the people in this country, have always abhorred sectionalism. They abhorred it before the war. They abhorred it in the war. They abhorred it during reconstruction. They abhor it now. [Applause.] And, thank God, they have got all the sectionalism now in front, and in the solid South. [Applause.] The sectionalism of the South has always been eager, joyous, aggressive, the pride and staple of their politics : with the North slow, sad, reluctant, defensive, never with a sword to attack, nothing but a shield to defend. We have defended the Union against sectionalism in arms. We have protected the Constitution against sectionalism in peace, and we will save the Government. [Great applause.] We will save the Government from passing into the hands of sectionalism next November, and four years hence, and eight years hence, and twelve years hence, and so on during the long roll of the history of the American people. [Applause.]

Keeping Faith With the Blacks.

Let us, then, understand that the freedom of suffrage to the black means the freedom of the suffrage to the white. I have not yet found anywhere, in any system of ethics or of morality, in any doctrine of religion, of any distinction between colors or race as to human rights. I have known them violated. I have known them trampled on, and I have known them re-asserted. I do not believe that a great party, and a noble party, that has kept its faith that it would preserve the Union, that it would preserve the Constitution, that it would pay its debts, that it would redeem

Its greenbacks—I do not believe that it will break the faith it has pledged to the poor and the defenceless, because they are poor and defenceless. [Applause.] The Democratic party may pass on the other side these poor sufferers of the South ; but the Republican party means to cheer with the wine of its protection and to soothe with the oil of its consolation these poor neighbors of ours that lie wounded and pillaged at our feet. [Applause.]

The Dignity of Labor.

There is another great interest of free government in American society—I mean the dignity of labor. We have undertaken on this continent of ours to build up a fabric of politics in which every laboring man had the same share, every ignorant man had the same share, every feeble man had the same share, in political power with the rich and the strong and the learned. And that system we mean to maintain ; and in order to maintain a system and dignity of labor which is known nowhere else in the world, and has never been known anywhere in the world till here and now, we mean to protect the wages of our workmen from competition with the pauper systems of Europe. [Applause.] Upon what a narrow and stupid basis do they discuss this American system of industry ! They speak of it as if it were protection of the mill-owners, of the mine-owners, of the proprietors and managers of furnaces and of railroads and of ships. Why, of course, they have their share in the workings of industry, but the object of it all, and the political reason of it all is that we mean to protect our wages from being beaten down by the peasantry or the laborers of foreign countries, whose dignity, whose manhood, whose equality is not preserved, or even that of any other systems of politics. [Applause.] That is what our system of wages and our barrier mean—the hands that we will protect—that dignity from being broken down. It is not for the rich nor the great.

And every laborer in this land ought to know—as many of them do know—that their interests are under the protection of the tariff system of the United States. They read in the Democratic platform that the Democratic party is opposed to that barrier, and opposed to anything that will save the laborers of America from the same poor pittance that the laborers of Europe and of China enjoy. [Applause.] You can see it as in a picture. When the Chinese come to California—full grown men without wives or children, without religion, without schools, without charities, without a share in the participation, or a desire for it, in this magnificent system of the dignity and glory of labor, then Denis Kearney and his friends can see that that impinges on their rates of wages. But the great mass of the Irish population of this country, that have come over to get rid of the crushing weight of taxes and of military expenses, and the Germans that have done the same, do not seem to see that they are voting for the lords of the loom and of the mine in Europe, to crush the competition of America and bring down the wages here, and then the wages there.

Relations with the South.

Now, this Democratic party is a very extraordinary thing. [Laughter.] Our relations to the South are to make them share and share alike with us in this Government, in the education, in the prosperity, in the wealth, in the liberty, in the happiness of this country. [Applause.] We draw no line. We want to diversify their industry. We want to fill out the forms of industry on them that are full with us. We want to build them up. We do not wish to keep them in subordination and paying tribute to us.

Now, let me read you what a great Democratic statesman tells the South, and what his plans for its benefits are. I mean Senator Wallace, of Pennsylvania, and that I may not be accused of taking it from an obscure newspaper, I take it from the *World*, published in the City of New-York. Who is Senator Wallace ? He is the power that made Hancock. He is a Pennsylvania Democrat. He is to Wallace what some other Presidential candidates were to the great statesman, Thurlow Weed. Wallace is the man that put Hancock on the course. Now, what has he said : " The genius of our people is progress, business and energetic life, and the parties that stand in their road will go down before the march of events." Here is some more : " Gen. Hancock is a representative of this unionism, and the Republican party are the exponents of the reverse. Their policy destroys our control [he was talking in Pennsylvania] of the manufacturing interests of the Republic, takes away from the North that peculiar control which has heretofore belonged to us, and builds factories, furnaces, rolling mills and workshops by every river in the South. The South has been agricultural : that is its natural sphere. Its enormous products from the soil have been and ought to continue to be the most important element in her progress and prosperity. Disunion, hatred, persecution, have forced them to depend upon themselves, and they have deprived us of what is and ought to continue to be our natural market."

Now, that is the view of the Democratic party on the tariff, that under the tariff industries have been fostered, and factories have been built up on every river in the South. Well, I think they will be, and if they will give us four years more of Republican administration the South will hum and buzz as Pennsylvania and Massachusetts do now. [Applause.] I have never heard of such folly avowed by a party that proposed and professed to be a friend of the solid South. Yes, keep them solid. Keep them clodhoppers. Keep them peasantry. Don't let Republicans get hold of them, or they will make them rich and prosperous, and your Pennsylvania Democrats will have to share their riches with them. As I said before, if the American people listen to such statesmanship as this, why, they will try a partnership in experience four years more.

What do the South say to-day ? I saw this only yesterday. I read now from the Atlanta *Constitution*, a leading newspaper of the Democratic party in Georgia. It quotes from the Memphis *Avalanche :* " Two thousand plows," says the Memphis *Avalanche*, " arrived on one steamer from the North. What this country wants is more plows and less politics to the acre." There is some sense in that—for the Memphis *Avalanche*. [Applause.] And then, says the Atlanta *Constitution*, " that is so, but we don't want more plows from the North, we want more plow factories and every kind of factories in the South, and make the articles we want." One would suppose that when the desiccated Democracy of the North says to the solid South, " We want to keep you clods, and sell you our wares," and the Republican party says, "We want you to make your own plows," and then the Atlanta *Constitution* says that it agrees that more plows and less politics to the acre would be a good thing, that they would like to have plow factories of their own, I say one would suppose the solid South would vote for the Republican party, and not for the desiccated Democracy. [Applause.] If the country has eaten of the "insane root" of this kind of reasoning and it is satisfactory to these sagacious statesmen, why, let it go.

What the Desiccated Democracy is.

Well, we had some experience about the relations of this desiccated Democracy, and why do I call it the "desiccated Democracy!" Why, because all the juices were taken out of it by the people that were opposed to the Lecompton bill, to Kansas and Nebraska, and the war against the Union, and the war against the public faith and the war against the suffrage. But now they say it is being revived by the transfusion of the warm blood of the Republican party in the person of Charles Francis Adams [applause] and Lyman Trumbull, of Illinois. This warm blood has been transfused into it, and since it got somewhat strengthened by the hot dose, with the still hotter one of Gen. Butler and Gen. Sickles and Gov. Shepherd, of the District of Columbia, until now this desiccated Democracy has become vigorated and enlivened, and is going through the motions of patriotism and reform. What a sacrifice these statesmen have been willing to make that they should, by the process of transfusion, revive a declining and decaying party, and be satisfied with the somewhat obscure though very useful function of corpuscles in their veins !

The Grumbling Solid South.

Now, the solid South and this allied North present very curious records. You know they had the House and the Senate and the committees, and more votes in both houses and everything, and one would suppose that they would be entitled to some show ; but the moment they wanted—I mean the solid South—wanted to choose a Speaker, why shouldn't they? I don't know why they shouldn't choose a Speaker. The law of our Government is, that the majority in a party should rule. They were not allowed to choose a Speaker. They must always have a Northern Democrat for Speaker, and so on in various measures, war claims and others. Oh, no, they must be silent. And then they turn around to this Northern Democracy and say, "Why, are not you the North? We thought you were the North." Oh, don't make such a terrible mistake as that. We are not the North. If you undertake to show your coun sels and your practices, you will find out who the North is. We are only the small boy that is put in at the side lights to let down the fastening, but the house-breaking will have to be done very silently and in the dark, and you must not make a noise.

Well, it is like the case, when they grumble about it, of the Government ship that was on the coast of Africa in slave-trading times to suppress the slave trade, that seized the crew of the American slavers,

and it was no doubt very hot, and when it came to night the Captain commanding the vessel, with such a raft of these fellows aboard, had to put on the hatches to keep them under there in the night-time—he could look after them in the day-time. Well, they came to him and said : "Well, this is pretty hot." " Yes," he says, "I know it is." And they said, "If you put on the hatches we can't sleep." "Well," said the Captain, "If I don't put on the hatches I can't sleep." And you may be sure that the hatches went on. And that is the ship that the South must be kept under the hatches of until the ship is delivered over, and the Democratic party then will come out from under the hatches and have a good time.

Democracy Helpless for Good.

Now, the Democratic party does not propose any thing. It proposes to be in power and undo. But I cannot see that it proposes to do any thing. It cannot help your currency. That is good enough. This country will ever be true to the greenbacks that saved them through their day of trial. When this Nation sat at the gate of victory and could not enter in, because the finances of the country could not be hurried up rapidly enough to carry on the immense transactions of the war, and when they cried for the financial aid of the country, the Government said to them, "Silver and gold have I none, but such as I have I give thee, and pledge the faith of this country. If you have faith in that, it will carry us through." And the crippled army leaped to its feet and entered the gate of victory. Will the American people ever asperse this greenback currency that represents the faith of the Nation? Will they ever frown upon its maintenance as equal to specie, as a part of the life-blood of the country's finances? I think not, as long as they remember the occasion which gave it birth and the great services it has performed.

I say, gentlemen, that I find nothing in the politics of the Democratic party that proposes any thing. It is to undo everything. It is to fight the war back from Appomattox to Sumter. It is to unravel the whole fabric of a noble and expanded nationality that the Republican party has woven for this people for a glory and a decoration forever. It is aimless. It is in the condition of the sage whom the youth, find ing an opportunity, thought it reasonable to consult as to how he had come to such wisdom and such fame, and asked him what was his aim in life. "Why," said the sage, "a little fire. I have not any aim. I have fired." Now the Democratic party has not any aim. It has fired. It has failed in its fire, and it has no aim that touches the honor or the growth or the prosperity of this country. Now, the party that I have upheld to you for its great achievements may be stricken down by the American people for what it has done, and in the only incomplete service that remains to fulfill its pledges and consummate your honor, it is resolved that there shall be a free ballot, a full vote and a fair count in this land—all over it. If it is to be stricken down by the American people for that resolve, so be it. "Such a party," to borrow the phrase of Lord Bolingbroke, "Such a party may fall, but if it fall, truth, liberty and reason will fall with it." [Applause.]—*From the New-York Times, Thursday, September 30,* 1880.

The Address of HENRY WARD BEECHER, *in the Cooper Union, New-York City, Wednesday evening, October 13, 1880.*

I hardly think that any man in this great assembly can feel the same joy that I feel in the tidings that come from the State where my youth was spent, and where the opening scenes of my public life took place. Indiana was my early home, and my elder children were from there, and the word "Hoosier" has never ceased to be music in my ears. [Applause.] When I went there, there was not an abolition speaker nor meeting from the North to the South in that State. I suppose that I delivered the first anti-slavery sermon that ever was delivered in the City of Indianapolis, the Capital of the State. My heart has gone to that State, and is with her, and while I to-night congratulate you I send to the far West, to her sons, and to her daughters, who inspired them to patriotism, my greeting, my thanks and my gratitude. [Applause.]

I am not thrilled with the victory in Ohio. When a great and good man does a good deed, no man lifts up his hand in surprise. Ohio is used to doing such things. [Laughter and applause.] It is a matter of course, [laughter,] and whenever an emergency takes place which involves really the national welfare, New-York is accustomed to do the same thing. [Applause and cheers.] She may amuse herself at intervals. [Laughter.] There is a good deal of her. [Laughter.] But when the times grow serious, and the thoughtful men and laboring men—mechanics, merchants, professional men—look out and see that the signs of storms are in the Heavens, all frolic ceases, and man joins his fellow man in high places and in low places through the whole State to rescue the nation and the National welfare. [Applause.]

This country, ladies and gentlemen, is better adapted for a harmonization of interests and opinions than any other country of which I have any knowledge. It is adapted on the great principle of reciprocal interests—it is adapted to the unity of the whole population. If it were all North, if it were all South, if it were all East, if it were all West, the identity of interests would create sluggishness of circulation ; but because the harvests of the South are one thing, and the harvests of the North are another, those of the East another, and the productive energies of the West another, the circulation is maintained which carries vigorous life throughout every part of this Union. And although we have a tribute paid us of its best citizens from every nation of the globe—in Europe, in Asia, in Africa—yet as long as liberty is being sought, and since liberty is here regulated by institutions ; since law and institutions in this land have been created by the people themselves, who knew the wants of the common people, I would have the emigrants find—wherever they come from—that for which they have pined, the want of which has nearly suffocated them in their own land. Because we have this vast people founded on institutions of liberty, designed to give scope and opportunity to every living man, we have a population that is inclined to friendship, to peace, to comity of interests ; and I hold that no party is worthy of one single hour's regard which does not aim at the harmonization of the interests of every part of this broad continent. [Great cheers.]

The Two Parties Compared.

Convince me that the Democratic party is more National than the Republican party ; convince me that their measures will really carry out peace more rapidly and more permanently than the measures of the Republican party, and I renounce my allegiance to the Republican party, and I go over to the Democrats. [Cheers.] But I don't go over. [Great cheers.] I don't at present see any likelihood of going over—neither I nor my children after me. [Renewed cheers.]

If the Republican party is in favor of sectional interests, of class interests ; if it overslaughs the laborer, whose hands are his capital ; if it disregards the poor and the needy ; if it goes in for the rich in contempt to the poor, for the North in derogation of the South, for the South at a mischief toward the North ; if it neglect the far Pacific States ; if it is not a party in whose very heart is the purpose to take care of the whole Nation, all its parts, all its interests and all its people—then I cannot ask you to vote for it. But it is because in my very heart of hearts I believe that it is a National party, seeking not alone nationality by controlling the Government, but having in its genius, in its history, in its inspirations, in its purposes, in its platform—in its platform and in all the legislation that will follow from it—having the interest of every section, of every class, of all conditions, North, South, East and West—it is for that reason that I am free to commend it to your suffrages. [Applause.]

I am here to-night, gentlemen, to dig out votes. [Laughter.] It might be a pleasant thing for me to make pleasant sentences for you, and to weave ingenious rhetoric, but I come on a practical errand, to urge you, not alone personally, but by your influence with every man around about you, to roll up such a majority as there shall never be an opportunity again to make the issues that torment us to-day. [Loud applause.] I have, in the earlier days, been slightly a controversionalist, and in all conflicts I have had one rule : So to strike a man when I struck him as never to need to strike twice. [Laughter and applause.]

I say to the people of this State of New-York, and through them to the people of my whole country, let these issues that have tormented us so long be settled, so that there shall never another politician come within gunshot of the question. [Applause.] Ladies and gentlemen, for fifty years past there has not sprung upon this nation one single disturbance through the North. [Applause.] We have been accused of being a sectional party and a Northern party. Now, I will defy the 'cutest historian or diplomat to show one great National disaster, jar or confusion that has sprung from the action of the

North. [Applause.] I go further, and declare that every one of the great conflicts that for twenty-five years have agitated this Nation, have sprung from the South, and not from the North. [Loud applause.] We have never vexed the West, we have never vexed the Northwest, nor they us. We have never vexed the Middle States, nor they us. We have defended ourselves against the South, but we never intruded upon them and they have intruded upon the National peace. [Loud cheers.]

Aggressions of the South.

When slavery began to lift a head of power, it, despite both the traditions and the solemn covenants of the United States, undertook to invade the free territory of the Northwest, and a great and hot debate ensued, which was settled by what was called the Missouri Compromise. That great national instrument came from the South and not from the North. As the growth of the South still went on with her prosperity, and her riches and her slaves, then it became important that the South should steal 'more territory, and it was the South that destroyed the Missouri Compromise, and abolished that line. It was the South that invaded Kansas, and brought on all those conflicts that resulted in so much bloodshed then and in the wars that followed since.

The Mexican war was not bred and hatched in the North. It was also one of the whelps of slavery. [Great applause.] The Fugitive Slave law was not enacted in Boston or New-York, though there were sneaking minions to execute it here. There never was so arrogant, so needless an insult thrown in the face of any people as the enactment of the Fugitive Slave law, and that we owe to the South. Then came the right proclaimed of Secession. Was it the North that precipitated the division of this country? Was it the North that drew the sword? The first declaration in a practical form was made from the shores of South Carolina when she bombarded Fort Sumter. And the whole great war was the product of Southern doctrine and Southern citizenship, and not of the North. [Applause.] Yet some men proclaim that the Republican party is a Northern party, and that the North is a section, and they are scheming to denationalize the country, and seeking to make our party an aristocratic party. These are the doctrines that have for the last twenty years ploughed this land as with a red-hot iron, and these have been from the South and not from the North. The Democratic party now in this impending conflict, in every ward, in every precinct, in every State, are declaring that there will be no peace in this land until the Democrats rule. They are saying that all the great mischiefs that have befallen this land have sprung from the reign of the Republican party.

National Mischiefs due to the Democrats.

They are not the first. There was something of the same sort that happened some 3,000 years ago. It was when old Elijah had stood for the liberty of his people and for the truth of the religion of God that he met Ahab, and Ahab said to him: "Art thou he that troubleth Israel?" Ahab had brought in the worship of idols and abolished the altars of Jehovah, and sought to put up Balaam's altars and fill the land with his praise. And old Elijah, with long locks and with a burning eye, exclaimed: "I have not troubled Israel. Thou hast forsaken the commandments of the Lord, and hast brought in the worship of Balaam."

And I say to the Democratic party, if there has been trouble on the continent, if there has been war, we are not to be charged with having played hyena to the lion, like those who during the war hung like dead-weights on the Union wheels, and who, in all the work of Governmental reconstruction, never raised so much as a little finger in the way of a possible settlement. Yes, gentlemen, the North has been ordained, I believe, by the Divine Providence, to stand for the continent and the whole Nation. The philosopher may tell you to-day that all the storms that ravage the Atlantic coast are bred in the great Caribbean Sea. All the storms that ravage this Nation have been bred in the Southern Caribbean Sea of the Gulf States. What, then, are Southern citizens? Are they worse than we are? Are we pedagogues whose mission is to punish fractious pupils? Are we the people with whom wisdom is alone reposed? Are we barbaric and they civilized? Individually the citizens of the South are as good as we are. [Applause.] As noble men live there as live in New-York State. Indeed, in social traits, in a high sense personal honor, in fidelity to their convictions, in standing up openly and in a manly way to that which they believe, they need no eulogy from me. Their courage is as good as our courage.

Ladies and gentlemen, there has not been a Boy in Blue that has been for four years in the South that has not learned to respect Southern courage. [Applause.] And there has not been a general in the South—whatever they may have become—there is not a Southern commander who has not learned to respect Northern courage. [Applause.] I have this to say: When the South went into the conflict of the war, they went in not only in earnest but they went in with a willingness to sacrifice property and life for their conviction, and, for two or three years the North did not half believe its own cause, and the South believed its own cause all the time: and I am not here to deprecate the South—I am not here to criticize in this respect. [Applause.] Their organized political action has not been wise. Their people are a noble people, and I am proud of them, and not the less so that now for the first time at the age of seventy years it would be safe for me to go to the South. [Laughter.] I am not here to make the breach wider, but to narrow and close it up; not by compromise, not by pretence or political jugglery, but by the advocacy of such principles as must become common to the whole land, or the whole land will be restless and disturbed for four years to come. [Great applause.] The whole mischief hitherto has arisen from the nature of an institution. It lay at the basis of the whole economy of the South, and it forced them to adopt the doctrine of State Sovereignty, and it forced upon them the consequences of the war, and certain results of that doctrine which have been disturbing to them and to us.

State Rights and State Sovereignty.

Now, the doctrine of State Rights must not be confounded with the doctrine of State Sovereignty. The South holds to State Sovereignty ; the North holds simply to State Rights, and that only. We deny that the North has ever interfered with the Southern States' rights, but it has denied State Sovereignty. The doctrines are alike up to a certain point. Nobody denies that there are certain local State rights which remain under the control of the citizens of a State. There are certain rights of every school district that the other districts cannot meddle with, and yet the town is superior to any of its districts. There are certain town rights not to be meddled with by the county, and yet the county is superior in many respects to the town. There are county rights which the Legislature cannot meddle with, and yet the State and its Legislature are superior to the county and its commissioners in every respect. There are certain rights of every State in this continent which cannot be meddled with with impunity, and yet the Nation is superior to the States. [Great applause.]

The sum of all the States, acting within certain defined and constitutional lines, is superior to the integral elements that constitute the sovereignty of the Nation. Yet the doctrine of the South has been that State rights were not only assured and guaranteed to them up to a certain line, but that when it is to the interest of a certain State to break up the confederacy of States, as they call it, the right to break up everything is inherent in them. It is as if a man should say : " I have hired a room in this common hotel, and if I like I will take the wall down on my side of the hotel for my room." [Great applause.] He has no right to let in the cold and weather for his own accommodation ; and no State has the right to break down the walls of the great Union anywhere to the damage of a majority of the States. Nowhere have State Rights a guarantee and privilege, a mission to do that which shall be for the damage of the whole Nation. [Tremendous cheers and applause.]

Now, it is supposed that the North don't believe in State Rights. Well, they don't believe in anything else, [laughter,] if one might say so. Where was the doctrine of State Rights born ? Georgia ? She didn't know anything about it long after it had attained its majority in New-England. [Laughter.] It was not in the Carolinas, nor was it in Virginia, nor in Delaware, nor in Maryland. It was in the old New-England colonies that State Rights first grew, and every year since, and never more than to-day, every single State of the North, New-England, New-York and all their progeny far West to the Pacific, were just as much in favor of the doctrine of State Rights as the South itself is ; but we discriminate between State rights within the Nation and State sovereignty over the Nation. [Applause.] When the colonists came, Plymouth colony was settled, and then Massachusetts Bay colony was established, and afterward Rhode Island and Connecticut, and so jealous were they of the rights of each colony that it was years and years before they could be brought into any kind of combined action for fear that the neighboring States would take advantage one of the other. They had just come out from England, where they had an arbitrary Church, that could step down into their conventicles and tell them what they must believe and what they must not believe, and they didn't like it. They had had an arbitrary State Government that went into their neighborhood and imposed most tyrannical conditions upon the liberty of citizens, and they didn't like it ; and they came to this country on purpose to establish the right of every community to take care of its own affairs. That was the very key-note, that was the very germ, of the colonies of New-England, and it was natural that they should carry it to excess. It was natural that Connecticut should say to Plymouth in 1643, when Connecticut proposed that there should be a combination of the New-England States, in view of Indian wars and the French war—it was very natural that Connecticut should say, " There cannot be any combination that don't reserve to us absolutely and totally every one of our rights. ' And then Massachusetts said, " But you are so jealous of your rights and we are jealous of ours." And Plymouth colony said, " We are just as jealous of ours ;" and they could not get them together, and the time went by, and it was not until a good many years later than that that they could get a temporary combination of the States of New-England to act in common against the Indian adversary. It was years and years, so jealous were they of the colonial rights ; and when at a later period there were various tentative efforts made to combine the colonies against the oppression of their mother country, it was only by taking the experience which at last had been wrought out in New-England, by which the rights of each colony were held compatibly with the rights of a common head to all the colonies—it was only then that we found out how to establish a nation upon the platform of separate individual States. And when people talk about State Rights as being Southern, I say it breathed the breath of life first in the colonies. It was rocked in the cradles of New-England. It went out with the children of New-England. It is the father of the doctrine of State Rights over this whole continent ; and it has never from that day to this died out of the jealous love of the people from whom it sprang. [Applause.]

Southern Belief not Changed.

But when it was found necessary for the sake of establishing the Federal Government, to make head against a foreign adversary, that something should be given up by every State, then, modified by a genuine National impulse, moved by a consideration of the general good, New-England modified and limited her doctrine of State Rights, so as to sacrifice something of her local rights for the sake of the general good to the whole of the nation. Just opposite to that was the way in which the cause of State Rights was treated in the South, not because by reason they had come to a different conclusion, but because there was in the midst of them a system at war with everything human and divine ; a system that degraded labor, made men like machinery and like cattle, and it was a system odious to God and to man, and lived only by the devil. [Laughter.] Now it became necessary to the South, as against the tendencies of Government, as against civilization—it became necessary to build up walls around about that black spot they had in their midst, and therefore the South narrowed, or rather enlarged, that doctrine of State Rights, and they maintained a more local State doctrine, namely, the doctrine of absolute sovereignty of every State, while New-England made herself compatible to all the States of the Union. [Applause.] The North, though maintaining her local rights, generously gave up so many of them as made all the States better; the South maintained local rights, and was not willing to give up one whit for the sake of the common good of this continent. That was the trouble that led to the war.

Now, it is said, why do you debate this question that was put to the arbitration of the sword, and the sword declared that the doctrine was false? [Applause.] Aye, gentlemen, the sword may slay, but the sword cannot convince; and Southern men are just as besotted with the doctrine of State sovereignty to-day as they were before they drew the sword of war. It is true, that so far as that was concerned, that issue was determined by the voice of the people of these United States, but the question has come back to-day, for you and me and all citizens to answer in this form: Will you stand up to the doctrine which you have vindicated by your sword? [Applause.] Has the war changed the belief of Southern citizens? Not a whit! They believe just as they did before. Has the war turned out of Southern seminaries, colleges and universities the men that teach the doctrines of Calhoun? Those doctrines are taught in every principal seminary and college of the South, just as before the war. The lawyers, doctors, ministers, politicians, that are being educated in Southern institutions, are educated in precisely the same doctrines as they were when they decided to stick to their own interest as against the common interests of the whole country. They have now taken to themselves the remnant of the Democratic party. [Applause.] If the Democrats should take possession of the General Government, will not the energy of this great nation be used to carry out Southern doctrines? If I was a Southern man home in the South, and I believed that it was good, I would use the Government by which to propagate and fortify it. Human nature is not so different on the two sides of Mason and Dixon's line. They may have victory to-day or to-morrow, but I tell you there never will be peace on this continent until the peace is founded on right doctrines. [Applause.] It used to be said when I was a younger man than I am now, "If you will only hold your peace, if the pulpit would not agitate it, if the Church would not agitate it, and if the lecture platform would not agitate it, and if you let commerce alone, we will settle the difficulties." And our cry to them was your cry of "Peace! peace! Why there is no peace." I say if the Democratic party go into an alliance with the Southern element, they enter again into the shadow of another penumbra, and that the men and the sons of the men that refuse to hold their peace and pour out discussion hot, their conscience will take up again their deplorable condition, and in the end there will be no peace until the doctrine of our forefathers will become the doctrine of the whole nation. [Long continued applause.] I will give you chance enough to applaud before I get through. [Applause and laughter.] Wait till I get out of breath if you want to. [Applause.]

Gentlemen—I would say ladies and gentlemen if ladies were allowed to vote [laughter]—the South for fifty years after the institutions of this country had been founded, the South dominated, for a long time very wisely, and not until slavery had developed itself, so as to poison them root and branch, did their wisdom forsake them. But for fifty years the counsels of the Southern men were a succession of blunders. There never were so many blunders since the Democrats were in power. But now the South seems determined to make one more great blunder. When the conflict had been settled by the sword, sagacious statesmen would have said, that if the South ever comes into power again it will be through an alliance with the men who conquered it and controlled it. But in truth, the South drew off suddenly and she refused the hand of friendship. When the Administration offered the olive branch, not one single State was willing to accept the proffered hand of President Hayes. [Applause.] That was a gigantic blunder. If the South had said, "We accept the situation," it would have been better for them. They should have said, "We will go with you and help maintain the Government on your principles;" the South then would have been all back again. The Democratic party had been defeated in the North, and also in the South, and these two defeated parties came together and undertook to assert the sovereignty of the South, and of this fragment of the Democratic party. They have come together to-day, and they are trying to control the Government under the old Southern doctrine, and we, the people, are determined that they shall not do it. [Loud and continued applause.] We are determined to fight it out on this line if it takes twenty-five summers. It is best for the Nation that Republican ideas of administering the Government shall prevail. [Applause.] It is best for the South that Republican ideas shall prevail. [Applause.] It will bring about that settlement which will never need to be settled again. [Hearty applause.]

The Question of Centralization.

But now comes Judge Black. [Laughter.] He and those who agree with him declare that the Republican party is about to betray this Nation by a centralization of this Government, and that we are, day by day, bringing in centralization. There are always two antagonistic forces to determine the course any people shall take. There is the force of the central Federal Government in its sphere, and that of the States in their sphere. There is a perpetual liability of conflict between the local independence of the State and the authority of the Nation. Sometimes one prevails a little too much and sometimes the other, but in the main the equilibrium between them is preserved. When Buchanan sat in the Presidential chair and declared that there was no power in the Constitution to coerce a sovereign State—there was the danger. [Applause.] The future of this Nation will depend on the authority, pre-eminence, and skill and efficiency of the central government. [Applause.] The mischiefs have never come from our own action of the Government. When the South committed burglary against this Nation, and the last Democratic President—I hope he will be the last [applause]—declared that he had no power—declared not only that, but that there was no power anywhere, Stanton convinced him that there was, and this great people stepped forward to prove it. [Applause.] I admit that there were, in the conduct of the Government, a good many mistakes. I remember Mr. Seward's little bell was commented upon. Mr. Seward was always in a hurry with unimportant things, and just the reverse with important things. No surgeon has any excuse, having a hospital and his own time and implements at his command, for cutting too wide or deep, and injuring where he should save. But when on the battlefield, while the battle rages and the sky is illumined by the fire of the enemy, the surgeon, seeing soldiers falling around him, finds a man who must be operated upon, if he cuts a little wide or too deep—why excuse him. [Applause.] If our Government, in the great emergency of the Nation, made a few mistakes, what they lacked in one direction they made up in another, and there was but very little mischief. [Applause.] And men are surprised that, in the settlement of the great conflict which took place afterward, the machine was not put together in a minute, and joined together as har moniously as an Italian organ. [Great laughter.] "Ah!" they say, "see how the Republican humbugs are bungling." It is as if the monkey on the machine should criticize the music of Beethoven and Mozart. [Tremendous laughter and applause.] It would not be more impertinent than for those who brought on the war to criticize the manner in which we took up the fragments and put them together and gave them life. [Great applause.] It was the Republican party which restored the Nation; not without some mistakes, but with fewer, when we consider the multitude of elements, the want of experience, than any nation in the world which has acted in such a drama as that could have done. And I look back upon the war and see the Nation come out of the drama and pay every dollar incurred in the struggle; I see the quick bringing back of the States into fellowship again, and when I see the leniency with which they were treated, I say that such a scene was never known on the face of the earth; and it cannot be known in any other nation than the humane, liberal American people. A war that destroyed a million of lives and six millions of property; which kept the Continent in a turmoil for five years, and yet, when it was settled, not a cord was stretched, not a stroke heard, not a drop of blood spilt. There was blood enough —blood enough, the people said; let there be an end of the executioner; and the man that loudest sang, "Let us hang Jeff Davis on a sour apple tree," would not have drawn the cord if he had it in his hand, [applause,] and flying in the garb of a woman, he would have appealed to honorable sympathies. [Tremendous laughter and applause.]

Views on Free Trade.

Now, gentlemen, I have had a tolerably good evidence of your kindness, but now I am going to say something, and I want to be at peace with you, and won't let you quarrel with me on the point I am going to make, and it is going to turn out better than you think when I open it. [Laughter.] The only point in which I disagree with the Republican party

campaign is on the tariff. I am a Free Trader. [cheers and hisses,] and I am a free speaker, too. [Applause.] I believe that the philosophy of the future is free trade. I believe that the nations should come to it just as fast as they can. I believe that as this Nation of forty States has no tariff between them, it is better, and the time will come when the nations of the earth will be in the condition when there will be no Custom Houses between them, but free trade amongst them from the North and South and the East and West. I preach that doctrine, and if in campaigns hereafter you find me speaking on the free trade platform, you must not be surprised or think that I go with my party in everything. But—but [laughter]—when the people, though they have mistaken a policy of political economy, have embarked in it; when the great body of our citizens have adjusted their business and capital upon the principle, though erroneous, we have no right to twitch from them the foundations on which they have builded, without giving them time. [Great applause.]

No policy of free trade, though it is the sound and true one, can ever prevail at once. Time must give it ripeness. When the other principle has prevailed for so long, it would be wanton, it would be not only unwise, but unutterable folly to make a sudden change. If a change is to be made, it must be made by cool men in cool times. How shall it be made? How fast? By what measures? It must be determined by ripe counsels of practical men. A tribunal of arbitrament for such questions should not be composed of a ferocious and tumultuous and headlong party. Look at the Court as constituted. Fourteen Southern States and a fragment of the Democratic party of the North. They are to sit in judgment upon and criticize a policy which has been followed for thirty or forty years, on which the foundations of the Nation have been built. Is that a proper tribunal—are these the right kind of men to judge? You cannot go into a fight for Free Trade, and influence the votes of men to-day. The world will not come to an end to-morrow. You must let the doctrine ripen.

"Ah," but a man would say, "if you think that you are doing wrong, should you not renounce it at once?" If it is a personal sin, I do—if a political mistake, I do not. When the captain of a ship unintentionally steers east, meaning to go south, and, running into a complicated channel on the east or north, when the fog breaks away he finds himself in peril, this man would then say: "Oh, you must go back—return the way you came." But that is not so. You could not in such a case go back with safety. You must find a channel in the direction in which you first set out. And, therefore, I say it is a fair appeal made to every man that is getting his day's wages: "Do not make a change suddenly." I say in behalf of every man who is engaged in manufactures, it is unwise and impolitic to force that issue upon capital and the industries of the country suddenly. I say to every man who is importing and selling, or using property for domestic happiness, no such sudden changes are safe or healthy, especially when they involve such enormous interests; and I don't think that it would be wise to get the Democrats to make them. [Great laughter.] Now, gentlemen, if you can advocate a tariff, and at the same time vote for no change of it more skilfully than that, I would like to see you get up here and try it. [Laughter.] Yet I think this policy is right and laid in solid grounds.

No Change Wanted.

Well, I hear those on the other side, young men—and some of them very young—say: "The Republicans have been in power long enough; it is time we had a change." Well, gentlemen, let us ask these men deliberately, what kind of a change do you want? Do you want a change in our foreign relations? We are in peace and amity with every Nation on the globe. You cannot change that state of things unless you go to war. Well, then, do you want a change in our finances? When a paper dollar is worth a gold dollar, I cannot see what change you want there; you cannot make it worth two dollars. Other men would say: "We want more paper dollars." Now a paper dollar represents property, and I have no objection to your increasing property, but I protest against your increasing that which represents it; you would find a very quick limit to the increase of the representative of property when there was no property to be represented. You have got gold and silver. We are generous of our gold and prodigal of our silver. We have a dollar, worth a dollar if it is gold, and we give about 80 cents or 85 cents for it if it is silver. [Laughter.] Gentlemen, we have got silver enough. I wish some of these men that are bothering about the polls were sent out to dig it; [laughter;] their counsel and their action at home are not very profitable.

In regard to everybody else there is universal content. If I go to the artist's he tells me: "There is a very large demand springing up for my pictures;" if I go to the builder's they tell me they are having house after house pressed upon them; I go to the mason, and his trowel clinks on the brick from early morning to late at night. I ask the loom and it says, "I am crowded to death with work;" I go to the plough—it shines as a mirror, rubbed through the furrows to bring out the harvests that all Europe and all the world wants; [applause;] I ask the compass and the rudder, and they say never were the seas more propitious; I ask commerce and agricul culture and manufacture; I ask the fine arts, scholarship and learning, and there comes an answer as of one voice from every interest—domestic, private, public—everywhere the Nation was never more prosperous than it is to-day. [Loud applause.]

And now you want a change. [Laughter.] To do what? A change to carry this prosperity forward faster would not be a wholesome change. In that way lies speculation, fictitious prosperity, the insanity of hope; moderation is on this side. The other change, and the only one is to go back to the dollar customs of the early days, when men did nothing but attend to politics. No, no. This Nation was never more blessed than it is to-day. [Loud applause.]

Now, National prosperity lasts about ten or fifteen years, and then the natural evolution of things brings matters to a point. We give men credit, as it were, for a period of ten to fifteen years; then we call upon every man to settle up. Settling up is called a crisis. [Laughter.] And it is. [Renewed laugh ter.] Then, when we have settled up we all start again, and generally there is a run of ten to fifteen years, according to the nation. If it is a vital nation, the settling up comes in about ten to fifteen years; in a conservative nation, like the British, it comes in about twenty years; if the nation is more phlegmatic, like the Dutch, it takes fifty years to do it. [Laughter.] But we are on the dawn of a day of prosperity such as has never been measured out to this land, [applause,] and the Republican party, having gone through the night; having carried the Nation safely through all its past difficulties; having suffered in every possible way; having vindicated its patriotism, and being now about to stretch out its hand and reach its just reward of quiet and peaceful comfort, which prosperity brings, the minions of Slaveocracy and Democracy start up and say, "Gentlemen, get down from the seat, and let us get up and drive." [Laughter.]

Where is there a guarantee for another four years of prosperity clearer than the four years that are running out to-day? Who is he that can inaugurate a kinder policy than President Hayes has done? [Applause.] Where can you pick out a Secretary who can manage the Treasury as Sherman does? [Applause.] When has there ever been a Cabinet, from the days of Washington cleaner in every member of it than the Cabinet that now consults in Washington? [Applause.] And yet men can say, looking at these four millennium years: "We want a change!" Do you want to go from good to bad? Do you want to go from prosperity backward? Ah, I know the answer of the Democratic party. They were the men that cried in the wilderness for the leeks and onions of Egypt, and they wanted to go back to Egypt for they hadn't enough to eat. [Laughter.] Gentlemen, the leeks and the onions are not for the Democratic party just yet. [Renewed laughter.] And yet I am a very great friend of the Democrats. [Laughter.] Whom I love I chasten. [Roars of laughter.]

They were doing a wise thing when they put up Hancock as their candidate. He is a very wise man. I do not think he is ordained to be the headpiece of the Democratic party—that is, I do not think he will be their President—but he is a very eminent man. He is a man who has earned the gratitude of his times for his services in the war. [Applause.] I have no sympathy with those that dissect his character to his disadvantage. I have no sympathy with those that throw mud at him. I have no sympathy not only with those who detract from him, and just as little with the party that goes down on its belly to write "329" on the sidewalks. [Roars of laughter.] Gentlemen, Ohio has given to us the interpretation of that mystic sign [applause]—329 cheers for Garfield. [Loud applause.]

Now, gentlemen, if this were meeting-time you would be asleep most of you. [Laughter.] But it is said of old that "the children of this world are wiser in their generation than the children of light," and you are wide awake to-night, and you will be to-morrow, and you will be in every subsequent day; and I have only one or two more points that I wish to make with you. [Cries of "Go on."] I am going on. [Laughter.] That's what I am here for. [Laughter.]

No Hatred toward the South.

I have one word to say, that I should be very glad to have carried to all the South—which, if I don't get old too fast, I mean to stump yet one day before I die; that is, that there is no feeling of animosity in the hearts of the North toward the Southern people. [Applause.] We recognize that the prosperity of the North itself depends on the prosperity of the South. [Applause.] We want their towns to be rebuilt; we want to see their industries re-established; we want to see them at peace with themselves; we want to see them at peace with their fellow-citizens throughout the whole of this Nation; we want the long catalogue of invectives, the long line of evil thoughts that have arisen through years gone by—we want them to go down like the dreams of the troubled and the fevered night. [Applause.] We want to take them by the hand as fellow-citizens. We want to see them brought back into Congress. They are there; and I take no part nor stock in the ridicule poured on the "Brigadiers." Gentlemen, when the South moved as one man into the war, as far as my observation went, with here and there single exceptions, the most honorable, wisest and best men went into the movement, and when she came back and her States were admitted again, if the South sent to Congress anybody, it was her interest and her duty to send her best men there; and when she selected her Brigadier-Generals she selected her best men and sent them there. She did well. I have no criticism to make.

More than that, I would fight just as soon for South Carolina as for my native State of Connecticut against anything that could destroy her local liberty and independence; [applause:] and what I would do for one State I would do for every State down there. All that I say is this: Restore, as they have had restored, their State rights; give them plenary liberty to transact their own affairs. For one, I believe that the time will come ere long when they will do justice to the black citizens there. If they do not do it at once, the Government of the United States cannot do it for them. That time has gone by. It might have been done earlier. I shall not go into that policy nor discuss that question; but at present it cannot be done by the Federal Government. Measures must be taken by which the South shall be so far divided as that there shall be in the Southern States two parties, one for and the other against, and then they will divide their colored voters between them, and they will respectively take care of them. [Applause.] In that way that question is yet to be settled. But now, I say, they have sent to Congress their best men. They have as much right to sit in Congress to-day as the members from New-York or the members from Boston. [Applause.] I want to detract no whit from their merit or their opportunities; but this is what I say: that while we restore to them their local independence, put their own State affairs absolutely into their hands, bring them back as counsellors into our National Congress, and treat them as fellow-citizens, I say that it is not time yet to give them the administration of the National Government, and for them to determine the policy of this Nation. [Applause.] They are not ripe for that. It belongs to the East; it belongs to the Northwest; it belongs to the North; it belongs to the Middle States; and the Southern States have got to lie in quarantine until the smell of yellow fever and black vomit is off from their garments. [Applause and laughter.]

Witnesses of the Struggle.

Now, gentlemen, it is not enough—and this is the second remark that I wish to make—for us, that we just squeeze through this election, and carry the country. If you wish to have the question settled without any resurrection, there ought to be such a testimony of the voters of these United States as shall forever more debar the entrance into politics of the questions that vex us to-day. Do your work strongly. Roll up such a majority in the State of New-York as shall make a man a lunatic that proposes ever to undertake to moot the question again. [Applause.] It is not enough for Indiana to roll up her 5,000 or 6,000. [Applause.] It is not enough for Ohio to give her 25,000. [Applause.] That does very well. New-York must come in with her 10,000 votes, [applause,] and it depends simply on the will —your will, and the will of men like you, who believe that the interests of this country are above every other interest; who believe they are called of God as well as of patriotism, to cleanse this Nation of its contaminations and put it upon a broad foundation, where there shall be a nationality without a North, without a South, without an East, without a West. [Applause.]

We are not working in a corner nor in a hole. If there ever was a Nation whose prosperity had attracted the thoughtful regard of wise men throughout the world, this is that Nation. If there has ever been surprise sprung upon men at the developments of human nature, the conduct of this Nation in the war, and after the war, and to this hour has given that surprise. Not only are we surrounded with a cloud of earthly witnesses in this great campaign, but all the men that landed with our fathers, in the misty distance, obscure to us but clear to them, are looking down upon us. It is the nation they founded, and if the rock could speak, as once the rock gushed forth with water for the famished crowd, old Plymouth Rock would give forth a voice to all the men of the Republican party and of the nation, saying: "Keep, build, fortify that which we founded." [Applause.]

Scarcely, like a reed blown from the wind in the sky, have they gone out of sight before we behold the reverent founders of the Constitution and the fathers of this nation. They, too, are the witnesses of their children, and they plead that this Constitution, which was ordained to Liberty, shall neither be undermined nor blackened, nor weakened, nor perverted into an instrument of tyranny by their posterity. Heed their voice. And scarcely have they gone out of sight when, gathering like armies, multitudinous as the drops of the storm-cloud, the men that laid down their lives for the Nation appear and lift up their voices and reach out airy hands to beseech us to preserve immaculate that for which they bled to gain. [Loud applause.] And high above them all, and most reverent, I behold the immortal form of the Father of his Country, a Southerner and loving the South. Methinks he turns his face from the North, and says to his brethren of the South: "Ye know not what ye do. Be at peace. Maintain the Government. Submit to the law; and let there be brotherhood in all the land, and your God and my God shall pour his blessing upon the Nation." [Tremendous applause, in the midst of which Mr. Beecher slowly retired.]—*From the New-York Tribune, Thursday October 14, 1880.*

The Speech of the Hon. EMERY A. STORRS, of Chicago, in the Cooper Union, New-York City, Wednesday night, October 20, 1880.

MR. CHAIRMAN—FELLOW CITIZENS : I am exceedingly gratified to meet so many Republicans of the great City of New-York under the circumstances under which I now meet them—presented by one of the most distinguished lawyers and one of the most distinguished Republicans of the country. [Applause.] I am delighted that one whom all this country, and indeed all the world, is proud to honor is here with us to-night. [Applause and cheers.] I am delighted that while I do not bring good tidings —you have heard them—yet I speak to the Republicans of this imperial City in the presence of the greatest success which our great party has ever achieved. [Applause.] I speak after two great strongholds have been carried, after the election has finally been determined, after Ohio has vindicated her fidelity to the cause by 20,000 majority, [applause,] after Indiana has spoken by 7,000 and rising. [Applause.]

I confess that in the presence of these great victories I feel a most solid and holy joy—a joy not unmixed with sadness in contemplating the great grief that has come over the very worthy gentlemen who are to-day busily engaged in crawling out from beneath the falling fragments of their old exploded machinery. [Laughter.] I commiserate that distinguished statesman from Massachusetts [laughter] who left our party a little too soon, and who joined the other party a little too quick. [Laughter.] I commiserate the two or three distinguished gentlemen from New-York City whose departure was well intended, but ill timed. [Laughter.] I commiserate Mr. Jerome and his Hancock Republican Club, and the general poverty that attends the treasury department of that club. [Great laughter.] And I commiserate all who have not already discovered that this is the wrong year to be a Democrat.

We have some solid serious work in front of us, and where a great splendid example has been set I like to follow it. I remember that we had a great General, who captured Vicksburg. [Cheers.] It was a Democratic stronghold. [Laughter.] The same distinguished gentleman also captured that solid Democratic city, Richmond. He did no hallooing over Richmond. He did not go into Richmond, any more than he did Vicksburg, but he passed right on, and made a little inconspicuous place, that never was known on the map at all—Appomattox—a place of everlasting renown, because there he corraled a Democratic town. [Applause.]

I have observed in the papers a great many gentlemen undertaking to diagnose this condition of things, seeking here and there for an explanation of Ohio and Indiana going Republican. I have a great variety of reasons for it. First, the Republican party was absolutely solidified and united, and it was absolutely right. [Applause.] Next, it has a magnificent history, and the other party has an absolutely infernal and diabolical history. I do not want to irritate Democrats here to-night by referring to their history. I know the enthusiastic displeasure with which they listen to the recital. I know if there is any thing that will drive the average Democrat straight out of a hall it is to read to him his last year's platform. [Laughter.] There are other reasons. The manufacturing instincts of this country, the business instincts, the agricultural instincts, were afraid of this Democratic party. The patriotic instincts that wanted a free ballot and a fair count were afraid of this Democratic party. Let me say right here that neither the tariff nor the currency question alone gave us this victory, for deeper down in the popular heart than either, solider than business, holier than the Spring trade, is the sentimental love of that blessed old banner—our flag ! [Great applause.] Hundreds of thousands of men were willing to die for it. You can't find anybody, Mr. President, that will die for a bank account or a corner lot ! Our blessed flag, with its stars and stripes and red, white and blue symbolizes all that there is noble in politics and glorious in history to us, [applause,] and we propose to wave it until no man stands on any foot of ground that cannot think just what he pleases, and vote just exactly as he wishes, and there will be none to molest or make him afraid. [Applause.]

Lesson in Democratic Harmony.

I talk to-night about the Democratic party. I have observed in looking over their sad and somewhat melancholy literature that we are enjoined to be "harmonious." If there is any thing the average Democrat likes it is harmony. [Laughter.] I am in favor of being harmonious about some things, but I am opposed to a harmonious stuffing of the ballot-box, to a harmonious false count, to harmonious assassinations and midnight raids as agents of political discussion, and to harmonious fraud in politics. I am in favor of harmonious equality, harmonious and universal enforcement of the laws and statutes. I know of nothing to do with a promise but to keep it, nothing in God's heavens to do with a national engagement but to fulfill it. I object to the Democratic party for a great variety of reasons. The life of man is limited to seventy years or thereabout, and you cannot expect me to consume that entire time in going into details concerning the record of the Democratic party. [Laughter.] I will cursorily leap from one summit to another as some great peak of criminality presents itself, descanting on it briefly, and pass on.

In the first place, can anybody tell me a promise that that party has made in twenty-five years in which the cause of good government was interested that it has kept ? Will somebody brush up his recollection, and refer me to an engagement that that party has entered into with the people that it has performed ? All along its pathway it is strewn with the skeletons, bleached and whitened, of broken pledges and violated faith. Tell me any great measure in our politics within the last quarter of a century which to-day we take pride in recounting, of which we are not ashamed, that the party proposed or organized or favored? You cannot one? Point me to a single great measure in the adoption of which we, as a people, are at all proud, that that party has not malignantly, steadily, persistently, solidly, diabolically, demagogically opposed. [Laughter.] Point me to a single statute, National or State, looking to the protection of the ballot-box against fraud that the party proposed. You will have to give it up. There is not one of that character that has been enacted and repealed where the repeal was not effected by a Democratic majority. [Applause.] That's a pretty foul sort of history. The trouble with it is, it's true!

What Democracy Represents.

All parties represent some interest. What does that party represent? Not the manufacturing interest. They have sought the destruction of it since 1832. It is not the financial interests of the country. They would overturn our entire system. Is it the educational interest? [Laughter.] That's a solemn question. I grieve to see it treated with so much levity. [Laughter.] Is it the moral interest? As representatives of great moral ideas, how does the average Democratic procession in the City of New-York look? [Prolonged laughter.] I am constrained to think they don't represent any interest. [A Voice—"The whiskey interest."] My friend is mistaken; that's not an interest. That is a calamity. They represent every single one of the calamities. They represent a stuffed ballot-box; they represent the assassination of revenue officers.

Has there been any change in that party? If so, when did it change? In the night? I remember in Western New-York, where I was born, we had a queer climate. I would go to bed at night when I was a school-boy, with the sky perfectly clear and the stars shining brightly in the heavens, and I would wake up in the morning and find it perfectly clear with snow on the ground, and a venerable old gentleman, disturbed a little at the frequency of transactions of that character, said that he sat up one night until about 2 o'clock, when he catched it at it! [Laughter.] Now, I have been sitting up late at night to catch this Democratic party at it, but I haven't succeeded. [Laughter.] They have all the same leaders that they had in 1860. Suppose we run over the list. It is an entertaining recital. They had Wade Hampton, Robert Toombs, Fort Pillow Forrest, Jefferson Davis (hisses) and Ben Hill, in the South in 1860, and haven't they got them now? They had in the North Horatio Seymour, Isaiah Rynders, Samuel J. Tilden, and William H. English, of Indiana; Tom Hendricks and Eaton, of Connecticut, and Ben Butler, of Massachusetts, and haven't they got them now? [Laughter.] Has the rank and file changed any? Don't the processions of 1880 look about as they did in 1860? Of course there has been some havoc in the ranks by casualties and delirium tremens, but they are filled up. [Laughter.] I am told you get your Democratic majorities from the toughest Wards in this city. Since Tweed has been called to his Democratic fathers has there been any essential change in the localities where there are large Democratic majorities? I take it not. Has there been any change in doctrine? They have taken great pains in 1880 to declare: "We pledge ourselves anew to the

constitutional doctrines and traditions of the Democratic party." I take them at their word, and I'll show you by and by what these doctrines and traditions are.

They want a change. So do I. I want a change from a Confederate to a loyal Congress, and we're going to have it. [Applause.] They claim they want a reform of the civil service. So do I; but the most important branch of the civil service is Congress, and I propose to reform it by hustling out every Democratic member, and putting a Republican in. What situation are they in to demand a change? In 1860 our national credit was so decrepit that we undertook to effect a little loan of a trivial few millions, and the bonds bore interest at 6 per cent., and the highest offer that could be got for them was 88 cents on a dollar, but in 1880 we are able to dispose of hundreds of millions of our bonds bearing 4 per cent. interest, at a premium of 10¾ per cent. [Applause.] Now, in 1860 the Democratic party was in power. Our bonds were 88 cents on the dollar, and they were opposed to a change. In 1880, when our bonds are 10¾ cents more than a dollar, they demand a change! In 1880 we have as fine a currency as there is in the world, which, like a Republican platform, is current everywhere. In 1860 we had "wild-cat" and "red-dog," and "stump tail"—the most variegated currency the world ever saw—like Democratic speeches, you have to change it as you cross the county line, [laughter,] and the Democratic party was opposed to a change. Now they demand it. Speaking of Democratic speeches, I sympathize with the Democratic orator who travels much, for Democratic doctrine is a climatic sort of thing, and a speech is affected by the temperature in which it is delivered. They have cold water and warm water speeches, and the Democrat who delivers a cold water speech, as Mr. Bayard did—the hardest kind of a hard-money speech—wakes up in the morning, after starting South, to find that his speech won't work. It is disagreeable to have to look at the thermometer before the meeting comes off to see what kind of a speech you've got to deliver. Down in Indiana that speech of Bayard played the very mischief, and it did not do any good here. Mr. Blackburn's orations on the tariff were superb down there, but they were destructive in Sandusky, Ohio.

What Democracy would Change.

I find in 1860 we had a foreign trade of $700,000,000, and in 1880 of $1,150,000,000; but in 1860 the Democrats opposed a change, now they demand it. In 1860 our imports exceeded our exports $20,000,000. In 1880 our exports exceed our imports $265,000,000, but the Democratic party opposed a change in 1860, and they demand a change in 1880. In 1860 we exported of wheat 4,000,000 bushels, and in 1880 175,000,000 bushels; in 1860, 3,000,000 bushels of corn; in 1880, 100,000,000 bushels. In 1860 the Democratic party opposed a change, now they demand it. In 1860, of rail-road iron we manufactured only 205,000 tons, and not a ton of steel, whereas in 1880 we manufactured 1,113,000 tons; yet, in 1860, they opposed a change; in 1880 they demand it. The fact is, to-day we stand in the midst of a most marvelous prosperity, and the glory of it all is that we have earned it. [Applause.] It is honest and well deserved. It is the prosperity that comes from wise legislation, from honest administration, from a steady upholding of the national faith, and a steady vindication of the national honor and credit. There's no luck about it. I know some Democratic orators have ascribed these good times to Providence. I have different views about the Lord. I don't think He interferes directly with financial legislation. I think He legislates in a general way, and, without being at all irreverent, let me say to you that you might take the best weather you ever saw, and our fields that ache with teeming harvests, and you put fiat money into it, and you could not have good times and the Lord altogether. Providence would not try to make good times out of any such combination.

The serious difficulty with the Democratic party is that if it ever favors the right thing it is at the wrong time. Thus, all through the war it was in favor of peace. You remember that. [Laughter.] And down South, when nobody can think, except to think as they think, when no one can speak save he speaks as they speak, when no man can vote except he votes as they vote, then they are in favor of free speech and free thought and a free vote. They claim in their platform that they are in favor of a free ballot, and there is something very eloquent in that platform, and it is what we have ample time here to-night to discuss, and nobody is in a hurry, and I would like to read just what they say :

"The right to a free ballot," the Democratic party says, "is a right preservative of all rights, and must and shall be maintained in every part of the United States."

In view of the fact that in 1868 they cast a great many thousands of fraudulent votes right in this town, and counted them, and carried the State by a fraud so conspicuous and impudent that nobody dares to deny it, the clatter for a " free ballot," and the claim that it is a " right preservative of all rights," and that it " must and shall be maintained in every part of the United States," is perhaps the cheekiest thing in political history. [Applause.] That fraud in 1868 constrained the loyal people of this country to pass the election laws, so called, and the party that now shrieks through the country for a free ballot has been industriously engaged in an effort to repeal those laws. Why? The repeal is not required at the South. The gentle agencies of assassination, terrorism, and violence and fraud, have repealed the statutes there, but in order that every barrier between the vote and fraud might be thrown down, so that by fraud New-York City and Brooklyn and Albany, and other great cities might give majorities sufficiently large to wheel these naturally Republican States into line with the solid South, and for those reasons alone was the attempt for the repeal of the election laws made, and so eager were they for that repeal that they were quite willing to starve the Government into submission, and to affix the repealing clauses to the appropriation bills.

A Terrible Arraignment.

It was a stupendous swindle, and the party, just from that dirty work, just from a scheme so fraudulent, so expansive and enlarged in its political scoundrelism, gets together in the City of Cincinnati, and declares that the right to a free ballot is a right preservative of all rights, and must and shall be main-

tained in all parts of the United States. The same party has to-day a solid South. In 1872 the Republicans cast 90,272 votes in Alabama, and in 1878 they did not cast a vote—not one. Do you suppose that that change was made through the marvelous efficacy of Mr. Tilden's Literary Bureau ? Was the subtle whisperer of Gramercy clothed with power so persuasive that, reaching over mountains and across prairies and plains, he converted the negro in six years, and the Republicans, so that 90,000 votes in 1872 dwindled to nothing in 1878 ? Terrorism did it, fraud did it, the false count and the no-count did it, the flaming cabin did it, the shot-gun did it, all of which convinces me that the right to a free ballot is a right preservative of all rights, and must and shall be maintained in every part of the United States. [Laughter and applause.]

Now, in 1872 the Republicans cast 41,000 votes in Arkansas, and in 1878 they cast 115. The shot-gun, terrorism, fraud, violence, did it, which makes me perfectly certain that the right to a free ballot is a right preservative of all rights, and must and shall be maintained in every part of the United States. [Applause.]

Now, in 1872, in the State of Mississippi, the Republicans cast 82,000 odd votes, and in 1878 they cast 1,168. The shot-gun reduced it ; the bludgeon reduced it ; the gentle ministrations of the White Leaguers and the Ku-Klux reduced it ; they act, where a free ballot has to be cast, as the old Romans did—they make a desert and they call it peace. How quiet it is in Mississippi ! How subdued it is in Arkansas ! How still it is in Alabama ! How restrained and calm it is in South Carolina ! Dixon has been convinced that he was wrong ; the argument was a slug fired at him in the back. Chisolm has been satisfied that he took incorrect views of the ordinance of 1870, and the argument was a body full of bullets. The dead negroes are very peaceable. All this assures me that the Democratic party has struck hard-pan when they declare that the right to a free ballot is the right preservative of all rights, and must and shall be maintained. Now, wonders will never cease with that wonderful party. There was an election in Alabama this year. The Democratic majority was very enthusiastic. It was 92,000—8,000 more than their entire vote. I am willing to concede that Mr. Tilden's Literary Bureau can convert Republicans. I do not believe that it can increase the population. [Laughter and applause.] Hence you see that the right to a free ballot is a right preservative, &c.

Where Bayonets Should be Used.

Now, Gen. Hancock has a word to say on this subject, and where we come to Gen. Hancock's utterances we strike something we can or cannot understand. I promise the reading by saying, that I never saw a Democratic Major-General that had not a horror of the bayonet. If there is any thing that a Democratic Major-General abhors and dislikes it is the bayonet. Hence, Major-Gen. Hancock says that the bayonet is not a fit instrument for collecting the votes of freemen. I do not know about that. [Applause.] I am told by experts that the bayonet is not much used in actual warfare, and that Sherman's men collected hams with bayonets on their march.

But if the ballot of the black men down South cannot be collected in any other way, except on the point of a bayonet, and cannot be put into the ballot-box by any other piece of machinery, I am in favor of employing the bayonet for just that purpose. [Loud applause.] If the Constitution-loving, law-abiding, God-fearing Democratic Inspectors behind the ballot-box cannot be brought to a knowledge of the truth as it is in the fourteenth and fifteenth constitutional amendments in any other way, I would like to have them, by the bayonet, punched into a lively appreciation of what they mean.

I have said to you that I thought that this free ballot was the supreme question in our politics. It is. The majorities in at least five States are disfranchised, and you know it and everybody knows it. In half this country there is no Republican that can vote as he wants to, and you know it and everybody knows it. And the organic law has declared that no one shall be deprived of his right to vote by reason of color, race or previous condition of servitude, and these solemn guarantees are unperformed, and you know it, and I think the time has come to perform them. [Applause.] I am in favor of the disturbance then. I am told that we will have trouble. Come trouble! I had rather have fifty years of earthquake, uproar and eclipse than any more disregard of great national engagements. Is there any real trouble about it? I take it not. Those amendments provide that Congress shall have power to enforce the provisions of those articles by appropriate legislation, and Congress judges what is appropriate. What do you think would be appropriate? That kind of legislation which would meet the truth, would not it? If this guaranteed privilege was interfered with by a shot-gun, I would not think that a hymn-book or a psalm or a song or a sermon would be an appropriate remedy, but I would say two shot-guns. And if it was interfered with by some armed men, I would not want any missionary work; I would meet those gentlemen with more armed men—even the Army of the United States. Coming right to something practical, your Chairman has indicated the method—a Republican Congress, courageous enough to take this great wrong right by the horns, enact statutes which will clothe the Executive with power to call out the Army of the United States to enforce those engagements, and a President that will do it when the time comes. [Loud applause.]

I confess I do not like to think of my country as a great, big, bullying, bragging, blustering, flunking Nation, that promises largely and does not perform. This is not the business of the States or of a State. The Republican party, by the organic law, has declared that we are all citizens of the United States, the grandest title that a man ever bore, and it has made of jarring States a Nation, and it has made that Nation free, and when the poor, trembling black man, given by this Nation his freedom, made by this Nation a citizen, takes the compact that Nation has made with him in his hand, and comes to the Nation, he can properly say, "Here is your engagement, you have made it, execute and carry out your contracts with me or quit business. [Applause.]

I like to think of my country sometimes as having material shape and form. This great, splendid Union of ours, so prosperous and so free—its future,

who can paint it? Its career, how glorious it has been! And I think of this Nation of mine and of yours, enthroned away above the clouds, among the stars, robed in her spotless garments, with the star of empire glittering on her forehead, hearing the cry of the lowest and the weakest and the poorest of her citizens, coming down from those glittering eminences, and with sword and shield taking the trembling black man or carpet-bagger by the hand through the ranks of his enemies, past his foes, and saying to him, "By the loving God, you shall cast an unconstrained ballot!" [Applause.] It is of such a Nation that I love to think; it is of such a Nation that I am proud.

Perhaps, by this time, you will reach the conclusion that I am a stalwart. Why? I know no degrees in Republicanism. There are none. A man is either a Republican or he is not. There are no conservative Republicans, or liberal Republicans, or independent Republicans now. We are Republicans! There is no free ballot—just a little; there is no fair—just a part of the time; there is no conservatism in fraud; we don't want any radicalism in wrong. We are Republicans.

Protection of our Industries.

Our doctrine, and the next doctrine to which I wish to address your attention without arguing it, is that of protection to our industries. Our party is committed to that system by its history and by its platform. The democratic party is committed in opposition to it by its platform and by its history. In its platform of 1880 it declared for a tariff for revenue only, and its candidate for the Presidency, General Hancock, declared in the most explicit manner his adhesion to the platform, and said that the principles therein enumerated were those that he had always cherished, and which he would maintain in the future. It is but fair that I should give General Hancock the full benefit of his own outpouring on this great question; and at the risk of being somewhat tedious I will read to you first his interview, and next his letter. I have seen political wisdom before now, but I never saw a stream of it come rushing with such a flood through the bung-hole, as it did in this interview. I have seen small bits of wisdom drop from the great summits and mountain peaks of thought, but when Gen. Hancock was interviewed great boulders of wisdom came rushing down. [Laughter.] Having read this document several times already, I am able to read it to you now without emotion. [Laughter.] I will read it as gently as possible, in small sections at a time, and with notes historical and explanatory, after the manner of Plutarch.

The representative of the Paterson (N. J.) *Guardian* wished to interview Gen. Hancock. After some general conversation, the reporter said: "There is one thing, General, I desire to speak about. The tariff question is creating a good deal of talk in Paterson, particularly among manufacturers." Now, I should suppose they would "talk" about it if anybody would. "Now," said the reporter, "how is that going to work?" How is the "talk" going to work, or the "question" going to work—which did he mean? Hancock, however, is up to the suggestion, and he responds in the words and figures following, that is to say: "The question," said the General, "cannot affect the manufacturing interests in the least." In the name of all that is good, will you be good enough to tell me what question can, if the tariff question cannot, affect manufacturing interests? Is it foreordination, or justification by faith, or immersion, or sprinkling, that can affect manufacturing interests? But the General is more entertaining as he proceeds: "My election can make no difference either one way or the other." As the celebrated Mr. Squeers said, "There's richness for you!" If a Democratic Congress should overturn our entire protective system, and Gen. Hancock should sign the bill, would that make any difference? Would it not make all the difference in the world? It would make just the difference between having protection and not having protection. But I go along: "The Paterson people need have no anxiety whatever that I will ever favor any thing that interferes with the manufacturing and industrial interests of the country The tariff is a local question."

I was about as much stunned when I read that as I would be in a mathematical debate if somebody had jumped up and disputed the multiplication table. If this is a local question, what is a general question? A tariff, for good or ill, affects not only every interest in this country, but in every other country on the face of the globe. But I understand his meaning. I catch his idea. He means, it is as local as this planet—that it does not affect the solar system generally—that it creates no disturbance among the fixed stars. In that sense certainly it is a local question, being confined merely to the globe on which we live. Then, as showing that he understands his subject, that he speaks by the card, he says: "The same question was brought up once in my native place in Pennsylvania." Now, if there is any thing in that State that they pull up by the hair at all times, it is the tariff question. They sit up with it nights; they get up with it early in the morning, and ever since 1812, every Pennsylvanian, when awake, has talked about the tariff. But that is not all. He says "it is a matter that the general Government seldom cares to interfere with." I ask, who do you suppose does interfere with it? He thinks they fix it up at Harrisburg, and after Don Cameron and the General and the rest of them have got it fixed, if there is any thing unsatisfactory about it, the general Government takes a lick at it.

Gen. Hancock's Conversion.

This interview brought about an irrepressible conflict between the Democratic orators and their candidate. Mr. Dorsheimer declares the tariff a destructive and not a protective measure. It shows the marvelous power of our party as a mere missionary concern, that we have converted Gen. Hancock within the last three weeks. [Laughter.] He started out on the platform with a tariff for revenue only. Clouds gathered in the sky—he had read my speech and Mr. Choate's, he had read the documents emanating from the National Committee—and, journeying as Paul was, he saw a great light in the sky, and the scales fell from his eyes, and he stands forth to-day probably the most enthusiastic all-wool, yard-wide protectionist on the Continent. [Laughter.]

Still, that interview was not quite satisfactory, and Mr. Randolph got troubled in his mind. In reply to him, Gen. Hancock says: 'In my letter of acceptance I expressed my sympathy with our American industries. I thought I spoke plainly enough to satisfy our Jersey friends.' Was he writing that letter of acceptance to our Jersey friends? [Laughter.] He spoke quite plainly. He said that the principles enumerated in the platform were those that he had always cherished, and that he was going to hold out faithful unto the end, and that he would always maintain them in the future, and the principles there were "tariff for revenue only." 'I am too sound an American," he says, "to defend any departure from the general features of a policy that has been largely instrumental in building up our industries and guarding the American from competition of the underpaid labor of Europe. If we intend to remain honest and pay the public debt, as good people of all parties do, and if we mean to administer the functions of government—[A Voice—Well, we do! Applause]—then we must raise the revenue in some way or other."

Was there ever a more unseemly lot of slop? To raise the revenue to be honest with! Raise the revenue for good people to be honest with! Raise the revenue to administer the functions of Government with! "With a united and harmonious country we shall certainly in time pay off the public debt, but the necessity for raising money for the administration of the Government will continue as long as human nature lasts." Not necessarily! I take issue there. We had human nature before we had a tariff. I think we are going to have a human nature after we have a tariff. Was there ever any thing in our history—to be serious about it—more utterly vapid? Is it not enough to make any man ashamed that he is expected to vote for a citizen, otherwise distinguished, who has made such a conspicuous and clamorous display of his utter inefficiency for the position which he seeks? [Applause.] I think that Gen. Hancock has swallowed the whole body of Democratic history—platform, record and all—in too solid a mass to be otherwise than exceedingly injurious to his digestion. Have you ever seen a more shameful abandonment of creed and doctrine than is displayed in these two documents?

Republicans completing the Edifice.

I shall not discuss the tariff. It is enough to say that behind the Republican party is more than twenty years of steady policy of the same character which we propose to pursue in future. I know what the Republican party will do. I know what James A. Garfield will do, and what, if he died, Chester A. Arthur will do. I know they believe in encouraging and maintaining American industry, and in maintaining our present system of currency. The Republican party took the old edifice, of which the Democrats spoke, and removed from it the decaying timbers of human chattelhood, and replaced them with the fullest guarantee of freedom. They found the old walls defaced, slimy all over will foul inscriptions. They found its presiding genius, not the great Nation that we now worship, but a bullying, cruel, blustering, bragging, dirt-eating sycophantic genius, carrying the Dred Scott decision in one hand and the Fugitive Slave law in the other, marching, not to the music of the Union, but to the music of the chain and the crack of the whip, and the baying of the bloodhound, and the appealing and imploring cry of the pursued. Thank God, Lincoln was our chieftain, and we wiped out all these foul records, and we have covered them with the shining and resplendent record of 4,000,000 of slaves lifted by one supreme effort from the night of savagery and chattelhood into the clear day of American citizenship. The world witnesses it, and hails and salutes it.

In this great party, that never made a promise it did not keep; that had crowded, if you count it by achievements, a thousand years of plenty into twenty years of time; whose banner is without stain; the hosts are gathering to-day, and the old imperial State shall lead these great hosts out of the night of the past into the free sunshine, up to the topmost heights of magnificent victory. [Applause.]—*From the New-York Times, Thursday, October* 21, 1880.

The Address of the Hon. WILLIAM M. EVARTS, *in the Brooklyn Academy of Music, Wednesday evening, October* 20, 1880.

MR. CHAIRMAN AND GENTLEMEN OF THE YOUNG REPUBLICAN CLUB, FELLOW CITIZENS, LADIES AND GENTLEMEN : It would give me great pleasure, as it has heretofore, to speak to the citizens of Brooklyn under any circumstances when they might do me the honor to be willing to listen to me. But, sir, I confess that the circumstances under which I now appear before them, under the auspices of your Club, give me greater pleasure, and I meet this welcome that is offered to me simply as your spokesman. You are of this community; you are known to it; you are recognized as young men who feel your duty to this country of ours, and mean to perform it. Your numbers have grown steadily, and are yet to increase; and when on election day, you do your duty at the polls, as up to that time you will do it in every form of activity among your fellow citizens, you will have made your Club an element in the canvass that cannot be overlooked wherever the honors and the congratulations of the triumph are bestowed. Where but here, where but in your neighboring city of New-York, should we expect this display of the zeal and animation of the young merchants and the young professional men of these great centres of influence in the country ? In the academic distribution it used to be said that to the Juniors belong the labor, and to the Seniors the honor. But in this combat honors never will be bestowed except upon those who have performed the labor, and if the Seniors wish to divide them with the Juniors they must share with them the labor in the public service. [Applause.]

A story is told of a great Massachusetts lawyer, Chief Justice Parsons, and a scarcely less distinguished merchant of Boston, Thomas H. Perkins, which, I think, illustrates the relation of the mercantile community to the prosperity and public service of the country. Chief Justice Parsons and Thomas H. Perkins were among the most eminent citizens of Boston, and were intimate friends and associates. One day, when Chief Justice Parsons was presiding at a jury trial, the name of Mr. Perkins was called, and the Sheriff deferentially stepped up to the bench and, laying down a fifty dollar bill before the Judge, said : " Mr. Perkins is particularly occupied to-day, and has desired me to present this and ask you to excuse him." The Chief Justice said to the Sheriff : " Did Mr. Perkins send that message to this Court ?" " Yes," said the Sheriff, "and he hoped you would excuse him." " Go down to Mr.

Perkins' counting-room and bring him here, and if he makes any further objection to coming, take a sufficient force to secure his attendance." And Mr. Perkins came up, and bowing to the Judge, said that he hoped he would be excused ; that he was fitting out a ship for the East Indies that day, and it was not convenient for him to attend upon the jury, and he had sent his fine. " Where did you get the money or the means to fit out a ship for the East Indies, Mr. Perkins ?" " Why, sir, you know my position and my relations to commerce." " Well," said the Chief Justice, " the means to fit out a ship for the East Indies you derived from the protection which the laws of your country give to you, and your prosperity is due to the obedience of the people to those laws." [Applause.] " Now," said he, " take your seat in the jury-box, Mr. Perkins, and let somebody else fit out your ship for the East Indies." [Applause.] And so it is, and so it must be, and I wish it were true—I wish it were true—that those who have received little may love but little, but that those who have received much from their country must love much. [Applause.]

What Suffrage consists in.

And now we are at the eve of an election, and of an election of President of the United States, and of an election by suffrage which belongs to the people. There is no power in this country that does not proceed from suffrage, and there is no authority that can be wielded by any citizen who is lifted into great office but what is recognized in him, because the free suffrages of the people have conferred the honor upon him. And what do we perceive at this election but this most extraordinary condition of things in this country ?—that all over this free country of ours, where loyalty and honor and duty to the Government of the country have been kept and preserved, there is animation, activity, discussion, spirit, pride, power, everywhere communicated and communicable. It is vital in every part, and in such a community "cannot but by annihilation die." [Applause.] But in one part of this country—alas ! severed from the rest by the same lines that divided revolt from fidelity to Government—the suffrage is dead. There is no discussion, there is no life, there is no love, there is no spirit, there is none of that movement of the popular heart, that exaltation of the popular minds, which belongs to a free people.

For the suffrage there is paralyzed; the suffrage there is subjugated. And what is the suffrage, and what does its paralysis and what its subjugation mean? Why, a free franchise is not the mere formality of the deposit of a vote. It is in its threefold capacity the great action of an intelligent, of an animated, of a loyal, government-loving people; and if it lacks these attributes, it is no suffrage at all.

The first of these attributes is, that the suffrage is a reflex of the moral and intellectual forces of the community, brought to a focus in this election of candidates, and the choice between them—and thus it is an act of sovereign intelligence and moral uprightness. The second feature is, that it stimulates and animates by public discussion the whole region of thought of a great people, and so is the greatest means and the greatest master of education that is free to the whole body of the people. The third great attribute is, that it consolidates the great mass into a strenuous community filled with interest, filled with passions, proud of their liberty, proud that they are the masters of the country. It consolidates them to the authority which the laws require to be obeyed by this great and strenuous community. It consolidates them to this authority because they have been consolidated, and have taken part in the transaction that has lodged the authority on law in the persons of those who have received the suffrage.

Dangers of a Solid South.

I need not say to you that if in any large part of this community these traits of the suffrage are not maintained, are not observed, are not potential—whether that portion of the community be reduced to obedience to the laws by force or not—they, for the time, and until these mischiefs are corrected, are struck out of American life, of American liberty, of American Government. [Applause.] And how long can that community, thus curtailed, thus impoverished, thus exhausted of the vitality of our institutions, maintain their freedom? I speak not now of any subject and inferior class that may have these dishonors and these contempts visited upon them; but I speak of what are called the ruling class, of what is spoken of as the intelligent class, and as including the material interests of that portion of the country; how long can the habit of violence, how long can the operations of cruelty, hold sway without in turn fastening a reign of terror, step by step, upon class after class and man after man? Believe me, no portion of the American people can afford to be without the life-blood of liberty and of justice, without itself succumbing in all its parts, in all its classes, to a final reign of terror and dominion of force. [Applause.]

And how long can the rest of the country tolerate this unequal partition of power? How long can it be maintained in this country, that 138 electoral votes are taken out of politics and are wielded, not by liberty and justice, but by power and oppression? [Applause.] How long can parties rest satisfied with peaceful discussions if there is to be thrown down into the arena a solid vote, uninfluenced by argument, by reason, by interests distributed in the community and openly proclaimed through the rest of the country? Whoever sides with this majestic mass

needs to get only forty-seven votes, and whoever dares to oppose it must get 185. [Applause.]

Now, is this free country of suffrage-loving and liberty-loving people to be told, that hanging over our manifold interests, brooding over our strong passion as freemen, and freedom-lovers, there is to be held this threat, that our opponents shall have the Government with 47 votes, and our friends cannot get the Government without the 185. [Applause.] How long will the right of suffrage be maintained in this country of ours if one-fifth of the freemen themselves are only necessary to carry the Presidency one way and four-fifths are necessary to carry it the other? Why, if the Emperor of Germany or the Czar of Russia wielded only 138 votes in our Electoral College of 369, and said to this people: "You may please yourselves with the equality and freedom of suffrage over the rest of the community, but those who vote with the Emperor or the Czar need only 47 votes, and those who vote against him need 185," how long would it be before we should see that there is not only no freedom in that 47 votes, but there cannot be long in the 185. [Applause.]

Liberty Better than Quiet.

And now that is the great problem that meets this people at the outset, and the alternatives are presented to us in the smooth speeches of Democratic statesmen and orators: "Why, don't you see how much easier it would be for you to yield to this wish of the South, and have it all peaceful and quiet, and give them the 47 votes without making a fuss about it? and don't undertake to rage through the country and ransack the conscience, the wisdom and the virtue of your people, in the hopeless task of getting the 185. [Applause.] Just for peace's sake and for good neighborhood, and to show that you value the repose of the community." [Laughter.] Well, gentlemen, I do not think that if the Czar of Russia or the Emperor of Germany wielded those votes, we would answer an argument of that kind by favoring the repose of this great and proud people at the sacrifice of its liberty and self-respect. [Applause.] I think that we will say, whenever that mass of political power is flaunted in our face and brandished over our heads, "If you want our liberties, come and take them." [Applause.] Come and get your forty-seven votes if you can, and we will submit; but we won't let you have Indiana, [applause,] which you were expecting to roll as a sweet morsel under your tongue; [laughter and applause:] and we won't let you have Ohio, [applause,] because we like to have the State where our candidate lives vote for him. [Applause.] And then they say, "Well, but the merchants of New-York, the merchants of Brooklyn, they surely won't make a fuss about liberty and honor and pride, and those sentimental vapors that are good enough for the agricultural classes. The merchants, knowing where the real interests of society rests, won't mind giving up the North to this demand of the South."

Well, gentlemen, these young people of the Republican Club have made up their minds, I believe, that so far as depends upon them, the vote of New-York shall not be surrendered to the consolidated South. [Loud applause.] These Southerners seem to think of the commercial classes somewhat as the great Lord

Chatham is said, in one of his most tremendous fulminations in Great Britain, at the time of our advancing revolution, to have spoken of the merchants of England. Now, Lord Chatham was a great friend of liberty and a great friend of America. He had dared to say, in the British Parliament, "I rejoice that America has resisted. Three millions of Whigs, with arms in their hands, cannot be put down by any force you can send against them." [Applause.] And when the commercial classes in England at that day wanted peace and repose, and trade in tea and other articles of consumption, and had ventured to throw themselves against Lord Chatham and against our liberty, what did Lord Chatham say? "Tell me not of the merchant. His counting-house is his temple; his desk is his altar; his ledger is his Bible, and money is his God." [Applause.]

Now, when the South, with arms in their hands, spoke to the merchants of New-York and Brooklyn, what answer did the merchants of New-York and Brooklyn make? They went to their ledgers and laid them on the altar of the country. They marked off one-half of their mercantile fortunes as lost by the rebellion of the South, and they carried the other half to the credit of the Government of the United States, to be drawn upon. [Applause.] And you may remember that it was then said of the merchants of New-York, that they sold their goods but not their principles. [Applause.] And now I am glad to know that old merchants and young merchants propose to take their places in the great jury-box that is now listening to argument, and in November, to give a verdict and to say, if necessary, "let other people fit out ships to the East Indies." [Applause.]

What the Solidarity of the South Means.

No, gentlemen, the people of this country have made up their minds that the answer to a "Solid South" is not, in any sense in which the South is solid, a "Solid North," but a deliberate, a manly, a persistent, a noble, a courageous effort to bring out the vote of this people, to maintain the suffrage all over this land. [Applause.] There is not the least objection to a solid vote for a candidate on one side or the other. There is no objection to Vermont, for instance, voting forever and forever on the right side. [Applause.] There has not been any great objection, except a moral one, to Indiana voting ever and again on the wrong side; but it was not a solid vote in the sense that the suffrage was suppressed and something else took its place. We are not accustomed to a report of the suffrage which brings in all the votes cast as being a majority of one party. [Laughter.] That we do not call an election, and the true phrase for the South is its solidarity. And let me read you the definition by Dr. Trench, the accomplished Archbishop of Dublin, who understands well the use of language, as to what this word solidarity means and where it comes from. Says Dr. Trench of solidarity: "A word which we owe to the French Communists, and which signifies a community of gain and loss, in honor and dishonor, a being, so to speak, all in the same bottom."

And that is what the solidarity of the South means. They are all in one bottom of honor and dishonor, of gain and loss. It is a cumulating, an aggregating, an iron-bound mass, from which every symptom of life in the suffrage has been expelled. And now, whenever they bring in the vote, and they find that the population have voted; and whenever they count the vote, and whenever they go through the sum in subtraction of taking the minority from the majority, and they have reported the vote against the Republican party, and in every one of the fifteen States—why, it is American suffrage, and we will submit to it! Whenever all the blacks, to whom we have given liberty, vote against liberty, we will submit to this wound, even in the house of our friends; but until that vote is taken we insist upon all the powers of the American people under the laws and the Constitution—all the moral and intellectual forces, all the pride in our institutions, all our duties as American citizens urging us one way: that we meet that solidarity of vote as now presented by solidity of moral and intellectual force, and of free suffrage that will destroy it forever as an agent and factor in American politics. [Applause.]

No Longer Propitiating the South.

Capt. Cook tells us in one of his voyages that in one of the South Sea Islands he found a race that had a peculiar idea of divinity; that they had a belief, to be sure, in a good God, and that it was the most powerful of the spirits, yet they recognized a devil also, and offered all their sacrifices to him. For they said: 'The good God, of his own goodness, will do what is right by us, but it is our business to propitiate this devil by the sacrifice of all that is dear to us." And now the Democratic orators and statesmen seem to think that Providence is on our side, and that this good and great, intelligent, free and manly community of the North would always do about what is right, and therefore the way is to propitiate this unmannerly—I use no harsher word—this unmannerly mass of our Southern fellow citizens. Well, we tried it before the war, and how many of our great statesmen went down to the grave with their heads bowed in shame! how many of the women of the land, how many of the Christian people, how many of the youth, suffered grief unutterable! How has all the land suffered for the shame of slavery! And then, when resistance in that same solidarity of slavery was raised by the vote and by arms, how many of our youth, how much of our treasure, did we sacrifice? But then, thank God, it was no longer in propitiation, but in a determination to destroy the enemies of American liberty. [Loud applause.] And now the appeal to the evil spirit that suppressed the suffrage no longer is heard by patient ears. If in Indiana they won't endure it, do you think they will endure it in Connecticut, in New-Jersey and in New-York. [Applause.] The whole stress of the battle finally rests upon us. The eyes of the whole country are concentrated here. Here is the trial, here in your own midst, here in the City of New-York. All the rest have spoken a tone not to be misunderstood. Does any body doubt how the State of New-York, outside of these great cities, feels and thinks, and how it will act? Does any body doubt that a hundred thousand majority of the free people of New-York State, outside of these great cities, are ranged with New-England, and the North-west, and Pennsylvania, and Indiana, [cheers.] and Ohio, and are saying with one voice, "We will submit to no such oppression any more?"

Well, now, it is said that there will be 100,000 majority in these two great cities, countervailing the free people of the rest of the State, and ranging us as the only State of the North on the side of this solidarity of the South. Why, gentlemen, who are to do it? We, ourselves, if it is done at all. Do you believe that the mass of this community, of your city, of which this is in numbers but a feeble representative, great as it is, but which in spirit and in work is the representative of the sober thought and manhood, education, morality and religion of the City of Brooklyn—do you believe that they can be stamped out as an inconsiderable item and crushed in a majority that will not make them worth counting? Not if they do their duty from now till November—not if they swear they will not leave this jury-box until the verdict is rendered for the right. [Applause.]

Choice Bits of Southern Oratory.

Now, some of the Democratic statesmen and orators have the advantage of making speeches at both ends of this country. Some of the Southern gentlemen we have heard, and they have wept at the corners of the streets and wiped their eyes in the newspapers [laughter] at the great dangers of oppressions to the suffrage of Brooklyn and in New-York. They seem to think that our adopted fellow-citizens do not have any chance in either of these cities [laughter]—that they are "put upon" [laughter], hustled at the polls, prevented from recording their votes, do not have their votes counted; and if any of them are set up for public office they are shot, I suppose in the back. [Laughter.] We have not perceived anything of that kind. I do not think that there are any of our Irish fellow-citizens either in your city or New-York that have ever complained that they did not have a fair share of the offices. I have never heard of any uprising on the part of our German fellow-citizens, because their Irish friends did not have a fair chance at the offices. [Laughter.] And I have never heard of any very general complaint among the native American population that injustice was done to our Irish fellow-citizens. I know that in our city of New-York three principal officers at the disposal of the local community—the Mayor, the Recorder and the Comptroller—are all able, excellent and spirited Irish fellow-citizens of ours in the ticket that they are proposing for the November election. And yet these Southern gentlemen in convention, by their votes, and in their speeches here, are greatly distressed lest this class in our community should not have a fair chance!

Now, one of the most intelligent and one of the ablest of the statesmen of the Democratic party, our friend, the distinguished Senator from Delaware, of whom so many people in New-York and in Brooklyn justly have such a high opinion, and for whom they feel a great regard, and whose disappointment at his failure to receive the nomination was conspicuous, and justly so, in their complaints, made a speech

down in South Carolina, and he came up to New-York and gave us an account of what he saw down in South Carolina. He didn't say anything in South Carolina about the enormity of depriving the people of their votes, not a word. But he did talk about the great fraud that had been committed four years ago in the electoral count for the President, and he wished that visited with condemnation. He also spoke of the great duty of the Democratic party to see that marshals at the polls do not deprive the people of the right to vote once, and that soldiers are not so thick about the polls as to deprive the people of that right, which is preservative of all rights—the Democratic platform says—the freedom of the suffrage. He said that he attended a Hancock meeting down there. There was a great number of men standing around on horseback, with red shirts, the most harmless and peaceable people in the world, for all the world just like the yeomanry of New-England and New-York and Pennsylvania. Well, that is new to the yeomanry at the North, that they are just like the red-shirted people of the South.

And then the blacks that he saw attending that Hancock meeting, why they looked cheerful and peaceable and quiet, not deprived of a single vote, and he talked with them. They came from a distance, some astride of horses and some astride of mules, and they even owned the animals on which they rode. Well, this is the evidence of an eye-witness that, in a Hancock meeting, the blacks that voted the Hancock ticket and the red-shirters were in perfect harmony, and all went smooth and merry as a marriage bell. [Applause.] And he would have you argue that as the Republicans are a quieter and more peaceable people, by so much greater reason a Republican meeting down there would have been even more quiet and more peaceful.

Now, in his own State of Delaware, in his own City of Wilmington, the other day, he made a speech, and he took up this subject of the freedom of the suffrage, and see what noble sentiments he utters, and how deeply he feels it. He said:

The question for each man to answer is simply, how shall the vote of each, that the laws of the land have given to him, be cast in November? It ought to be cast just as its owner desires it should be; and if every man is true to himself it can be so cast. No man has the power, in this country, to control another man's vote, if the voter will but do his duty. It is not merely a man's duty to cast his free and untrammelled ballot, but it is his high privilege to exercise that privilege as the dignified duty of a freeman. To unresistingly allow another to rob him of it is to exhibit the disgraceful qualities of a coward. When any one seeks to control the vote of another by any other than the legitimate means of argument he goes beyond the spirit of an American citizen, and exhibits the spirit of a tyrant.

Now why didn't he make that speech down in South Carolina? [Applause and laughter.]

But in Wilmington he had heard that there was such an excitement on the question of labor that Democrats thought really of voting against the Democratic ticket; and he thought that ought to be put a stop to, and that the oppression and intimidation and suppression of the suffrage that the people of the North were threatening to practice ought to be resisted, for any man who attempted it was a tyrant. And yet all over the South the rule is ostracism—social ostracism—for the whites and exclusion from patronage and from livelihood of the blacks who vote the Republican ticket. Why didn't he make his speech in South Carolina? Probably the red-shirt men would not have been as peaceable as the Northern yeoman. [Applause.]

Well, I don't know how people can go around this country with a grave face talking in this way. Whenever I hear such a speech as that at the North, from a Democratic statesman, somehow or other I expect to see the screen that he would hold up between you and his Southern allies fall to the floor, and disclose that Southern virago, "the little French Milliner"—the *Lady Teazle* of this comedy of "Democracy" behind the screen—[applause and laughter]—with a tunic—she is in full dress, of course—with a tunic cut in the fashion of a red shirt, with a jupon whose warp and woof are the principles of Lee and Stonewall Jackson, with a scarlet overskirt and a deep black fringe—in bullion. I think the ladies call it—of the murders of Hamburg, Yazoo and Kemper County.

Let us have a fair understanding with our public men; let them have none of these noble sentiments so much out of place.

Shall the Present Prosperity Continue?

Well, gentlemen, this country is in abundant prosperity in all corners of the land. North, South, East and West; and a people in possession of these great blessings of civilization and Christianity, of these magnificent fruits of their Government and the principles on which it rests, are called upon to cast their suffrage for the continuance of that rule that has brought it about, or for the reversal of that rule and the chances of what may follow.

I see that a very intelligent writer on Political Economy, Mr. Atkinson, of Boston, in counting with great gratification, as we all do, the magnificence of the cotton crop—five millions of bales and odd—says that this shows that labor has its rewards in the South, and that violence is not the general rule. The general rule? Why we didn't suppose they shot all the people at the South. [Laughter.] We should have very little trouble in the suffrage if that was so; we should have it all one way. But I cannot tolerate this method of talking about the rights of our Southern friends. Not the general rule? Why, who made all this cotton? The black Republicans did the work and the white Democrats have the politics. Good heavens! do you suppose, if the yeomanry of the North had made a crop of five million bales of cotton, that it would be considered a most grateful and agreeable fact to notice that they owned the animals on which they rode. [Laughter.] Why, they would own the farms [applause] as they would own the cotton, and they would own the fruits of their labor. But the truth is, the South is divided into three classes: Those who labor, and they are Republicans; those who make politics, and they are Democratic statesmen; and a large class intermediate, that abhors labor and adores politics. [Laughter.] So the Republican blacks pick all the cotton of the

Democratic whites, and the Democratic whites pick all the votes of the Republican blacks. [Loud laughter and long applause.]

Now, gentlemen, we must talk plainly of and to these countrymen of ours. To take the political strength in Congress and in the Electoral Colleges which makes this arduous concentration and aggregation in the free parts of the country and overcome it—to take those votes, and then take from the blacks, to whom they were counted out, *per capita*, as it were—to take the suffrage from them, cannot be respectable in the contemplation of God or man. [Applause.] All the reasoning about it, all the rhetoric, all the screens in the world, cannot hide that ghastly fact, that a great mass of our countrymen takes the power, in comparing suffrage with you, that was meant for the blacks, and robs them, who would vote with you, of being counted in the suffrage. As Junius said of certain unworthy characters in English politics: "Such conduct can never escape censure except when it escapes observation." [Applause.] I think the sober judgment of the people of this country—yes, I think the sober judgment of a great portion of the white people of the South takes precisely the same view of that transaction that I have submitted to you; and I beg of you, by your manhood, and your firmness and your solidity, to help this recurrence of honor and duty and pride in the Southern people, so that it shall not be trampled out by your surrender to the pretensions of the solidarity of the South. [Loud applause.]

But now what about this pretence that, as it is not a general rule that violence is offered, therefore it is unbecoming in us to make so much ado about the instances in which these rights are suppressed and this violence is exhibited. What is the measure of it? As *Mercutio* said of his wound: "It is not as wide as a church door; it is not as deep as a well, but as the life-blood flows from it, it will do; it will do." There is enough of exhibition, and enough of perpetration to answer the purpose of suppressing the wound and reducing the solidity of the South. It will do; it will do. Hume, having once written a treatise which brought upon him the condemnation of the religious portion of the English people, complained bitterly that he was visited with so much vituperative criticism when he had only written one bad treatise, and had written so many good works; to which a gentleman engaged in the conversation said to him: "Why, Mr. Hume, your reasoning is like that of the French notary, who, when he had been detected in a forgery and was sent to the galleys for it, thought it very hard that a man that had written so many genuine signatures should be punished for one forgery." [Laughter.]

But, as I have said, the country is prosperous, and I think I may be permitted to add, that the Republican administration now present to the observation of the people, and in the sight of whose conduct of affairs the people are to determine whether their servants shall be changed and another party put in possession of a lease of power—I think I may be permitted to say, that the actual conduct of the affairs of the country is irreproachable. [Great applause.] I have not heard any Democratic criticism of this administration or of the present conduct of affairs. And yet I submit to you that the real issue before an intelligent people, abounding in prosperity and having no fault to find with the conduct of affairs, is really this and no wider : Do you wish for the next four years that the affairs of this country should be carried on as they have been for the last four years ? [Applause.]

I have observed some criticism, to be sure, when attacks are made upon the Republican party in the way that these statesmen and orators—and within their right—make, not of the actual conduct of affairs, but of the past and of the party. A complaint is made that the principal officers of the Government should find it their duty to speak to their fellow-citizens of the States in which they live of the facts and of the nature of the prospects of the issue that is before them. I never have known yet in any of the experience of English politics, or in any of the experience of ours, that when the question was between a party in administration and a party in opposition seeking power, there was not a right to canvass the question on one side as well as on the other. [Applause.] I am ready to account for any right that I may exercise whenever the citizens of New-York or the citizens of Brooklyn are ready to do me the honor to listen to what I have to say. [Applause.]

A Democratic Suggestion Answered.

You will observe that theoretic politics, dogmas, historic points, to an intelligent, manly people like ours, cease to have an interest when the present issue is one of the simple nature that I have explained to you. Our people know whether they like the administration of affairs as now exhibited by the party in power. They know whether they are pleased with the harvest of this sowing, of this culture ; and as to such a question, thus rigidly observed, there can be no answer unless the people have lost their senses. Our Democratic friends are fond of saying, " Oh, if you had only renominated President Hayes we should not have been able to make any headway against him. When the country is so prosperous and he is so upright and he is so considerate of the rights of all—when he loves the whole country and serves the whole country, it would be ungrateful for the Democratic part of our fellow citizens not to recognize Hayes' Administration as worthy of their praise." Well, gentlemen, supposing that the identical shape of the canvass is not the presentation of his claim, I ask the Republicans—I ask the Democrats—of the country, which is nearest like him, and which promises more nearly to follow in the path that he has trod, of this prosperity—James A. Garfield [immense applause and repeated cheering] and the Republican party behind him, and the solid North behind it, or General Hancock and the Democratic party behind him, with the solid South behind it ?

Well, there may be some force in the suggestion that the Democratic party could not stand against the renomination of President Hayes, but I think they will find that they cannot stand against the nomination of James A. Garfield. [Great applause.] Among the curses denounced by divine authority against the people of Israel, if they should swerve from the right path and from their duty to their God,

was this, that, in war, they should go out in one way against their enemy and should flee in seven ways. It seems to me, if I can look over the field of battle, that the Democratic party has come out one way against the Republican party behind Gen. Hancock, and is now fleeing seven ways. [Applause.] And so near a route has it become that all the leaders of the different arms of the service, so far as I can see, are firing into one another. [Applause and laughter.]

Well, gentlemen, as the Democrats will insist upon getting away from this issue and going back a little ways into history, what are the grievances ? Why is the South solid against the prosperity of the country and the party that has produced it ? Why is it ? And what answer do you get ? What answer do you get that does not go back to the memories and the resentments of the war that was waged against this Union—that does not go back to the grievances in the processes of reconstruction ; that does not go back to the retaliation and the reaction that wishes to place in power the same party, under the same lead and with the same make-up in which it was driven from power. And yet, and yet when they go back, if they will go back, to the source, to the cause, to the responsibility and to the guilt which has produced all these disturbances, all these obligations and all these disasters to them and to us, they say it is a cruel recalling of the issues of the war. But if they go back to the halting or the stumbling or the errors in this grievous process of reconstruction, why that is nothing but becoming self-respect. But I have looked in vain for an identification of the mischief that induced this solidarity, and I find that the only thing a man can put his finger on is presented by a very intelligent statesman of Virginia and by Gen. Hampton, in a speech which he made in the streets of New-York, that when in 1866, I think it was in Virginia and in some of the more Southern States, they chose a very intelligent, a very patriotic and a very respectable body of old Whigs and sent them to Congress, Congress refused to receive them ; and that justifies the solidarity of the South until they have put their foot on our necks and restored themselves as they were before the war. [Applause.]

The Statesmanship of the Plough.

But there is one argument which they have to parry, the prosperity of the country, and that is by ascribing it all to Providence ; and there is a phrase which Governor Seymour has produced, and which Mr. Bayard has applauded in one of his speeches, that it was not the statesmanship of the Republican party that did all these great things for the public credit, for the public honor and for the public prosperity, but it is what Governor Seymour calls the statesmanship of the plough. Well, let us choose the plough as President. [Laughter and applause.] There were ploughs in this country before this prosperity came, and there was not any statesmanship in the plough then. But what speeds the plough ? What stops it from rusting in the furrow, or the crops from rotting in the field ? What, but that step by step the Republican party pacified the South at the outset of its administration, and has restored the public credit, has reduced the public burdens and has made a demand for the crops that the plough produces. This is the part that statesmanship plays; and the plough might slumber under the disasters of an administration that might follow just as the plough slumbered before we had unsnarled our finances and reduced our burden of troubles that the great war had brought upon us.

Chief Justice Chase used to delight in telling a story of a journey he made, when a young man, in going to Cincinnati to establish himself in life, and passing through the magnificent scenery in the upper part of Virginia. As the passengers waked up in the morning, after their night's sleep, and looked out upon it, a gentleman mentioned, "Why, just here is the birthplace of Patrick Henry." And Mr. Chase, fresh from college and full of enthusiasm, broke out in a rhapsody—"How could he fail to have had that magnificent gift of eloquence, that genius of liberty, when he was born in the midst of this magnificent scenery, that would inspire any one with those gifts." The Chief Justice said that a sober and respectable gentleman spoke to him from another seat in the stage, and said: "Young man, this scenery has been here ever since Patrick Henry was born, and there haven't been any more Patrick Henrys since." [Laughter.] And I think this statesmanship of the plough that pleases our Democratic friends is very like the genius and eloquence being the production of the magnificent scenery of Virginia.

Now, I think I have never heard that it was wise for a people to wish to change their rulers upon the single argument that Providence seems to have been on their side. [Laughter.] I do not think that that by itself is a good reason for trying somebody else that peradventure Providence might not be on the side of. [Laughter.] But it is the only argument that I have heard brought forward by our Democratic friends against giving the Republican party the renewal of power that belongs to the party that has carried the country through unheard of disaster,and brought it out to unexampled prosperity. [Loud applause.] I think that the American people would rather keep this prosperity in the hands of the Republican party and Providence, rather than give it into the hands of the Democratic party and take their chance of what Providence might do. [Laughter and applause.] I know there is one bitter curse denounced upon that people that calls evil good, and good evil, and I have heard from no side, except the Democratic, any praise of the abominable oppressions that are practiced in a large part of this country.

A Party and a Candidate that "Don't Know."

Well, gentlemen, the Democratic party, having been up for examination several times during the last twenty years, [laughter,] has now presented itself once more. You may have seen the story of the schoolmaster down in Texas who offered himself for the examination of the school board, to be trusted with the charge of the education of the young people of the neighborhood. Well, he had got all the political divisions of the world by the ears, had thrown the multiplication table into confusion, and the solar system into absolute disorder and destruction by the answers that he made, and he was rejected. But he

prevailed upon the kind-hearted board to give him a chance at another examination, and he was rejected again. His friends said to him, "Why, you didn't pass this time!" "No," says he "how could I? They asked me the same questions as before." [Roars of laughter.] And that is the disastrous position of the Democratic party is in now. People have asked them the same questions as they did four years ago, and eight years ago, and twelve years ago, and sixteen years ago; how can they reply satisfactorily when they are asked the same questions every time. [Laughter.] Hereafter let me advise them to follow the example of a student in a certain academic examination. He was coming out, looking, as we called it in those days, 'badly plucked," and was asked by his classmates how he had fared. "Fared?" says he, "I didn't pass at all, and yet I answered every question correctly; and they asked me a great many questions." "Why, how could that be, that you didn't pass the examination if you answered every question correctly?" "Why," he replied, "to every question they asked me I answered that I didn't know." [Laughter.]

Now, I think that when General Hancock is asked what he thinks about the war claims, he had better answer that he don't know; what he thinks about suffrage at the South—whether it is likely to be befriended at all, or any good come out of it—that he don't know; and when he is asked about the tariff question—[laughter]—that he don't know. He has answered, not in those words, but in a manner that his countrymen, under a charitable construction of his answer, have considered as equivalent to saying it. [Applause.]

Parties and Candidates on the Tariff.

Well, now that we are on this subject of "examinations," let us see. The subject of examination was the platforms of the two parties on the subject of the tariff. The Democratic party said in 1876: "We demand that all custom-house taxation shall be only for revenue;" in 1880, "A tariff for revenue only." The Republican platform of 1880 says that the reviving industries should be further promoted, and that the commerce, already so great, should be steadily encouraged. We affirm the belief avowed in 1876, that the duties levied for the purpose of revenue should so discriminate as to favor American labor. [Applause.]

Gen. Hancock, in passing the examination on the Democratic platform, answers: "The principles enumerated by the Convention are those I have cherished in the past and shall endeavor to maintain in the future." [Laughter.] Garfield says in reference to our customs laws: "A policy should be pursued which will bring revenues to the treasury, and will enable the labor and capital employed in our great industries to compete fairly in our own markets with the labor and capital of foreign producers." We legislate for the people of the United States and not for the whole world, and it is our glory that the American laborer is more intelligent and better paid than his foreign competitor. [Applause.]

Now, Gen. Hancock, when informed that his

countrymen were nearly interested in this question of whether American labor was to be pauperized or not, and that there was an impression that the Democratic party had declared for a well-known principle and a well understood principle, says that there should not be the swerving of a hair's breadth to the right or to the left in the laying of customs, but that the most money from the largest importations and the largest gains on the skilled labor imported from abroad was to be the rule of the American people. Does anybody ever hear of revenue increasing on the mere principle of the lowest rate that will bring in revenue that does not flood the market with foreign goods? That is an intelligible principle; it has been understood for fifty years. Well, now, Gen. Hancock says, having had an interview with a Paterson editor [laughter]—which Governor Randolph didn't think did him justice, but which has not been retracted, as far as I can discover—he said that it was in vain to think that anything that the Federal Government could do about a tariff would affect the industries of the country; that it was a local issue, came up about once in a half a century in Pennsylvania, and that it was all right. He was astonished that anybody should be so stupid as to suppose that it was of any consequence what the opinions of the candidate for the Presidency were on the subject of the tariff. [Much laughter.] And then, when that was not quite satisfactory to his intelligent countrymen, too many of them being stupid, I suppose, he comes out with the saying that he is too sound an American to ever have it supposed that he would do anything that did not help and favor American industry in comparison with industry abroad.

But the people say, "What we wanted was not to know whether you are too sound an American to have that opinion, because that is the very question that we are going to determine—whether you are too sound an American—what we wanted was to know whether you were, as Garfield is, for a system of duties that will protect the dignity of American labor as a more intelligent body, and better paid than foreign labor?" [Applause.] "If you will tell us that," say the laborers all over this country, "then we will know whether to vote for you or not." Well, having the war claims all right, he entertains the view that nothing can be done to hurt the North, that the suffrage is to be protected to the extent of a "free ballot, a full vote and a fair count," all over the country. And now, having said that he is "too sound an American," what is there left to undervalue American labor, what is there left for him but to write one more letter, [laughter and applause,] and address it to Mr. English, of Indiana, [laughter,] conceived somewhat in this way:

MY DEAR SIR,—There seems to be an impression prevailing in the minds of some of our countrymen that I am running on the same ticket with you. [Laughter and applause.] I am astonished that anybody should give credit to such a bugbear. [Laughter.] For myself, I denounce it. There also seems to be an impression that I am running on the Democratic platform. I am too sound an American to do that—and this is the last letter that I shall write, [laughter,] and not only is this the last letter that I shall write, but the last that I was ever expected to write. [Uproarious laughter.]

The truth is that when a man in the public gaze of the whole country stands upon a platform, and plank after plank of it breaks down, so that there is not a wide enough spot in it to stand upon except on one leg, it gets to be very irksome and very awkward. It is true you can shift from one leg to the other, [laughter,] but still it is not graceful and it is very tiresome. [Great laughter.] Then come down from the platform! Come down from the candidacy, and let us have the return of the votes all for General Garfield and the Republican ticket. [Hearty applause.]

Manhood of the American Laborer.

Now, gentlemen, there are a great many things in this country that are of interest to the people of it, and among other things of great interest to the people of this country is the question of the labor of the country. The labor of the country holds in its hand, by the gift of the suffrage, the political power of the country—that is to say, in that part of the country where the laborers are allowed to vote. Starting as we did, a poor, sparse people, without great inequalities of rank, we put suffrage upon *manhood*, and said that the man is greater than his circumstances or his property. Pericles had some such idea about a man, when he advised the young women of Athens to marry a man without an estate rather than an estate without a man. [Laughter and applause.] I think the ladies of this country have generally followed that advice—partly, perhaps, because there are more men than there are estates. [Laughter.] But, nevertheless, that is our proposition; and the laws of this country are intended to preserve the dignity of labor. The South never desired the dignity of labor to be preserved under the old system—I do not see that they have much care to preserve its dignity under the new. But in this country of ours, where intelligence and thrift and domestic virtue and personal pride are just as generally and just as clearly the possession of the laboring men as they are of the learned and the powerful and the rich, no peace, no prosperity can exist if we undertake to put our labor in the system of the world upon the level of the labor of countries where its dignity and its political power are not accorded. [Applause.] Any party, any people, in this country that undertake to say that upon the mere economic question of whether a broadcloth coat for a gentleman, or a Worth dress for a lady, can be bought cheaper or dearer, is the great problem of American statesmanship, will find that the laborers of this country do not agree with him. [Applause.] They mean to have it understood—and they are right—that having education open to them; that having equality in politics their right and their heritage, that having the hopes of the future and all the delights of home, its purity, its dignity, their possession, for which they will vote, and for which they will fight, they will tolerate no party that subjects this manhood of the American laborer to the necessities or conveniences of wealth and luxury.

It is not a question of the manufacturer or of the merchant. It is not a question of the foreman or of the master-workman merely. It is a question of all the common people who take part in the magnificence of your commerce and of your manufactures, and who bear their share of the taxation and the burdens, in peace and in war; that uphold this country. And now, when it is found out that whether the Scribes and the Pharisees do or do not understand this problem of the tariff to protect labor, the laborers understand it. You may be sure that the votes of those laborers will settle the question in the great strenuous industries of those great States of Connecticut, New-York and New-Jersey in favor of the dignity and the security of American labor. [Loud applause.] And if General Hancock don't fully understand the subject now, on the 3d day of November he will see through it clearly. [Laughter.]

Well, gentlemen, we are to come to the great judgment. Parties are to be judged; people are to be judged. We lawyers have a maxim that in our trials the judge is condemned if the guilty escape; and by the same rule the judge is condemned if the innocent are condemned. And this people, looking at these two parties, are quite as much in judgment as they, the parties, are. If this people deliberately drives from power a party with the record of the Republican party, and with the fruits of the strenuous labors and courage in the field, of its soldiers, from Grant down

to the private soldier, [applause,] and in civil life from Garfield down to the common artisan; [applause;] if they put in power the opposite party, with such a record as that of the Democratic party, in the field, from Jefferson Davis down to the common soldier, and in statesmanship, from the men that betrayed their trust to the common people that they deluded to their ruin, it is not the Republican party that is guilty, but the people are guilty of a desertion of their trust. [Applause.] Let us understand this matter. Let us hasten on the judgment of this people that follows close a flying foe. Let us hear already the glad shouts of the American people renewing power in the name and in the persons of the Republican party and their candidates. [Applause.] Let us hear, deserved by us,

Omnium consensu capax imperii quia imperavit:

that in the judgment of foreign nations, in the judgment of all this people, in the judgment of the learned and the wise, in the judgment of the feeble and the poor, this party is capable of the trust of government because it has discharged it. [Applause.]—*From the New-York Tribune, Thursday, October 21, 1880.*

The great Speech of Colonel ROBERT G. INGERSOLL, *in the Cooper Union, New-York City, Saturday evening, October 23, 1880.*

LADIES AND GENTLEMEN: Years ago I made up my mind that there was no particular argument in slander. [Applause.] I made up my mind that for parties, as well as for individuals, honesty in the long run is the best policy. [Applause.] I made up my mind that the people were entitled to know a man's honest thoughts, and I propose to-night to tell you exactly what I think. [Applause.] And it may be well enough, in the first place, for me to say that no party has a mortgage on me. [Applause.] I am the sole proprietor of myself. [Laughter and applause.] No party, no organization, has any deed of trust on what little brains I have, and as long as I can get my part of the common air, I am going to tell my honest thoughts. [Applause.] One man in the right will finally get to be a majority. [Laughter.] I am not going to say a word to-night that every Democrat here will not know is true, and, whatever he may say with his mouth, I will compel him in his heart to give three cheers. [Applause.]

In the first place, I wish to admit that during the war there were hundreds of thousands of patriotic Democrats. I wish to admit that if it had not been for the War Democrats of the North we never would have put down the rebellion. [Applause.] Let us be honest. I further admit that had it not been for other than War Democrats there never would have been a rebellion to put down. [Great applause.] War Democrats! Why did we call them War Democrats? Did you ever hear anybody talk about a War Republican? We spoke of War Democrats to distinguish them from those Democrats who were in favor of peace upon any terms.

I also wish to admit that the Republican party is not

absolutely perfect. [Laughter.] While I believe that it is the best party that ever existed, [applause,] while I believe it has, within its organization, more heart, more brain, more patriotism than any other organization that ever existed beneath the sun, I still admit that it is not entirely perfect. I admit, in its great things, in its splendid efforts to preserve this Nation, in its grand effort to keep our flag in heaven, in its magnificent effort to free four millions of slaves, [applause,] in its great and sublime effort to save the financial honor of this Nation, I admit that it has made some mistakes. In its great effort to do right it has sometimes, by mistake, done wrong. And I also wish to admit that the great Democratic party, in its effort to get office, has sometimes by mistake done right. [Laughter.] You see that I am inclined to be perfectly fair. [Applause and laughter.] I am going with the Republican party because it is going my way; but if it ever turns to the right or left, I intend to go straight ahead.

In every government there is something that ought to be preserved; in every government there are many things that ought to be destroyed. Every good man, every patriot, every lover of the human race, wishes to preserve the good and destroy the bad; and every one in this audience who wishes to preserve the good will go with that section of our common country—with that party in our country that he honestly believes will preserve the good and destroy the bad. [Applause.] It takes a great deal of trouble to raise a good Republican. [Laughter.] It is a vast deal of labor. The Republican party is the fruit of all ages—of self-sacrifice and devotion. [Applause.] The Republican party is born of every good thing that was ever done in this world. [Applause.] The Republican party is the result of all martyrdom, of all heroic bloodshed for the right. It is the blossom and fruit of the great world's best endeavor. [Applause.] In order to make a Republican you have got to have school-houses. [Applause.] You have got to have newspapers and magazines. [Applause.] A good Republican is the best fruit of civilization, of all there is of intelligence, of art, of music and of song. [Applause.] If you want to make Democrats, let them alone. [Laughter.] The Democratic party is the settlings of this country. [Laughter.] Nobody hoes weeds. Nobody takes especial pains to raise dog fennel, and yet it grows under the very hoof of travel. The seeds are sown by accident and gathered by chance. But if you want to raise wheat and corn you must plough the ground. You must defend and you must harvest the crop with infinite patience and toil. It is precisely that way—if you want to raise a good Republican, you must work. If you wish to raise a Democrat, give him wholesome neglect. [Laughter.] The Democratic party flatters the vices of mankind. That party says to the ignorant man, "you know enough." It says to the vicious man, "you are good enough."

The Republican party says, "you must be better next year than you are this." A man is a Republican because he loves something. Most men are Democrats because they hate something. A Republican takes a man, as it were, by the collar and says, "you must do your best, you must climb the infinite hill of human progress as long as you live." Now and then one gets tired. He says, "I have climbed enough, and so much better than I expected to do that I don't wish to travel any further." Now and then one gets tired and lets go all hold, and he rolls down to the very bottom, and as he strikes the mud he springs upon his feet transfigured, and says, "Hurrah for Hancock." [Great laughter.]

No Free Speech in the South.

There are things in this Government that I wish to preserve, and there are things that I wish to destroy; and in order to convince you that you ought to go the way that I am going, it is only fair that I give to you my reasons. This is a Republic founded upon intelligence and the patriotism of the people, and in every Republic it is absolutely necessary that there should be free speech. ["Good," "good," and applause.] Free speech is the gem of the human soul. Words are the bodies of thought, and liberty gives to those words wings, and the whole intellectual heavens are filled with thought. [Applause.] In a Republic every individual tongue has a right to the general ear. In a Republic every man has the right to give his reasons for the course he pursues to all his fellow-citizens, and when you say that a man shall not speak, you also say that others shall not hear. When you say a man shall not express his honest thoughts, you say his fellow-citizens shall be deprived of honest thoughts; for of what use is it to allow the attorney for the defendant to address the jury, if the jury has been bought? Of what use is it to allow the jury, if they bring in a verdict of "not guilty," if the defendant is to be hanged by a mob? I ask you to-night, is not every solitary man here in favor of free speech? Is

there a solitary Democrat here who dares say he is not in favor of free speech? In what part of this country are the lips of thought free—in the South or in the North? What section of our country can you trust to the inestimable gem of free speech with? Can you trust it to the gentlemen of Mississippi or to the gentlemen of Massachusetts? Can you trust it to Alabama or to New-York? Can you trust it to the South or can you trust it to the great and splendid North? Honor bright—[laughter]—honor bright, is there any freedom of speech in the South? There never was, and there is none to-night—and let me tell you why.

They had the institution of human slavery in the South, which could not be defended at the bar of public reason. It was an institution that could not be defended in the high forum of human conscience. No man could stand there, and defend the right to rob the cradle—none to defend the right to sell the babe from the breast of the agonized mother—none to defend the claim that lashes on a bare back are a legal tender for labor performed. Every man that lived upon the unpaid labor of another knew in his heart that he was a thief. [Applause.] And for that reason he did not wish to discuss that question. [Laughter.] Thereupon the institution of slavery said, "You shall not speak; you shall not reason," and the lips of free thought were manacled. You know it. Every one of you. [Laughter.] Every Democrat knows it as well as every Republican. There never was free speech in the South.

And what has been the result? And allow me to admit right here, because I want to be fair, there are thousands and thousands of most excellent people in the South—thousands of them. There are hundreds and hundreds of thousands there who would like to vote the Republican ticket. [Applause.] And whenever there is free speech there, and whenever there is a free ballot there, they will vote the Republican ticket. [Great applause.] I say again, there are hundreds of thousands of good people in the South; but the institution of human slavery prevented free speech, and it is a splendid fact in nature that you cannot put chains upon the limbs of others without putting corresponding manacles upon your own brain. [Applause.] When the South enslaved the negro, it also enslaved itself, and the result was an intellectual desert. No book has been produced, with one exception, that has added to the knowledge of mankind; no paper, no magazine, no poet, no philosopher, no philanthropist, was ever raised in that desert. [Great applause.] Now and then some one protested against that infamous institution, and he came as near being a philosopher as the society in which he lived permitted. [Laughter.] Why is it that New-England, a rock-clad land, blossoms like a rose? Why is it that New-York is the Empire State of the great Union? I will tell you. Because you have been permitted to trade in ideas. Because the lips of speech have been absolutely free for twenty years. [Applause.] We never had free speech in any State in this Union until the Republican party was born. [Applause.] That party was rocked in the cradle of intellectual liberty, and that is the reason I say it is the best party that ever existed in the wide, wide world. [Applause.] I want to preserve free speech, and, as an honest man, I look about me and I say,

"How can I best preserve it?" By giving it to the South or North; to the Democracy or to the Republican party? And I am bound, as an honest man, to say free speech is safest with its earliest defenders. [Applause.] Where is there such a thing as a Republican mob to prevent the expression of an honest thought; where? The people of the South are allowed to come to the North; they are allowed to express their sentiments upon every stump in the great East, the great West and in the great Middle States; they go to Maine, to Vermont, and to all our States, and they are allowed to speak, and we give them a respectful hearing, and the meanest thing we do is to answer their argument. [Applause.]

I say to-night that we ought to have the same liberty to discuss these questions in the South that other Southerners have in the North. And I say more than that, the Democrats of the North ought to compel the Democrats of the South to treat the Republicans of the South as well as the Republicans of the North treat them. [Applause.] We treat the Democrats well in the North; [laughter;] we treat them like gentlemen in the North; and yet they go in partnership with the Democracy of the South, knowing that the Democracy of the South will not treat Republicans in that section with fairness. A Democrat ought to be ashamed of that. If my friends will not treat other people as well as the friends of the other people treat me, I'll swap friends. [Applause and laughter.]

First, then, I am in favor of free speech, and I am going with that section of my country that believes in free speech; I am going with that party that has always upheld that sacred right. When you stop free speech, when you say that a thought shall die in the womb of the brain—why, it would have the same effect upon the intellectual world that to stop springs at their sources would have upon the physical world. Stop the springs at their sources and they cease to gurgle, the streams cease to murmur, and the great rivers cease rushing to the embrace of the sea. So you stop thought. Stop thought in the brain in which it is born, and theory dies; and the great ocean of knowledge to which all should be permitted to contribute, and from which all should be allowed to draw, becomes a vast desert of ignorance. [Applause.]

I have always said, and I say again, that the more liberty there is given away, the more you have. There is room in this world for us all; there is room enough for all of our thoughts; out upon the intellectual sea there is room for every sail, and in the intellectual air there is space for every wing. [Applause.] A man that exercises a right that he will not give to others is a barbarian. A State that does not allow free speech is uncivilized, and is a disgrace to the American Union. [Applause.]

The Party of an Honest Ballot.

I am not only in favor of free speech, but I am also in favor of an absolutely honest ballot. There is one king in this country; there is one emperor; there is one supreme Czar; and that is the legally expressed will of a majority of the people. [Applause.] The man who casts an illegal vote, the man who refuses to count a legal vote, poisons the fountain of power, poisons the springs of justice, and is a traitor to the only king in this land. The Government is upon the edge of Mexicanization through fraudulent voting. The ballot-box is the throne of America; the ballot-box is the ark of the covenant. Unless we see to it that every man who has a right to vote votes, and unless we see to it that every honest vote is counted, the days of this Republic are numbered.

When you suspect that a Congressman is not elected; when you suspect that a judge upon the bench holds his place by fraud, then the people will hold the law in contempt, and will laugh at the decisions of courts, and then come revolution and chaos. It is the duty of every good man to see to it that the ballot-box is kept absolutely pure. It is the duty of every patriot, whether he is a Democrat or Republican—and I want to further admit that I believe a large majority of Democrats are honest in their opinions, and I know that all Republicans *must* be honest in their opinions. [Applause.] It is the duty, then, of all honest men of both parties to see to it that only honest votes are cast and counted. Now, honor bright, which section of this Union can you trust the ballot-box with? Honor bright, can you trust it with the masked murderers who rode in the darkness of night to the hut of the freedman and shot him down, notwithstanding the supplication of his wife and the tears of his babe? Can you trust it to the men who since the close of our war have killed more men, simply because those men wished to vote, simply because they wished to exercise a right with which they had been clothed by the sublime heroism of the North—who have killed more men than were killed on both sides in the Revolutionary War; than were killed on both sides during the War of 1812; than were killed on both sides in both wars? Can you trust them? Can you trust the gentlemen who invented the tissue-ballot? [Laughter.] Do you wish to put the ballot-box in the keeping of the shot-gun, of the White Liners, of the Ku Klux? Do you wish to put the ballot-box in the keeping of men who openly swear that they will not be ruled by a majority of American citizens if a portion of that majority is made of black men? [Applause.] And I want to tell you right here, I like a black man who loves this country better than I do a white man who hates it. [Applause.] I think more of a black man who fought for our flag than for any white man who endeavored to tear it out of heaven! [Applause.] I like black friends better than white enemies. [Applause.] And I think more of a man black outside and white inside than I do of one white outside and black inside. [Applause.]

I say, can you trust the ballot-box to the Democratic party? Read the history of the State of New-York! [Laughter.] Read the history of this great and magnificent city—the Queen of the Atlantic—read her history and tell us whether you can implicitly trust Democratic returns? [Laughter.] Honor bright! [Laughter.]

I am not only, then, for free speech, but I am for an honest ballot; and in order that you may have no doubt left upon your minds as to which party is in favor of an honest vote, I will call your attention to this striking fact. Every law that has been passed in every State of this Union for twenty long years, the object of which was to guard the American ballot-box, has been passed by the Republican party, [applause,] and in every State where the Republican party has introduced such a bill for the purpose of making it a law ; in every State where such a bill has been defeated, it has been defeated by the Democratic party. [Applause.] That ought to satisfy any reasonable man to satiety.

Who Shall Collect the Revenue?

I am not only in favor of free speech and an honest ballot, but I am in favor of collecting and disbursing the revenues of the United States. I want plenty of money to collect and pay the interest on our debt. I want plenty of money to pay our debt and to preserve the financial honor of the United States. [Applause.] I want money enough to be collected to pay pensions to widows and orphans and to wounded soldiers. [Applause.] And the question is, what section in this country can you trust to collect and disburse that revenue ? Let us be honest about it. [Laughter.] What section can you trust? In the last four years we have collected $467,000,000 of the internal revenue taxes. We have collected, principally from taxes upon high wines and tobacco, $418,000,000, and in those four years we have seized, libelled and destroyed in the Southren States 3,874 illicit distilleries. And during the same time the Southern people have shot to death twenty-five revenue officers and wounded fifty-five others, and the only offence that the wounded and dead committed was an honest effort to collect the revenues of this country. [Applause.] Recollect it—don't you forget it. [Laughter.] And in several Southern States to-day every revenue collector or officer connected with the revenue is furnished by the Internal Revenue Department with a breech-loading rifle and a pair of revolvers, simply for the purpose of collecting the revenue. I don't feel like trusting such people to collect the revenue of my Government.

During the same four years we have arrested and have indicted 7,084 Southern Democrats for endeavoring to defraud the revenue of the United States. Recollect —3,874 distilleries seized, 25 revenue officers killed, 55 wounded, and 7,084 Democrats arrested. [Applause.[Can we trust them?

The State of Alabama in its last Democratic Convention passed a resolution that no man should be tried in a Federal Court for a violation of the revenue laws—that he should be tried in a State Court. [Laughter.] Think of it—he should be tried in a State Court ! Let me tell you how it will come out if we trust the Southern States to collect this revenue. A couple of Methodist ministers had been holding a revival for a week, and at the end of the week one said to the other that he thought it time to take up a collection. When the hat was returned he found in it pieces of slate pencils and nails and buttons, but not a single solitary cent [laughter]—not one—and his brother minister got up and looked at the contribution, and he said, "Let us thank God !" [Laughter.] And the owner of the hat said, "What for ?" And the brother replied, "Because you got your hat back." [Roars of laughter and applause.] If we trust the South we won't get our hat back. [Laughter and cheers.]

Honest Money and an Honest Nation.

I am next in favor of honest money. I am in favor of gold and silver, and paper with gold and silver behind it. [Applause.] I believe in silver, because it is one of the greatest of American products, and I am in favor of anything that will add to the value of an American product. [Applause.] But I want a silver dollar worth a gold dollar, even if you make it or have to make it four feet in diameter. [Great laughter.] No Government can afford to be a clipper of coin. [Applause.] A great Republic cannot afford to stamp a lie upon silver or gold. [Great applause.] Honest money, an honest people, an honest Nation ! [Renewed applause.] When our money is only worth 80 cents on the dollar, we feel 20 per cent. below par. [Great laughter.] When our money is good, we feel good. When our money is at par, that is where we are. [Applause and laughter.] I am a profound believer in the doctrine that for nations as as well as men, honesty is the best, always, everywhere and forever. [Tremendous applause.]

What section of this country, what party will give us honest money—honor bright—honor bright ? [Laughter.] I have been told that during the war we had plenty of money. I never saw it I lived years without seeing a dollar. I saw promises for dollars, but not dollars. [Applause.] And the greenback, unless you have the gold behind it, is no more a dollar than a bill of fare is a dinner. [Great laughter.] You cannot make a paper dollar without taking a dollar's worth of paper. We must have paper that represents money. I want it issued by the Government, and I want behind every one of these dollars either a gold or a silver dollar, so that every greenback under the flag can lift up its hand and swear, "I know that my redeemer liveth." [Great laughter.]

When we were running into debt, thousands of people mistook that for prosperity, and when we began paying, they regarded it as adversity. [Laughter.] Of course we had plenty when we bought on credit. No man has ever starved when his credit was good, if there were no famine in that country. [Laughter.] As long as we buy on credit we shall have enough. The trouble commences when the pay-day arrives. [Laughter.] And I do not wonder that after the war thousands of people said, "Let us have another inflation." What party said, "No, we must pay the promise made in war ?" [Great applause.] Honor bright ! The Democratic party had once been a hard money party, but it drifted from its metallic moorings and floated off in the ocean of inflation, and you know it ! [Laughter.] They said, "Give us more money," and every man that had bought on credit and owed a little something on what he had purchased, when the property went down, he commenced crying, or many of them did, for inflation. I understand it. A man, say, bought a piece of land for $6,000 ; paid $5,000 on it ; gave a mortgage for $1,000, and suddenly, in 1873, found that the land would not pay the other thousand. The land had resumed. [Much laughter.] And then he said, looking lugubriously at his note and mortgage, "I want another inflation." And I never heard a man call for it that did not also say, " If it ever comes, and I don't unload, you may shoot me." [Great laughter.]

It was very much as it is sometimes in playing poker, and I make this comparison knowing that hardly a person here will understand it. [Great laughter. A voice—"Honor bright!" Renewed laughter.] I have been told [laughter] that along toward morning [laughter] the man that is ahead suddenly says, "I have got to go home. [Great laughter.] The fact is, my wife is not well." [Great laughter.] And the fellow who is behind says, "Let us have another deal." [Laughter.] I have my opinion of the fellow that will jump a game. And so it was in the hard times of 1873. They said : "Give us another deal ; let us get our driftwood back into the centre of the stream." And they cried out for more money. But the Republican party said : "We do want more money, but not more promises. We have got to pay this first, and if we start out again upon that wide sea of promise we may never touch the shore." [Applause.]

The Fallacy and Folly of Fiat Dollars.

A thousand theories were born of want ; a thousand theories were born of the fertile brain of trouble ; and these people said after all : "What is money ? why it is nothing but a measure of value, just the same as a half bushel or yard stick." True. And consequently it makes no difference whether your half bushel is of wood, or gold, or silver or paper ; and it makes no difference whether your yard stick is gold or paper. But the trouble about that statement is this : A half bushel is not a measure of value ; it is a measure of quantity, and it measures rubies, diamonds and pearls, precisely the same as corn and wheat. The yard stick is not a measure of value ; it is a measure of length, and it measures lace, worth $100 a yard, precisely as it does one cent tape. And another reason why it makes no difference to the purchaser whether the half bushel is gold or silver, or whether the yard stick is gold or paper, you don't buy the yard stick ; you don't get the half bushel in the trade. And if it was so with money—if the people that had the money at the start of the trade, kept it after the consummation of the bargain—then it wouldn't make any difference what you made your money of. But the trouble is the money changes hands. And let me say to-night, money is a thing— it is a product of nature—and you can no more make a "fiat" dollar than you can make a fiat star. I am in favor of honest money. Free speech is the brain of the Republic ; an honest ballot is the breath of its life, and honest money is the blood that courses through its veins. [Applause.]

If I am fortunate enough to leave a dollar when I die, I want it to be a good one ; I don't wish to have it turn to ashes in the hands of widowhood, or become a Democratic broken promise in the pocket of the orphan ; I want it money. I saw not long ago a piece of gold bearing the stamp of the Roman Empire. That Empire is dust, and over it has been thrown the mantle of oblivion, but that piece of gold is as good as though Julius Cæsar were still riding at the head of the Roman Legion. [Applause.] I want money that will outlive the Democratic party. They told us —and they were honest about it—they said, "when we have plenty of money, we are prosperous." And

I said, "When we are prosperous, we have plenty of money." When we are prosperous, then we have credit, and credit inflates the currency. Whenever a man buys a pound of sugar and says, "Charge it," he inflates the currency ; whenever he gives his note, he inflates the currency ; whenever his word takes the place of money, he inflates the currency. The consequence is that when we are prosperous, credit takes the place of money, and we have what we call "plenty." But you cannot increase prosperity simply by using promises to pay. Suppose you should come to a river that was about dry, and there you would see the ferryboat, and the gentleman who kept the ferry, high on the sand, and the cracks all opening in the sun filled with loose oakum, looking like an average Democratic mouth listening to a Constitutional argument, and you should say to him, "How is business ?" [Applause and laughter.] And he would say, "Dull." And then you would say to him, "Now, what you want is more boat." He would probably answer, "If I had a little more water I could get along with this one." [Laughter.]

But I want to be fair, [laughter,] and I wish to-night to return my thanks to the Democratic party. You did a great and splendid work. You went all over the United States and you said upon every stump that a greenback was better than gold. You said, "We have at last found the money of the poor man. Gold loves the rich ; gold haunts banks and safes and vaults ; but we have got money that will go around inquiring for a man that is dead broke. [Great laughter.] We have finally found money that will stay in a pocket with holes in it." [Laughter.] But after all, do you know that money is the most social thing in this world ? [Laughter.] If a fellow has got $1 in his pocket, and he meets another with two, do you know that dollar is absolutely homesick until it gets where the other two are ? [Laughter.] And yet the Greenbackers told us that they had finally invented money that would be the poor man's friend. They said, "It is better than gold, better than silver," and they got so many men to believe it that when we resumed and said, "Here is your gold for your greenback," the fellows who had the greenback said, "We don't want it. The greenbacks are good enough for us." Do you know, if they had wanted it we could not give it to them ? [Laughter.] And so I return my thanks to the Greenback party. But allow me to say in this connection, the days of their usefulness have passed forever. [Applause.]

Now, I am not foolish enough to claim that the Republican party resumed I am not silly enough to say that John Sherman resumed. But I will tell you what I do say. I say that every man who raised a bushel of corn, or a bushel of wheat, or a pound of beef or pork for sale, helped to resume. [Applause.] I say that the gentle rain and the loving dew helped to resume. The soil of the United States impregnated by the loving sun helped to resume. The men that dug the coal and the iron, and the silver and the copper and the gold, helped to resume. And the men upon whose foreheads fell the light of furnaces helped to resume. And the sailors who fought with the waves of the seas helped to resume.

I admit to-night that the Democrats earned their share of the money to resume with. All I claim in God's world is that the Republican party furnished the honesty to pay it over. [Great applause.] That is what I claim; and the Republican party set the day, and the Republican party worked to the promise. That is what I say. And had it not been for the Republican party this nation would have been financially dishonored. [Applause.] I am for honest money, and I am for the payment of every dollar of our debt, and so is every Democrat now, I take it. But what did you say a little while ago? Did you say we could resume? No: you swore we could not, and you swore our bonds would be as worthless as the withered leaves of winter. And now, when a Democrat goes to England, and sees an American four per cent. quoted at 110 he kind of swells up. [laughter.] and he says: "That's the kind of man I am." [Great laughter.] In that country he pretends he was a Republican in this. And I don't blame him. And I don't begrudge him enjoying respectability when away from home. [Laughter.] The Republican party is entitled to the credit for keeping this nation grandly and splendidly honest. [Applause.] I say, the Republican party is entitled to the credit of preserving the honor of this nation. [Applause.]

The Struggle after the Panic.

In 1873 came the crash, and all the languages of the world cannot describe the agonies suffered by the American people from 1873 to 1879. A man who thought he was a millionaire came to poverty; he found his stocks and bonds ashes in the paralytic hand of old age. Men who expected to have lived all their lives in the sunshine of joy found themselves beggars and paupers. The great factories were closed, the workmen were demoralized, and the roads of the United States were filled with tramps. In the hovel of the poor and the palace of the rich came the serpent of temptation, and whispered in the American ear the terrible word, "Repudiation." But the Republican party said, "No; we will pay every dollar. [Applause.] No; we have started toward the shining goal of resumption, and we never will turn back." [Applause.] And the Republican party struggled until it had the happiness of seeing upon the broad shining forehead of American labor the words, "Financial Honor." [Applause.]

The Republican party struggled until every paper promise was as good as gold. [Applause.] And the moment we got back to gold then we commenced to rise again. We could not jump up until our feet touched something that they could be pressed against. And from that moment to this we have been going, going, going, going higher and higher, more prosperous every hour. [Applause.] And now they say, "Let us have a change." [Laughter.] When I am sick I want a change; when I am poor I want a change; and if I were a Democrat I would have a personal change. [Laughter.] We are prosperous to-day, and must keep so. We are back to gold and silver. Let us stay there; and let us stay with the party that brought us there. ["Good," "good," and applause.]

A Nation, Not a Confederacy.

Now, I am not only in favor of free speech and an honest ballot-box and an honest collection of the revenue of the United States and an honest money, but I am in favor of the idea of the great and splendid truth that this is a nation one and indivisible. [Great applause.] I deny that we are a confederacy bound together with ropes of cloud and chains of mist. This is a nation, and every man in it owes his first allegiance to the grand old flag for which more brave blood was shed than for any other flag that waves in the sight of heaven. [Great applause.]

The Southern people say this is a confederacy, and they are honest in it. They fought for it. they believed it. They believe in the doctrine of State Sovereignty, and many Democrats of the North believe in the same doctrine. No less a man than Horatio Seymour—standing it may be at the head of Democratic statesmen—said, if he has been correctly reported, only the other day, that he despised the word "Nation." I bless that word. [Applause.] I owe my first allegiance to that Nation, and it owes its first protection to me. [Great applause.] I am talking here to-night, not because I am protected by the flag of New-York. I would not know that flag if I should see it. [Laughter.] I am talking here, and have the right to talk here, because the flag of my country is above us. [Applause.] I have the same right as though I had been born upon this very platform. I am proud of New-York because it is a part of my country. I am proud of my country because it has got such a State as New-York in it. [great applause.] and I will be prouder of New-York on a week from next Tuesday than ever before in my life. [Great cheering.] I despise the doctrine of State Sovereignty. I believe in the rights of the States, but not in the sovereignty of the States. States are political conveniences. Rising above States as the Alps above valleys are the rights of man. Rising above the rights of the Government even in this Nation are the sublime rights of the people. [Loud applause.] Governments are good only so long as they protect human rights. But the rights of a man never should be sacrificed upon the altar of the State or upon the altar of the Nation. [Applause.]

State Sovereignty and Human Slavery.

Let me tell you a few objections that I have got to State Sovereignty. That doctrine has never been appealed to for any good. The first time it was appealed to was when our Constitution was made. And the object then was to keep the slave trade open until the year 1808. The object then was to make the sea the highway of piracy—the object then was to allow American citizens to go into the business of selling men and women and children, and feed their cargo to the sharks of the sea, and the sharks of the sea were as merciful as they. That was the first time that the appeal to the doctrine of State Sovereignty was made, and the next time was for the purpose of keeping alive the inter-State slave trade, so that a gentleman in Virginia could sell his slave to the rice and cotton plantations of the South. Think of it! It was made so they could rob the cradle in the name of the law. Think of it! Think of it! And the next time they appealed to the doctrine of State Sovereignty was in favor of the Fugitive Slave law—a law that made a bloodhound of every Northern man; that made charity a crime. A law that made love a State prison offence; that branded the forehead of charity as if it were a felon. Think of it! A law that, if a woman ninety-nine one-hundredths white had escaped from slavery, had traversed forests, had been torn by briars, had crossed rivers, had travelled at night and in darkness, and had finally got within one step of free soil, with the whole light of the North star shining in her tear-filled eyes, with her little babe on her withered bosom—a law that declared it the duty of Northern men to clutch that woman and turn her back to the domination of the hound and the lash. [Tremendous applause.] I have no respect for any man living or dead who voted for that law. I have no respect for any man who would carry it out. I never had.

The next time they appealed to the doctrine of State Sovereignty was to increase the area of human slavery, so that the bloodhound, with clots of blood dropping from his loose and hanging jaws, might traverse the billowy plains of Kansas. Think of it! The Democratic party then said the Federal Government had a right to cross the State line. And the next time they appealed to that infamous doctrine was in defence of secession and treason; a doctrine that cost us six thousand millions of dollars; a doctrine that cost four hundred thousand lives; a doctrine that filled our country with widows, our homes with orphans. And I tell you the doctrine of State Sovereignty is the viper in the bosom of this Republic, and if we do not kill that viper it will kill us. [Long continued applause.]

The Democrats tell us that in the olden time the Federal Government had a right to cross a State line to put shackles upon the limbs of men. It had the right to cross a State line to trample upon the rights of human beings, but now it has no right to cross those lines upon an errand of mercy or justice. We are told that now, when the Federal Government wishes to protect a citizen, a State line rises like a Chinese wall, and the sword of Federal power turns to air the moment it touches one of those lines. I deny it, and I despise, abhor and execrate the doctrine of State Sovereignty. [Applause.] The Democrats tell us if we wish to be protected by the Federal Government we must leave home. [Laughter.] I wish they would try it [applause] for about ten days. [Great laughter.] They say the Federal Government can defend a citizen in England, France, Spain or Germany, but cannot defend a child of the Republic sitting around the family hearth. I deny it. A Government that cannot protect its citizens at home is unfit to be called a Government. [Applause.] I want a Government with an ear so good that it can hear the faintest cry of the oppressed wherever its flag floats. [Applause.] I want a Government with an arm long enough and a sword sharp enough to cut down treason wherever it may raise its serpent head. [Applause.] I want a Government that will protect a freedman, standing by his little log hut, with the same alacrity and with the same efficiency that it would protect Vanderbilt, living in a palace of marble and gold. [Applause.] Humanity is a sacred thing, and manhood is a thing to be preserved. Let us look at it. For instance, here is a man, and the Federal Government says to a man, "We want you," and he says, "No, I don't want to go," and then they put a lot of pieces of paper in a wheel, and on one of those pieces is his name, and another man turns the crank, and then they pull it out and there is his name, and they say, "Come," and so he goes. [Laughter.] And they stand him in front of the brazen-throated guns; they make him fight for his native land, and when the war is over he goes home, and he finds the war has been unpopular in his neighborhood, and they tramp upon his rights, and he says to the Federal Government, "Protect me." And he says to that Government, "I owe my allegiance to you. You must protect me." What will you say of that Government if it says to him, "You must look to your State for protection." "Ah, but,' he says, "my State is the very power trampling upon me," and, of course, the robber is not going to send for the police. [Applause.] It is the duty of the Government to defend even its drafted men; and if that is the duty of the Government, what shall I say of the volunteer, who for one moment holds his wife in a tremulous and agonized embrace, kisses his children, shoulders his musket, goes to the field, and says, "Here I am, ready to die for my native land." [A voice, "Good."] A nation that will not defend its volunteer defenders is a disgrace to the map of this world. A flag that will not protect its protectors is a dirty rag that contaminates the air in which it waves. [Applause.] This is a Nation. Free speech is the brain of the Republic; an honest ballot is the breath of its life; honest money is the blood of its veins; and the idea of nationality is its great beating, throbbing heart. [Applause.] I am for a Nation. And yet the Democrats tell me that it is dangerous to have centralized power. How would you have it? I believe in the localization of power; I believe in having enough of it localized in one place to be effectively used; I believe in a localization of brain. I suppose Democrats would like to have it spread all over your body, [applause and laughter,] and they act as though theirs was.

Protecting American Labor.

There is another thing in which I believe: I believe in the protection of American labor. The hand that holds Aladdin's lamp must be the hand of toil. This Nation rests upon the shoulders of its workers, and I want the American laboring man to have enough to wear; I want him to have enough to eat; I want him to have something for the ordinary misfortunes of life; I want him to have the pleasure of seeing his wife well dressed; I want him to see a few blue ribbons fluttering about his children; I want him to see the flags of health flying in their beautiful cheeks: I want him to feel that this is his country, and the shield of protection is above his labor. [Applause.]

And I will tell you why I am for protection, too. If we were all farmers we would be stupid. If we were all shoemakers we would be stupid. If we all followed one business, no matter what it was, we would become stupid. Protection to American labor diversifies American industry, and to have it diversified touches and develops every part of the human brain. Protection protects ingenuity; it protects intelligence; and protection raises sense; and by protection we have greater men and better looking women and healthier children. [Applause.] Free Trade means that our laborer is upon an equality with the poorest paid labor of this world. And allow me to tell you that for an empty stomach, "Hurrah for Hancock" is a poor consolation. [Laughter.] I do not think much of a Government where the people do not have enough to eat. [Applause.] I am a materialist to that extent; I want something to eat. I have been in countries where the laboring man had meat once a year; sometimes twice—Christmas and Easter. And I have seen women carrying upon their heads a burden that no man in this audience could carry, and at the same time knitting busily with both hands, and those women lived without meat; and when I thought of the American laborer, I said to myself, "After all, my country is the best in the world." [Applause.] And when I came back to the sea and saw the old flag flying in the air, it seemed to me as though the air from pure joy had burst into blossom. [Applause.]

Labor has more to eat and more to wear in the United States than in any other land of this earth. [Applause.] I want America to produce everything that Americans need. I want it so if the whole world should declare war against us, so if we were surrounded by walls of cannon and bayonets and swords, we could supply all our human wants in and of ourselves. [Applause.] I want to live to see the American woman dressed in American silk; the American man in everything from hat to boots produced in America, [applause,] by the cunning hand of American toil; I want to see the workingman have a good house, painted white, grass in the front yard, carpets on its floor, pictures on the wall, [applause.] I want to see him a man feeling that he is a king by the divine right of living in the Republic. [Applause.] And every man here is just a little bit a king, you know. Every man here is a part of the sovereign power. Every man wears a little of purple; every man has a little of crown and a little of sceptre; and every man that will sell his vote for money or be ruled by prejudice is unfit to be an American citizen. [Applause.]

I believe in American labor, and I will tell you why. The other day a man told me that we had produced in the United States of America one million tons of steel rails. How much are they worth? Sixty dollars a ton. In other words, the million tons are worth $60,000,000. How much is a ton of iron worth in the ground? Twenty-five cents. American labor takes twenty-five cents of iron in the ground and adds to it $59.75. [Applause.] One million tons of rails, and the raw material not worth $24,000. We build a ship in the United States worth $500,000, and the value of the ore in the earth, of the trees in the great forest, of all that enters into the composition of that ship bringing $500,000 in gold is only $20,000; $480,000 by American labor. American muscle, coined into gold; American brains made a legal-tender the world around. [Applause.]

Source of the Free Trade Doctrine.

I propose to stand by the Nation. I want the furnaces kept hot. I want the sky to be filled with the smoke of American industry, and upon that cloud of smoke will rest forever the bow of perpetual promise. ["Good," "good;" great cheers.] That is

what I am for. [A voice—"So are we all."] Yes, sir. [Laughter.] Where did this doctrine of a tariff for revenue only come from? From the South. The South would like to stab the prosperity of the North. They had rather trade with Old England than with New England. They had rather trade with the people who were willing to help them in war than those who conquered the rebellion. [Great cheers.] They knew what gave us our strength in war. They knew that all the brooks and creeks and rivers of New-England were putting down the rebellion. They knew that every wheel that turned, every spindle that revolved, was a soldier in the army of human progress. It won't do. [Great applause.] They were so lured by the greed of office that they were willing to trade upon the misfortunes of a Nation. It won't do. I don't wish to belong to a party that succeeds only when my country fails. I don't wish to belong to a party whose banner went up with the banner of rebellion. I don't wish to belong to a party that was in partnership with defeat and disaster, I don't. [Applause.] And there isn't a Democrat here but what knows that a failure of the crops this year would have helped his party. [Applause.] You know that an early frost would have been a godsend to them, [Laughter.] You know that the potato-bug could have done them more good than all their speakers. [Great applause.]

I wish to belong to that party which is prosperous when the country is prosperous. I belong to that party which is not poor when the golden billows are running over the seas of wheat. I belong to that party that is prosperous when there are oceans of corn, and when the cattle are upon the thousand hills. I belong to that party which is prosperous when the furnaces are aflame; and when you dig coal and iron and silver; when everybody has enough to eat; when everybody is happy; when the children are all going to school, [applause;] and when joy covers my Nation as with a garment. [Applause.] That party which is prosperous, then, is my party.

Now, then, I have been telling you what I am for. I am for free speech, and so ought you to be. I am for an honest ballot, and if you are not, you ought to be. I am for the collection of the revenue. I am for honest money. I am for the idea that this is a Nation forever. [Great applause.] I believe in protecting American labor. [Great applause.] I want the shield of my country above every anvil, above every furnace, above every cunning head and above every deft hand of American labor. [Applause.]

Now, then, what section of this country will be the more apt to carry these ideas into execution? What party will be the more apt to achieve these grand and splendid things? Honor bright? [Laughter.] Now we have not only to choose between sections of the country; we have to choose between parties. Here is the Democratic party, and I admit there are thousands of good Democrats who went to the war, and some of those that stayed at home were good men; and I want to ask you, and I want you to tell me in reply what that party did during the war when the War Democrats were away from home. What did they do? That is the question. I say to you that every man who tried to tread our flag out of heaven was a Democrat. [Applause.] The men who wrote the ordinances of secession, who fired upon Fort

Sumter; the men who starved our soldiers, who fed them with the crumbs that the worms had devoured before, they were Democrats. The keepers of Libby, the keepers of Andersonville were Democrats; Libby and Andersonville, the two mighty wings that will bear the memory of the Confederacy to eternal infamy. And when some poor, emaciated Union patriot, driven to insanity by famine, saw, in an insane dream, the face of his mother, and she beckoned him, and he followed, hoping to press her lips once again against his fevered face, and when he stepped one step beyond the dead line the wretch that put the bullet through his loving, throbbing heart was a Democrat. [Great applause.] The men who wished to scatter yellow fever in the North, and who tried to fire the great cities of the North, knowing that the serpents of flame would devour the women and babes—they were all Democrats. [Applause.] He who said that the greenback would never be paid, and he who slandered sixty cents out of every dollar of the nation's promises, were Democrats. Who were joyful when your brothers and your sons and your fathers lay dead on a field of battle, that the country had lost? They were Democrats. The men who wept when the old banner floated in triumph above the ramparts of Rebellion——they were Democrats. You know it. The men who wept when slavery was destroyed, who believed slavery to be a Divine institution, who regarded bloodhounds as apostles and missionaries, and who wept at the funeral of that infernal institution—they were Democrats. Bad company—bad company! [Laughter and applause.]

And let me implore all the young men here not to join that party. Do not give new blood to that institution. The Democratic party has a yellow passport. On one side it says "dangerous." They imagine they have not changed, and that is because they have not intellectual growth. That party was once the enemy of my country, was once the enemy of our flag, and more than that, it was once the enemy of human liberty, and that party to-night is not willing that the citizens of the Republic should exercise all their rights irrespective of their color. And allow me to say right here that I am opposed to that party. [Loud applause.]

Candidates of the Two Parties.

We have not only to choose between parties, but to choose between candidates. The Democracy have put forward as the bearers of their standard General Hancock and William H. English. [Hisses.] No, no, no. They will soon be beyond hissing. [Roars of laughter.] But let us treat them respectfully. When I am by the side of the dying, I never throw up their crimes. I feel to-night as though standing by the open grave of the Democratic party, [great laughter,] and allow me to say, that I feel as well as could be expected. [Much laughter.]

That party has nominated General Winfield S. Hancock, and I am told that he is a good soldier. I admit it. I don't know whether he is or not. I admit it. [Laughter.] That was his reputation before he was nominated, and I am willing to let him have the advantage of all he had before he was nominated. He had a conversation with General Grant. [Great ap-plause.] It was a time when he had been appointed at the head of the Department of the Gulf. In that conversation he stated to General Grant that he was opposed to "nigger domination." Grant said to him, "We must obey the laws of Congress. [Applause.] We are soldiers." And that meant, the military is not above the civil authority. [Applause.] And I tell you to-night, that the army and the navy are the right and left hands of the civil power. [Applause.] Grant said to him: "Three or four million ex-slaves, without property and without education, cannot dominate over thirty or forty millions of white people, with education and with property." General Hancock replied to that; "I am opposed to 'nigger domination.'" Allow me to say that I do not believe any man fit for the Presidency of the great Republic who is capable of insulting a downtrodden race. [Great applause.] I never meet a negro that I do not feel like asking his forgiveness for the wrongs that my race has inflicted on his. [Applause.] I remember that from the white man he received for 200 years agony and tears; I remember that my race sold a child from the agonized breast of a mother; I remember that my race trampled, with the feet of greed, upon all the holy relations of life; and I do not feel like insulting the colored man; I feel rather like asking the forgiveness of his race for the crimes that my race have put upon him. "Nigger domination." What a fine scabbard that makes for the sword of Gettysburg. It won't do. [Laughter.]

What is General Hancock for, besides the Presidency? [Laughter.] How does he stand upon the great questions affecting American prosperity? [Cries of "Give it up." "Give us an easier one." Laughter.] He told us the other day that the tariff is a local question. The tariff affects every man and woman, live they in hut, hovel or palace; it affects every man that has a back to be covered or a stomach to be filled, and yet he says it is a local question. [Laughter.] So is death. [Laughter.] He also told us that he heard that question discussed once, in Pennsylvania. [Great laughter.] He must have been "eavesdropping." [Great laughter.] And he tells us that his doctrine of the tariff will continue as long as Nature lasts. [Laughter.] Then Senator Randolph wrote him a letter. I don't know whether Senator Randolph answered it or not; [laughter;] but that answer was worse than the first interview; and I understand now that another letter is going through a period of incubation at Governor's Island, upon the great subject of the tariff. It won't do. [Applause and laughter.]

They say one thing they are sure of, he is opposed to paying Southern pensions and Southern claims. He says that a man that fought against this Government has no right to a pension. Good! I say a man that fought against this Government has no right to office. [Loud and prolonged applause.] If a man cannot earn a pension by tearing our flag out of the sky, he cannot earn power. [A voice—"How about Longstreet?"] Longstreet has repented of what he did. Longstreet admits that he was wrong. And there was no braver officer in the Southern Confederacy. [Applause.] Every man of the South who will say, "I made a mistake"—I don't want him to say that he knew he was wrong—all I ask him to say is, that he now thinks he was wrong, and every man of the South to-day who says he was wrong, and who says from this day forward, henceforth and forever, he is for this being a Nation, I will take him by the hand. [Renewed applause.] But while he is attempting to do at the ballot-box what he failed to accomplish upon the field of battle, I am against him ; while he uses a Northern General to bait a Southern trap, I won't bite. I will forgive men when they deserve to be forgiven ; but while they insist that they were right, while they insist that State Sovereignty is the proper doctrine, I am opposed to their climbing into power.

Hancock says that he will not pay these claims ; he agrees to veto a bill that his party may pass ; he agrees in advance that he will defeat a party that he expects will elect him ; he, in effect, says to the people, " You can't trust that party, but you can trust me." He says, " Look at them ; I admit they are a hungry lot ; I admit that they haven't had a bite in twenty years ; I admit that an ordinary famine is satiety compared to the hunger they feel. But between that vast appetite known as the Democratic party and the public treasury I will throw the shield of my veto." [Applause.] No man has a right to say in advance what he will veto, any more than a judge has a right to say in advance how he will decide a case. [Applause.] The veto power is a distinction with which the Constitution has clothed the Executive, and no President has a right to say that he will veto until he has heard both sides of the question. [Applause.] But he agrees in advance, [Laughter.]

I would rather trust a party than a man. Death may veto Hancock, and death has not been a successful politician in the United States. [Laughter.] Tyler, Fillmore, Andy Johnson—[laughter]—I don't wish Death to elect any more Presidents ; and if he does, and if Hancock is elected, William H. English becomes President of the United States. [Hisses.] No, no, no ! All I need to say about him is simply to pronounce his name ; [laughter ;] that is all. You don't want him. Whether the many stories that have been told about him are true or not I don't know, and I will not give currency to a solitary word against the reputation of an American citizen unless I know it to be true. [Applause, and cries of " Good !"] What I have got against him is what he has done in public life. When Charles Sumner, [loud applause,] that great and splendid publicist—Charles Sumner, the philanthropist, one who spoke to the conscience of his time and to the history of the future—when he stood up in the United States Senate, and made a great and glorious plea for human liberty, there crept into the Senate a villain and struck him down, as though he had been a wild beast. That man was a member of Congress, and when a resolution was introduced in the House to expel that man, William H. English voted " No." [Hisses.] All the stories in the world could not add to the infamy of that public act. [Applause.] That is enough for me, and whatever his private life may be—let it be that of an angel—never, never, never will I vote for a man that would defend the assassin of free speech. [Applause.] General Hancock, they tell me, is a statesman ; [laughter ;] that what little time he has had to spare from war he has given to the tariff, [laughter,] and what little time he could spare from the tariff he has

given to the Constitution of his country ; showing under what circumstances a Major-General can put at defiance the Congress of the United States. It won't do. But while I am upon that subject it may be well for me to state that he never will be President of the United States. [Loud applause.] Now, I say that a man who, in time of peace prefers peace, and prefers the avocations of peace ; a man who, in the time of peace, would rather look at the corn in the air of June, rather listen to the hum of bees, rather sit by his door with his wife and children ; the man who, in time of peace, loves peace, and yet when the blast of war flows in his ears, shoulders the musket, and goes to the field of war to defend his country, and when the war is over goes home, and again pursues the avocations of peace—that man is just as good, to say the least of him, as a man who in a time of profound peace makes up his mind that he would like to make his living killing other folks. To say the least of it, he is as good.

The Republican Standard-Bearers.

The Republicans have named as their standard-bearers James A. Garfield, [tremendous cheers, again and again renewed, the men standing up, waving their hats and the ladies their handkerchiefs.]—James A. Garfield [cheers] and Chester A. Arthur. [Great cheers and applause.] James A. Garfield was a volunteer soldier, and he took away from the field of Chickamauga as much glory as any one man could carry. [Great applause.] He is not only a soldier—he is a statesman. [Applause.] He has studied and discussed all the great questions that affect the prosperity and well-being of the American people. His opinions are well known, and I say to you to-night that there is not in this Nation, there is not in this Republic a man with greater brain and greater heart than James A. Garfield. [Great cheers.] I know him and I like him. [Applause.] I know him as well as any other public man, and I like him. The Democratic party say that he is not honest. I have been reading some Democratic papers to-day, and you would say that every one of their editors had a private sewer of his own, [laughter,] into which had been emptied for a hundred years the slops of hell. [Laughter and applause.] They tell me that James A. Garfield is not honest. Are you a Democrat ? Your party tried to steal nearly half of this country. [Applause.] Your party stole the armament of a Nation. Your party was willing to live upon the unpaid labor of four millions of people. [Applause.] You have no right to the floor for the purpose of making a motion of honesty. [Applause.] Sit down. [Laughter and applause.] James A. Garfield has been at the head of the most important committees of Congress ; he is a member of the most important one of the whole House. He has no peer in the Congress of the United States. [Applause.] And you know it. He is the leader of the House. With one wave of his hand he can take millions from the pocket of one industry and put it into the pocket of another ; with a motion of his hand he could have made himself a man of wealth, but he is to-night a poor man. [Applause.] But he is rich in honor, [applause,] in integrity he is wealthy, [applause,] and in brain he is a millionaire. [Great applause.] I know him and I like him. [Cheers.] He is as genial as May and he is as generous as Autumn. [Applause.] And the men for whom he has done unnumbered favors, the men whom he had pity enough not to destroy with an argument, the men who, with his great generosity, he has allowed, intellectually, to live, are now throwing filth at the reputation of that great and splendid man. [Cheers.]

Several ladies and gentlemen were passing a muddy place around which were gathered ragged and wretched urchins. And these little wretches began to throw mud at them; and one gentleman said, "If you don't stop I will throw it back at you." And a little fellow said, "You can't do it without dirtying your hands." [Laughter and applause.] And it doesn't hurt us, anyway. [Renewed laughter.]

In ever was more profoundly happy than on the night of that 12th day of October, when I found that between an honest and a kingly man and his maligners, two great States had thrown their shining shields. [Great applause.] When Ohio said, "Garfield is my greatest son, and there never has been raised in the cabins of Ohio a grander man," [tremendous and prolonged applause and cheers;] and when Indiana [loud cheers]—and when Indiana held up her hands and said, "Allow me to endorse that verdict," I was profoundly happy, because that said to me. "Garfield will carry every Northern State;" that said to me, "The solid South will be confronted by a great and splendid North." [Cheers.]

I know Garfield—I like him. [Laughter and cheers.] Some people have said, "How is it that you support Garfield, when he was a minister?" [Laughter.] "How is it that you support Garfield, when he is a Christian?" I will tell you. There are two reasons. The first is, I am not a bigot; and secondly, James A. Garfield is not a bigot. He believes in giving to every other human being every right he claims for himself. He believes in an absolute divorce between Church and State. He believes that every religion should rest upon its morality, upon its reason, upon its persuasion, upon its goodness, upon its charity, and that love should never appeal to the sword of civil power. He disagrees with me in many things; but in the one thing, that the air is free for all, we do agree. I want to do equal and exact justice everywhere. I want the world of thought to be without a chain, without a wall. James A. Garfield, believing with me as he does, disagreeing with me as he does, is perfectly satisfactory to me. I know him and I like him.

Men are to-day blackening his reputation, who are not fit to blacken his shoes. [Applause.] He is a man of brain. Since his nomination he must have made forty or fifty speeches, and every one has been full of manhood and genius. He has not said a word that has not strengthened him with the American people. He is the first candidate who has been free to express himself, and who has never made a mistake. [Great applause.] I will tell you why he don't make a mistake; because he spoke from the inside out. [Applause.] Because he was guided by the glittering Northern Star of principle. Lie after lie has been told about him. Slander after slander has been hatched and put in the air, with its little short

wings, to fly its dirty day, and the last lie is a forgery. [Great applause.]

I saw to-day the *fac simile* of a letter that they pretend he wrote upon the Chinese question. I know his writing; I know his signature; I am well acquainted with his writing. I know handwriting, and I tell you to-night that letter and that signature are forgeries. [Long and continued applause.] A forgery for the benefit of the Pacific States; a forgery for the purpose of convincing the American working-man that Garfield is without heart. I tell you, my fellow citizens, that cannot take from him a vote. [Applause.] But Ohio pierced their centre and Indiana rolled up both flanks, and the rebel line cannot reform with a forgery for a standard. [Applause.] They are gone. [Laughter.]

Not Preaching a Gospel of Hate.

Now, some people say to me, "How long are you going to preach the doctrine of hate?" I never did preach it. In many States of this Union it is a crime to be a Republican. I am going to preach my doctrine until every American citizen is permitted to express his opinion and vote as he may desire in every State of this Union. [Applause.] I am going to preach my doctrine until this is a civilized country. That is all. I will treat the gentlemen of the South precisely as we do the gentlemen of the North. I want to treat every section of the country precisely as we do ours. I want to improve their rivers and their harbors; I want to fill their land with commerce; I want them to prosper; I want them to build school-houses; I want them to open the lands to immigration to all people who desire to settle upon their soil. I want to be friends with them; I want to let the past be buried forever; I want to let by-gones be by-gones, but only upon the basis that we are now in favor of absolute liberty and eternal justice. [Great applause.] I am not willing to bury nationality or free speech in the grave for the purpose of being friends. Let us stand by our colors; let the old Republican party that has made this a Nation—the old Republican party that has saved the financial honor of this country—let that party stand by its colors.

Let that party say, "Free speech forever!" Let that party say, "An honest ballot forever." Let that party say, "Honest money forever; the Nation and the flag forever." And let that party stand by the great men carrying her banner, James A. Garfield and Chester A. Arthur. [Applause.] I had rather trust a party than a man. If General Garfield dies, the Republican party lives; if General Garfield dies, General Arthur will take his place—a brave, and honest and intelligent gentleman, upon whom every Republican can rely. [Applause.] And if he dies, the Republican party lives, and as long as the Republican party does not die, the great Republic will live. As long as the Republican party lives, this will be the asylum of the world. Let me tell you, Mr. Irishman, this is the only country on the earth where Irishmen have had enough to eat. Let me tell you, Mr. German, that you have more liberty here than you had in the Fatherland. Let me tell you, all men, that this is the land of humanity.

Oh! I love the old Republic, bound by the seas, walled by the wide air, domed by heaven's blue, and lit with the eternal stars. I love the Republic; I love it because I love liberty. Liberty is my religion, and at its altar I worship and will worship. [Long-continued applause.]—*From the New-York Tribune "Extra," No. 73, Tuesday, October 26, 1880.*

The Speech of Colonel ROBERT G. INGERSOLL, *in front of the Sub-Treasury in Wall Street, New-York City, Thursday afternoon, October 28, 1880.*

FELLOW-CITIZENS OF THE GREAT CITY OF NEW-YORK : This is the grandest audience I ever saw. [Great applause.] This audience certifies that General James A. Garfield, [tremendous cheers,] that General James A. Garfield is to be the next President of the United States. [Renewed cheers.] This audience certifies that a Republican is to be the next Mayor of the City of New-York. [Great cheers.] This audience certifies that the business men of New-York understand their interests, and that the business men of New-York are not going to let this country be controlled by the rebel South and the rebel North. [Cheers.] In 1860 the Democratic party appealed to force; now it appeals to fraud. [Applause.] In 1860, the Democratic party appealed to the sword; now it appeals to the pen. [Tremendous cheers and laughter.] It was treason then ; it is forgery now. [Great cheers.] The Democratic party cannot be trusted—[A voice : "No, no, it cannot !"]—with the property or with the honor of the people of the United States. [Applause.] The City of New-York owes a great debt to the country. Every man that has cleared a farm has helped to build New-York; every man who helped to build a railway helped to build up the palaces of this city. [Applause.] Where I am now speaking are the terminii of all the railways in the United States. They all come here. New-York has been built up by the labor of the country, [applause,] and New-York owes it to the country to protect the best interest of the country. [Applause.] The farmers of Illinois depend upon the merchants, the brokers and the bankers, upon the gentlemen of New-York, to beat the rabble of New-York. [Great cheers.] You owe to yourselves ; you owe to the great Republic ; and this city that does the business of a hemisphere—this city that will in ten years be the financial centre of this world, [applause,] owes it to itself to be true to the great principles that have allowed it to exist and flourish. [Great applause.]

The Republicans of New-York ought to say that this shall be forever a free country. The Republicans of New-York ought to say that free speech shall forever be held sacred in the United States. [Applause.] The Republicans of New-York ought to see that the party that defended the Nation shall still remain in power. [Applause.] The Republicans of New-York should see that the flag is safely held by the hands that defended it in war. [Applause.] The Republicans of New-York know that the prosperity of the country depends upon good government, and they also know that good government means protection to the people—rich and poor, black and white. [Applause.] The Republicans of New-York know that a black friend is better than a white enemy. [" Good !

good !" and cheers.] They know that a negro while fighting for his Government is better than any white man who will fight against it. [Great cheers.] The Republicans of New-York know that the colored party in the South, which allows every man to vote as he pleases, is better than any white man who is opposed to allowing a negro to cast his honest vote. [Applause.] A black man, in favor of liberty, is better than a white man in favor of slavery. [Applause.] The Republicans of New-York must be true to their friends. [Applause.] This Government means to protect all its citizens, at home and abroad, or it becomes a by-word in the mouths of the Nations of the world.

Now, what do we want to do ? [A voice—" Vote for Garfield." Great cheers and laughter.] Of course. We are going to have an election next Tuesday, and every Republican knows why he is going to vote the Republican ticket ; while every Democrat votes his without knowing why. [Great laughter.] A Republican is a Republican because he loves something ; a Democrat is a Democrat because he hates something. [Great applause.] A Republican believes in progress ; a Democrat in retrogression. A Democrat is a " has been." He is a " used to be." [Great laughter.] The Republican party lives on hope ; the Democratic on memory. [Renewed laughter.] The Democrat keeps his back to the sun and imagines himself a great man because he casts a great shadow. [Laughter.] Now there are certain things we want to preserve—that the business men of New-York want to preserve—and, in the first place, we want an honest ballot. [Applause.] And where the Democratic party has power there never has been an honest ballot. You take the worst ward in this city, and there is where you will find the greatest Democratic majority. [Applause.] You know it, [laughter,] and so do I. [Laughter.] There is not a university in the North, East or West that has not in it a Republican majority. [Applause.] There is not a penitentiary in the United States [tremendous laughter and cheers: cries of " good ! good !"]—how did you know what I was going to say ?—[Great cheers and laughter]—there is not a penitentiary, I say, [great cheers,] in the United States that has not in it a Democratic majority, [outbursts of laughter,] and they know it. [Great laughter.] Two years ago about 283 convicts were in the Penitentiary of Maine. Out of that whole number there was one Republican, [laughter,] and only one. [A voice—" Who was the man ?"] Well, I don't know, but he broke out. [Great laughter.] He said that he didn't mind being in the Penitentiary, but the company was a little more then he could stand. [Renewed laughter.]

The Party that Needs the "Change."

You cannot rely upon that party for an honest ballot. Every law that has been passed in this country in the last twenty years to throw a safeguard around the ballot-box, has been passed by the Republican party. [Applause.] Every law that has been defeated has been defeated by the Democratic party. [Applause.] And you know it. [Laughter.] Unless we have an honest ballot the days of the Republic are numbered; and the only way to get an honest ballot is to beat the Democratic party forever. [Cheers.] And that is what we are going to do. [Applause.] That party can never carry its record; that party is loaded down with the infamies of twenty years; yes, that party is loaded down with the infamies of fifty years. [Applause.] It will never elect a President in this world. I give notice to the Democratic party to-day that it has got to change its name before the people of the United States will change the administration. [Cheers.] You will have to change your natures; [applause;] you will have to change your personnel, and you will have to get enough Republicans to join you and tell you how to run a campaign. [Applause.] If you want an honest ballot—and every honest man does—then you will vote to keep the Republican party in power. [Applause.] What else do you want? You want honest money, [applause,] and I say to the merchants and to the bankers and to the brokers, the only party that will give you honest money is the party that resumed specie payments. [Applause.] The only party that will give you honest money is the party that has said a greenback is a broken promise until it is redeemed with gold. [Cheers.] You can only trust the party that has been honest in disaster. [Applause.] From 1863 to 1879—sixteen long years—the Republican party was the party of honor and principle, and the Republican party saved the honor of the United States. [Cheers.] And you know it. [Applause.] During that time the Democratic party did what it could to destroy our credit at home and abroad. [Applause.] We are not only in favor of free speech and an honest ballot, and honest money, but we go in for law and order. [Applause.] What part of this country believes in free speech—the South or the North? [A voice—"the North."] The South would never give free speech to the country; there was no free speech in the City of New-York until the Republican party got into power. [Applause.] The Democratic party has not intelligence to know that free speech is the germ of this Republic. [Applause.] The Democratic party cares little for free speech because it has no argument to make. [Laughter.] No reasons to offer. [Applause.] Its entire argument is summed up and ended in three words—"Hurrah for Hancock." [Great laughter.] The Republican party believes in free speech because it has got something to say; because it believes in argument; because it believes in moral suasion; because it believes in education. [Great applause.] Any man that does not believe in free speech is a barbarian. [Applause.] Any State that does not support it is not a civilized State. [Applause.]

What Republicanism Means.

I have a right to express my opinion, and the right in common with every other human being, and I am willing to give to every other human being the right that I claim for myself. [Applause.] Republicanism says that out upon the great intellectual sea there is room for every sail; Republicanism says that in the intellectual air there is room enough for every wing. [Applause.] Republicanism means justice in politics. Republicanism means progress in civilization. [Applause.] Republicanism means that every man shall be an educated patriot and a gentleman. [Applause.] And I want to say to you to-day that the Republican party is the best that ever existed. [Applause.] I want to say to you to-day, that it is an honor to belong to it. [Applause.] It is an honor to have belonged to it for twenty years; it is an honor to belong to the party that elected Abraham Lincoln President. [Great applause.] And let me say to you that Lincoln was the greatest, the best, the purest, the kindest man that has ever sat in the Presidential chair. [Great applause.] It is an honor to belong to the Republican party that gave 4,000,000 of men the rights of freemen; it is an honor to belong to the party that broke the shackles from 4,000,000 of men, women and children. [Great applause.] It is an honor to belong to the party that declared that bloodhounds were not the missionaries of civilization. [Applause.] It is an honor to belong to the party that said it was a crime to steal a babe from its mother's breast. [Applause.] It is an honor to belong to the party that swore that this is a Nation forever, one and indivisible. [Great applause.] It is an honor to belong to the party that elected U. S. Grant President of the United States. [Tremendous cheers.] It is an honor to belong to the party that issued thousands and thousands of millions of dollars in promises—that issued promises until they became as thick as the withered leaves of winter; an honor to belong to the party that issued them to put down a rebellion; an honor to belong to the party that put it down; an honor to belong to the party that had the moral courage and honesty to make every one of the promises, made in war, in peace as good as shining, glittering gold. [Great applause.] And I tell you that if there is another life, and if there is a day of judgment, all you need say upon that solemn occasion is, "I was in life and in my death a good square Republican." [Roars of laughter and great applause.]

The Doctrine of State Rights.

I hate the doctrine of State Sovereignty because it fostered State pride; because it fostered the idea that it is more to be a citizen of a State than a citizen of this glorious country. [Applause.] I love the whole country. I like New-York because it is a part of the country, and I like the country because it has got New-York in it. [Great applause.] I am not standing here to-day because the flag of New-York floats over my head, but because that flag for which more heroic blood has been shed than for any other flag that is kissed by the air of heaven waves forever over my head. [Great applause.] That is the reason I am here. The doctrine of State Sovereignty was appealed to in defence of the slave trade; the next time in defence of the slave trade as between the States; the next time in favor of the fugitive slave law; and if there is a Democrat in favor of the fugitive slave law he should be ashamed [applause]—if not of himself—of the ignorance of the time in which he lived. [Laughter.] That fugitive slave law was a compromise so that we might be friends of the South. They said in 1850-'52: "If you catch the slave we will be your friend;" and they tell us now: "If you let us trample upon the rights of the black man in the South, we will be your friend." I don't want their friendship on such terms. [Applause.] I am a friend of my friend, and an enemy of my enemy. [Applause.] That is my doctrine. We might as well be honest about it. [Laughter.] Under that doctrine of State Rights, such men as I see before me—bankers, brokers, merchants, gentlemen—were expected to turn themselves into hounds and chase the poor fugitive that had been lured by the love of liberty and guided by the glittering Northern star. [Great applause.]

The Democratic party wanted you to keep your trade with the South, no matter to what depths of degradation you had to sink, and the Democratic party to-day says if you want to sell your goods to the Southern people, you must throw your honor and manhood into the streets. [Applause. Cries of "No; never."] The patronage of the splendid North is enough, to support the City of New-York. [Applause.]

In Favor of Protection.

There is another thing. Why is the city here filled with palaces, covered with wealth? Because American labor has been protected. [Great applause.] I am in favor of protection to American labor, everywhere. [Applause.] I am in favor of protecting American brain and muscle; I am in favor of giving scope to American ingenuity and American skill. [Great cheers.] We want a market at home, and the only way to have it is to have mechanics at home; and the only way to have mechanics is to have protection; and the only way to have protection is to vote the Republican ticket. [Great cheers.] You business men of New-York know that General Garfield [tremendous cheers] understands these great— [A voice—"Three cheers for General Garfield!"] These were given with vigor.] I was going to say that he knows what the tariff means; he understands the best interests not only of New-York, but the entire country. [Applause.] And you want to stand by the men who will stand by you. What does a simple soldier know about the wants of the City of New-York? What does he know about the wants of this great and splendid country? If he does not know more about it than he knows about the tariff, he doesn't know much. [Great laughter.] I don't like to hit the dead. [Renewed laughter.] My hatred stops with the grave, and I tell you we are going to bury the Democratic party next Tuesday. [Cheers.] The pulse is feeble now, [laughter,] and if that party proposes to take advantage of the last hour, it is time that it goes into the repenting business. [Great laughter.] Nothing pleases me better than to see the condition of that party to-day. What do the Democrats know on the subject of the tariff. They are frightened; they are ratting. [Great laughter.] They swear

their plank and platform meant nothing. They say in effect: "When we put that in we lied; and now, having made that confession, we hope you will have perfect confidence in us from this out." [Great cheers and laughter.] Hancock says that the object of the party is to get the tariff out of politics. That is the reason, I suppose, why they put that plank in the platform. [Laughter.] I presume he regards the tariff as a little local issue, but I tell you to-day that the great question of protecting American labor never will be taken out of politics. [Applause.] As long as men work, as long as the laboring man has a wife and family to support, just so long will he vote for the man that will protect his wages. ["Good, good," and cheers.] And you can no more take it out of politics than you can take the question of Government out of politics. [Cheers.] I don't want any question taken out of politics. [Applause.] I want the people to settle these questions for themselves, and the people of this country are capable of doing it. [Great cheers.] If you don't believe it, read the returns from Ohio and Indiana. [Great cheers.] There are other persons who would take the question of office out of politics. [Great laughter.] Well, when we get the tariff and office both out of politics, then, I presume, we will see two parties on the same side. It won't do. [Laughter.]

David A. Wells has come to the rescue of the Democratic party on the tariff, and shed a few pathetic tears over scrap iron. But it won't do. [Laughter.] You cannot run this country on scraps. [Laughter.] We believe in the tariff because it gives skilled labor good pay. We believe in the tariff because it allows the laboring man to have something to eat. We believe in the tariff because it keeps the hands of the producer close to the mouth of the devourers. [Applause.] We believe in the tariff because it developed American brain; because it builds up our towns and cities; because it makes Americans self-supporting; because it makes us an independent Nation. [Applause.] And we believe in the tariff because the Democratic party don't. [Laughter.] That plank in the Democratic party was intended for a dagger to assassinate the prosperity of the North. The Northern people have become aroused, and that is the plank that is broken in the Democratic platform; and that plank was wide enough when it broke to let even Hancock through. [Laughter.]

Desperate Resorts of the Democrats.

Gentlemen, they are gone. ["Honor bright?"] They are gone—honor bright. [Laughter.] Look at the desperate means that have been resorted to by the Democratic party, driven to the madness of desperation. Not satisfied with having worn the tongue of slander to the very tonsils, not satisfied with attacking the private reputation of a splendid man, not satisfied with that, they have appealed to a crime; a deliberate and infamous forgery has been committed. [Loud applause—"Hit him hard."] That forgery has been upheld by some of the leaders of the Democratic party; that forgery has been defended by men calling themselves respectable. ["Give it to them."] Leaders of the Democratic party have stood by and said that they were acquainted with the handwriting of James A. Garfield; and that the handwriting in the forged letter was his, when they know that it was absolutely unlike his. They knew it, and no man has certified that that was the writing of James A. Garfield who did not know that in his throat of throats he told a falsehood. [Applause.]

Every honest man in the City of New-York ought to leave such a party if he belongs to it. [" Go for Hewitt."] Every honest man [repeated cries of " Go for Hewitt] ought to refuse to belong to the party that did such an infamous crime. [" Go for Hewitt."] What is the use of my going for Hewitt, when all New-York is going for Hewitt? [Laughter.] And there is no man in this city going for Hewitt like Hewitt himself.

Senator Barnum, Chairman of the Democratic Committee, has lost control. He is gone, and I will tell you what he puts me in mind of. There was an old fellow used to come into town every Saturday and get drunk. He had a little yoke of oxen, and the boys, out of pity, used to throw him into the wagon and start the oxen for home. Just before he got home they had to go down a long hill, and the oxen, when they got to the brow of it, commenced to run. Now and then the wagon struck a stone and gave the old fellow an awful jolt, and that would wake him up. After he had looked up and had one glance at the cattle, he would fall helplessly back to the bottom, and always say, "Gee a little, if any thing." [Laughter.] And that is the only order that Barnum has been able to give for the last two weeks—"Gee a little," if any thing. [Laughter.] I tell you now, that forgery makes doubly sure the election of James A. Garfield. [Applause.] The people of the North believe in honest dealing; the people of the North believe in free speech and in an honest ballot. [Applause.] The people of the North believe that this is a Nation; the people of the North hate treason; the people of the North hate forgery; [tremendous cheering;] the people of the North hate slander. The people of the North have made up their minds to give to General Garfield a vindication of which any American may be forever proud. [Loud applause.]

General Garfield's Career.

I will tell you why I am for Garfield. [Laughter.] I know him, and I like him. [" Good enough."] No man has been nominated for the office since I was born, by either party, who had more brains and more heart than James A. Garfield. [Loud applause.] He was a soldier, he is a statesman. In time of peace he preferred the avocations of peace; when the bugle of war blew in his ears he withdrew from his work and fought for the flag, [cheers,] and then he went back to the avocations of peace. And I say to-day that a man who, in a time of profound peace, makes up his mind that he would like to kill folks for a living [laughter] is no better, to say the least of it, than the man who loves peace in the time of peace, and who, when his country is attacked, rushes to the rescue of her flag. [Loud cheers.]

James A. Garfield is to-day a poor man, and you know that there is not money enough in this magnificent street to buy the honor and manhood of James

A. Garfield. [Enthusiastic applause.] Money can not make such a man, and I will swear to you that money cannot buy him. [Renewed applause.] James A. Garfield to-day wears the glorious robe of honest poverty. He is a poor man; but I like to say it here in Wall-street; I like to say it surrounded by the millions of America; I like to say it in the midst of banks and bonds and stocks; I love to say it where gold is piled—that, although a poor man, he is rich in honor, in integrity he is wealthy, and in brain he is a millionaire. [Loud applause.] I know him, and I like him. [" So do we," and renewed applause.] So do you all, gentlemen. Garfield was a poor boy; he is a certificate of the splendid form of our Government. Most of these magnificent buildings have been built by poor boys ; [" That's so ;"] most of the success of New-York began almost in poverty. You know it. The kings of this street were once poor, and they may be poor again ; [laughter ;] and if they are fools enough to vote for Garfield, they ought to be. [Loud laughter and cheers.] Garfield is a certificate of the splendor of our Government, that says to every poor boy, "All the avenues of honor are open to you." I know him, and I like him. He is a scholar; he is a statesman ; he was a soldier; he is a patriot ; and above all, he is a magnificent man ; [loud cheers ;] and if every man in New-York knew him as well as I do, Garfield would not lose a hundred votes in this city. [" We will all be true to him," and cheers.] And yet this is the man against whom the Democratic party has been howling its filth ; this is the great and good man whom the Democrats have slandered from the day of his nomination until now ; this, the statesman, the soldier, the scholar, the patriot, is the man against whom the Democratic party was willing to commit the crime of forgery.

Compare him with Hancock, and then compare General Arthur with William H. English. [" Oh !" " Oh !" and laughter.] If there ever was a pure Republican in this world, General Arthur is one. [Cheers.] Now, gentlemen, [" Give us something about English,"] there is no use my talking about English. I have made up my mind to avoid unpleasant subjects. [Laughter]

What would follow Hancock's Election.

You know in Wall-street there are some men always prophesying disaster ; there are some men always selling "short." [Laughter.] That is what the Democratic party is doing to-day. You know as well as I do that if the Democratic party succeeds, every kind of property in the United States will depreciate. [" That's so ;" "true enough."] You know it. There is not a man on the street who, if he knew Hancock was to be elected, would not sell the stocks and bonds of every railroad in the United States "short." [Laughter.] I dare any broker here to deny it. There is not a man in Wall or Broad streets, or in New-York, but what knows the election of Hancock will depreciate every share of railroad stock, every railroad bond, every Government bond in the United States of America. And if you know that, I say it is a crime to vote for Hancock and English. [Loud cheers.]

I belong to a party that is prosperous when the country is prosperous. That's me. [Laughter.] I belong to the party that believes in good crops; that is glad when a fellow finds a gold mine; that rejoices when there are forty bushels of wheat to the acre; that laughs when every railroad declares dividends; that claps both its hands when every investment pays; when the rain falls for the farmer, when the dew lies lovingly upon the grass. I belong to the party that is happy when the people are happy; when the laboring man gets $3 a day; when he has roast beef on his table; [laughter;] when he has a carpet on the floor; when he has a picture of Garfield on the wall. [Laughter and applause.] I belong to the party that is happy when everybody smiles; when we have plenty of money, good horses, [that's you,] good carriages; when our wives are happy and our children feel glad. [Loud applause.] I belong to the party whose banner floats side by side with the great flag of the country; that does not grow fat on defeat. [Laughter.] The Democratic party is a party of famine; it is a good friend of an early frost; [laughter;] it believes in the Colorado beetle and in the weevil. [Renewed laughter.] When the crops are bad the Democratic mouth opens from ear to ear with smiles of joy; it is in partnership with bad luck; a friend of empty pockets; rags help it. I am on the other side. The Democratic party is the party of darkness; I belong to the party of sunshine, and to the party that even in darkness believes that the stars are shining and waiting for us. [Applause.]

Why the Republican Party Should be Supported.

Now, gentlemen, I have endeavored to give you a few reasons for voting the Republican ticket, and I have given enough to satisfy any reasonable man. And you know it. [Laughter.] Don't you go with the Democratic party, young man. You have got a character to make. You cannot make it, as the Democratic party does, by passing a resolution. [Laughter.] If your father voted the Democratic ticket that is disgrace enough for one family. [Roars of laughter.] Tell the old man that you can stand it no longer. Tell the old gent that you have made up your mind to stand with the party of human progress; and if he asks you why you cannot vote the Democratic ticket, you tell him: "Every man that tried to destroy the Government, every man that shot at the holy flag in heaven, every man that starved our soldiers, every keeper of Libby, Andersonville and Salisbury, every man that wanted to burn the negro, every one that wanted to scatter yellow fever in the North, every man that opposed human liberty, that regarded the auction-block as an altar, and the howling of the bloodhounds as the music of the Union, every man who wept over the corpse of slavery, that thought lashes on the naked back were a legal tender for labor performed, every one willing to rob a mother of her child—every solitary one was a Democrat." [Applause.]

Tell him you cannot stand that party. Tell him you have to go with the Republican party; and if he asks you why, tell him it destroyed slavery; it preserved the Union; it paid the National debt; it

made our credit as good as that of any nation on the earth. ["Better," and applause.] Tell him it makes a four per cent. bond worth $1.10; that it satisfies the demands of the highest civilization; that it made it possible for every greenback to hold up its hand and swear: "I know that my Redeemer liveth." [Laughter and applause.] Tell the old man that the Republican party preserved the honor of the Nation; that it believes in education; that it looks upon the school-house as a cathedral. [Applause.] Tell him that the Republican party believes in absolute intellectual liberty, in absolute religious freedom, in human rights, and that human rights rise above States. Tell him that the Republican party believes in humanity, justice, human equality, and that the Republican party believes this a Nation for ever and ever; [applause;] that an honest ballot is the breath of the Republic's life; ["good, good;"] that honest money is the blood of the Republic, and that nationality is the great throbbing beat of the heart of the Republic. [Great cheers.] Tell him that; and tell him that you are going to stand by the flag that the patriots North carried upon the battle-field of death. [Cheers.] Tell him you are going to be true, to the martyred dead; that you are going to vote exactly as Lincoln would have voted were he living. ["Good, good," and cheers.] Tell him that every traitor dead, were he living now, there would issue from his lips of dust, "Hurrah for Hancock;" [laughter;] that could every patriot rise he would cry for Garfield and liberty, [cheers,] for union and for human progress everywhere. [Great cheers.] Tell him that the South seeks to secure by the ballot what it lost by the bayonet; ["No, no, never!"] to whip by the ballot those who fought it in the field. But we saved the country, and we have got the heart and brains to take care of it. [Cheers.] I will tell you what we are going to do. We are going to treat them in the South just as well as we treat the people in the North. [Great cheers.] Victors cannot afford to have malice. [Cheers.] The North is too magnanimous to have hatred. [Cheers.] We will treat the South precisely as we treat the North. [Applause.] There are thousands of good people there. [Good! good! and cheers.] Let us give them money to improve their rivers and harbors; I want to see the sails of their commerce filled with the breezes of prosperity; [cheers;] their fences rebuilt; [applause;] their houses painted. ["Good! good!"] I want to see their towns prosperous; I want to see school-houses in every town; ["Good! good!" and cheers;] I want to see books in the hands of every child, and papers and magazines in every house; [cheers;] I want to see all the rays of light of the civilization of the nineteenth century enter every home of the South; [cheers;] and in a little while you will see that country full of good Republicans. [Roars of laughter.] We can afford to be kind; we cannot afford to be unkind. [Cheers.] I will shake hands cordially with every believer in human liberty; I will shake hands with every believer in Nationality. [Applause.] I will shake hands with every man who is the friend of the human race. [Cheers.] This is my doctrine. I believe in the great Republic; in this magnificent country of ours. [Cheers.] I believe in the great people of the United

States. [Cheers.] I believe in the muscle and brain of America, in the prairies and forests. I believe in New-York. [Cheers.] I believe in the brain of your city. I believe that you know enough to vote the Republican ticket. [Great applause.] I believe that you are grand enough to stand by the country that has stood by you. [Cheers.] But whatever you do, I shall never cease to thank you for the great honor you have conferred upon me this day. [Great and long continued cheering.]—*From the New-York Tribune, Friday, October 29, 1880.*

A Speech by President HAYES, *delivered at Cleveland, Ohio, Thursday evening, November 4, 1880.*

MR. PRESIDENT, FELLOW-CITIZENS, AND PEOPLE OF THE UNITED STATES OF ALL PARTIES AND OF ALL SECTIONS: We have all many solid reasons for rejoicing over the result of Tuesday's election. At this late hour of the night and in this weather I shall not delay you to enumerate them. I will allude to one or two of them. We rejoice that the majority for Gen. Garfield is so decided, so large, that there is no room to question his election. You all remember how, four years ago, the business of the country for weeks and months was interrupted and almost suspended by the doubts incurred of the election. Possibly the weakest point in our system is that it does not adequately provide for the ascertainment and declaration of the result of a Presidential election when it is close and doubtful and disputed. And, therefore, my friends, it is a subject for congratulation and rejoicing by all men of all parties that this question is settled, and that in one or two days or weeks we shall all be pursuing our usual avocations, and business will be going on as it has been going on for the last six or eight months. A less important point, perhaps, is also that we are able to rejoice in the fact demonstrated by this election, that no amount of calumny and personal attack upon a Presidential candidate, of really high character, affects him in the least in the judgment of the good people. As citizens of Cleveland, of the Western Reserve of Ohio, and neighbors of Gen. Garfield, we rejoice, because we know that he is worthy of the success he has achieved. How many and how great are the laurels that now encircle his brow. He stands to-day the Representative of the Nineteenth Congressional District, in his ninth term, his eighteenth year as Representative of that district, a district composed of the counties of Ashtabula, Trumbull, Geauga and Portage, a community not surpassed in intelligence and patriotism anywhere on earth. He is their representative to-day, sustained by them through all these years, elected again and again nine times, in spite of opposition and calumny. More than that, he is to-day Senator elect for a six years' term, a position that sought him, unsought by him, un-bought, receiving it spontaneously and without effort, he is Senator from Ohio, and now the President elect from the 4th of March next of the United States. In all our history no such combination of civil honors have rested upon the head of any man, and we rejoice, as I said, to know that he is worthy of these honors.

Looking through the history of our public men we find that he is a model self-made man. In our history we can see in the past Franklin, Lincoln, and then comes Garfield as the self-made man of the United States, the best illustration and example of what under our institutions may occur to the humblest boy, the humblest child of the Republic—an example of what can be done where all have a fair start and an equal chance in the race of life. Finally, my friends, we rejoice because we feel assured that in the wise, firm and moderate administration of Gen. Garfield, our country is to attain an era of prosperity not surpassed in any country on the face of the globe. Under his broad and liberal and generous administration, every section of this country will be fairly and justly dealt with. He will say to the mistaken men of the South, "You will be treated precisely as the citizens of my own State of Ohio are to be treated. All we ask of you is that you shall faithfully obey the Constitution as it now is, regarding the new parts as equal parts, and equally sacred, with the old." Doing this to the Administration of General Garfield, every liberal and generous act required on his part will be cheerfully and gladly done. Extending to every State its State's Rights, he requires of them that they shall accord to every citizen his individual rights. With this done, with harmony restored throughout the Union, throughout all classes, I say again that the blessings of the victory gained on Tuesday by you are blessings alike and equally to the Republicans and to the Democrats, and to the Southern man and to the Northern man, and to whosoever is a citizen of the United States. I thank you for your hearing.—*From the New-York Times, Friday, November 5, 1880.*

PATRIOTIC SENTIMENTS.

"WE are citizens of a Republic. We govern ourselves. Here no pomp of eager array in chambers of royalty awaits the birth of boy or girl to wield a hereditary sceptre whenever death or revolution pours on the oil of coronation. We know no sceptre save a majority's constitutional will. To wield that sceptre in equal share is the duty and the right, nay, the birthright of every citizen. The supreme, the final, the only peaceful arbiter here is the ballot-box ; and in that urn should be gathered, and from it should be sacredly recorded, the conscience, the judgment, the intelligence of all. The right of free self-government has been in all ages the bright dream of oppressed humanity ; the sighed-for privilege to which thrones, dynasties and powers have so long blocked the way. France seeks it by forced marches and daring strides. Mr. Forster, Secretary for Ireland, tells the peerage of England it must take heed lest it fall, and Westminster and England ring with dread echoes of applause. But in the fullness of freedom the Republic of America is alone in the earth ; alone in its grandeur ; alone in its blessings ; alone in its promises and possibilities, and, therefore, alone in the devotion due from its citizens."— Senator ROSCOE CONKLING.

"We have undertaken on this Continent of ours to build up a fabric of politics, in which the laboring man had the same share, every ignorant man had the same share, every feeble man had the same share in political power with the rich and the strong and the learned. And that system we mean to maintain ; and in order to maintain a system and dignity which is known nowhere else in the world, and has never been known anywhere in the world till here and now, we mean to protect the wages of our workmen from competition with the pauper systems of Europe."—Hon. WILLIAM M. EVARTS.

"This country is better adapted for a harmonization of interests and opinions than any other country of which I have any knowledge. It is adapted on the great principle of reciprocal interest—it is adapted to the unity of the whole population. If it were all North, if it were all South, if it were all East, if it were all West, the identity of interests would create sluggishness of circulation ; but because the harvests of the South are one thing, and the harvests of the North are another, those of the East another, and the productive energies of the West another, the circulation is maintained which carries vigorous life throughout every part of this Union. And although we have a tribute paid us of its best citizens from every nation of the globe—in Europe, in Asia, in Africa—yet as long as liberty is being sought, and since liberty is here regulated by institutions ; since law and institutions in this land have been created by the people themselves, who knew the wants of the common people, I would have the emigrants find— wherever they come from—that for which they have pined, the want of which has nearly suffocated them in their own land. Because we have this vast people founded on institutions of liberty, designed to give scope and opportunity to every living man, we have a population that is inclined to friendship, to peace, to comity of interests ; and I hold that no party is worthy of one single hour's regard which does not aim at the harmonization of the interests of every part of this broad continent."—Rev. HENRY WARD BEECHER.

"If the Republican party is in favor of sectional interests, of class interests ; if it overslaughs the laborer, whose hands are his capital ; if it disregards the poor and the needy ; if it goes in for the rich in contempt for the poor, for the North in derogation of the South, for the South at a mischief toward the North ; if it neglects the far Pacific States ; if it is not a party in whose very heart is the purpose to take care of the whole nation—all its parts, all its interests and all its people—then I cannot ask you to vote for it. But it is because in my very heart of hearts I believe that it is a National party, seeking not alone nationality by controlling the Government, but having in its genius, in its history, in its inspirations, in its purposes, in its platform and in all the legislation that will follow from it—having the interest of every section, of every class, of all conditions, North, South, East and West—it is for that reason that I am free to commend it to your suffrages." —Rev. HENRY WARD BEECHER.

"It is enough to say, that behind the Republican party is more than twenty years of steady policy of the same character which we propose to pursue in future. I know what the Republican party will do. I know what James A. Garfield will do, and what, if he died, Chester A. Arthur will do. I know they believe in encouraging and maintaining American industry, and in maintaining our present system of currency.

The Republican party took the old edifice, of which the Democrats spoke, and removed from it the decaying timbers of human chattelhood, and replaced them with the fullest guarantee of freedom. They found the old walls defaced, slimy all over with foul inscriptions. They found its presiding genius, not the great Nation that we now worship, but a bullying, cruel, blustering, bragging, dirt-eating sycophantic genius, carrying the Dred Scott decision in one hand and the Fugitive Slave law in the other, marching, not to the music of the Union, but to the music of the chain and the crack of the whip, and the baying of the bloodhound, and the appealing and imploring cry of the pursued. Thank God, Lincoln was our chieftain, and we wiped out all these foul records, and we have covered them with the shining and resplendent record of 4,000,000 of slaves, lifted by one supreme effort from the night of savagery and chattelhood into the clear day of American citizenship. The world witnesses it, and hails and salutes it."—Hon. EMERY A. STORRS.

"I wish to admit that the Republican party is not absolutely perfect. While I believe that it is the best party that ever existed, while I believe it has, within its organization, more heart, more brain, more patriotism than any other organization that ever existed beneath the sun, I still admit that it is not entirely perfect. I admit, in its great things, in its splendid efforts to preserve this Nation, in its grand effort to keep our flag in heaven, in its magnificent effort to free four millions of slaves, in its great and sublime effort to save the financial honor of this Nation, I admit that it has made some mistakes. In its great effort to do right it has sometimes, by mistake, done wrong. And I also wish to admit that the great Democratic party, in its great effort to get office, has sometimes by mistake done right. You see that I am inclined to be perfectly fair. I am going with the Republican party because it is going my way ; but if it ever turns to the right or left, I intend to go straight ahead."—Col. ROBERT G. INGERSOLL.

"The Republican party is the fruit of all ages—of self-sacrifice and devotion. The Republican party is born of every good thing that was ever done in this world. The Republican party is the result of all martyrdom of all heroic bloodshed for the right. It is the blossom and fruit of the great world's best endeavor."—Col. ROBERT G. INGERSOLL.

"I believe in the protection of American labor. The hand that holds Aladdin's lamp must be the hand of toil. This Nation rests upon the shoulders of its workers, and I want the American laboring man to have enough to wear; I want him to have enough to eat; I want him to have something for the ordinary misfortunes of life; I want him to have the pleasure of seeing his wife well-dressed; I want him to see a few blue ribbons fluttering about his children; I want him to see the flags of health flying in their beautiful cheeks; I want him to feel that this is his country, and the shield of protection is above his labor."—Col. ROBERT G. INGERSOLL.

"I wish to belong to that party which is prosperous when the country is prosperous. I belong to that party which is not poor when the golden billows are running over the seas of wheat. I belong to that party that is prosperous when there are oceans of corn, and when the cattle are upon the thousand hills. I belong to that party which is prosperous when the furnaces are aflame; and when you dig coal and iron, and silver; when everybody has enough to eat; when everybody is happy; when the children are all going to school, and when joy covers my Nation as with a garment. That party which is prosperous, then, is my party."—Col. ROBERT G. INGERSOLL.

"Oh! I love the old Republic, bound by the seas, walled by the wide air, domed by heaven's blue, and lit with the eternal stars. I love the Republic; I love it because I love liberty. Liberty is my religion, and at its altar I worship and will worship."— Col. ROBERT G. INGERSOLL.

"I have a right to express my opinion, and the right in common with every other human being, and I am willing to give to every other human being the right that I claim for myself. Republicanism says, that out upon the great intellectual sea there is room for every sail; Republicanism says, that in the intellectual air there is room enough for every wing. Republicanism means justice in politics. Republicanism means progress in civilization. Republicanism means that every man shall be an educated patriot and a gentleman. And I want to say to you to-day, that the Republican party is the best that ever existed. I want to say to you to-day, that it is an honor to belong to it. It is an honor to have belonged to it for twenty years; it is an honor to belong to the party that elected Abraham Lincoln President. And let me say to you, that Lincoln was the greatest, the best, the purest, the kindest man that has ever sat in the Presidential chair. It is an honor to belong to the Republican party that gave 4.000,000 of men the rights of freemen; it is an honor to belong to the party that broke the shackles from 4,000,000 of men, women and children. It is an honor to belong to the party that declared that bloodhounds were not the missionaries of civilization. It is an honor to belong to the party that said it was a crime to steal a babe from its mother's breast. It is an honor to belong to the party that swore that this is a Nation forever, one and indivisible. It is an honor to belong to the party that elected U. S. Grant President of the United States. It is an honor to belong to the party that issued thousands and thousands of millions of dollars in promises—that issued promises until they became as thick as the withered leaves of winter; an honor to belong to the party that issued them to put down a rebellion; an honor to belong to the party that put it down; an honor to belong to the party that had the moral courage and honesty to make every one of the promises, made in war, in peace as good as shining, glittering gold. And I tell you that if there is another life, and if there is a day of judgment, all you need to say upon that solemn occasion is, 'I was in life and in my death a good, square Republican.'"—Col. ROBERT G. INGERSOLL.

"We are not working in a corner nor in a hole. If there ever was a Nation whose prosperity had attracted the thoughtful regard of wise men throughout the world, this is that Nation. If there has ever been surprise sprung upon men at the developments of human nature, the conduct of this Nation in the war and after the war, and to this hour, has given that surprise. Not only are we surrounded with a cloud of earthly witnesses in this great campaign, but all the men that landed with our fathers, in the misty distance, obscure to us but clear to them, are looking down upon us. It is the Nation they founded, and if the rock could speak as once the rock gushed forth with water for the famished crowd, old Plymouth Rock would give forth a voice to all men of the Republican party and of the Nation, saying, 'Keep, build, fortify that which we founded.'"—Rev. HENRY WARD BEECHER.

"Scarcely, like a reed blown from the wind in the sky, have they gone out of sight before we behold the reverent founders of the Constitution and the fathers of this Nation. They, too, are the witnesses of their children, and they plead that this Constitution, which was ordained to Liberty, shall neither be undermined nor blackened, nor weakened, nor perverted into an instrument of tyranny by their posterity. Heed their voice. And scarcely have they gone out of sight, when, gathering like armies, multitudinous as the drops of the storm-cloud, the men that laid down their lives for the Nation appear and lift up their voices and reach out airy hands, to beseech us to preserve immaculate that for which they bled to gain. And high above them all, and most reverent I behold the immortal form of the Father of his Country, a Southerner and loving the South. Methinks he turns his face from the North, and says to his brethren of the South: 'Ye know not what ye do. Be at peace. Maintain the Government. Submit to the law; and let there be brotherhood in all the land, and your God and my God shall pour his blessing upon the Nation.'"—Rev. HENRY WARD BEECHER.